PATIENT DARKNESS

A BROODING CITY NOVEL

TOM SHUTT

Published by Red Eagle

Visit us at www.redeaglepublishing.com

This is a work of fiction. Names, characters, places, and incidents either are the product of the author's imagination or are used fictitiously, and any resemblance to actual persons, living or dead, business establishments, events, or locales is entirely coincidental.

Copyright © 2015 Tom Shutt

All rights reserved.

ISBN: 978-1-7334810-1-4

Cover design by Mibl Art (www.miblart.com)

This book is protected under the copyright laws of the United States of America. Any reproduction or other unauthorized use of the material or artwork herein is prohibited without the express written permission of the author.

Thank you for buying an authorized edition of this book and for complying with copyright laws by not reproducing, scanning, or distributing any part of it in any form without permission.

DEDICATION

The family of Tom Shutt dedicates this novel to his eternal memory, following his abrupt physical departure from this world at age 25. Thomas passed away peacefully from an unexplained sudden cardiac arrhythmia while working on a new novel, less than a year after landing on the *New York Times* Bestseller List. He is profoundly missed and infinitely loved.

The novel that you're currently holding includes updated cover art designed before his passing, but never released until now. Aside from that change, everything you're about to read is exactly what he wrote for you to enjoy.

Proceeds from all book sales go directly to the Thomas J. Shutt Memorial Foundation, a registered 501(c)(3) nonprofit dedicated to supporting the next generation of great storytellers through scholarships and grants. You can learn more about the foundation at www.thomasjshuttmemorialfoundation.org.

CONTENTS

	Acknowledgments	i
1	Chapter One	1
2	Chapter Two	13
3	Chapter Three	17
4	Chapter Four	27
5	Chapter Five	37
6	Chapter Six	44
7	Chapter Seven	57
8	Chapter Eight	65
9	Chapter Nine	71
10	Chapter Ten	80
11	Chapter Eleven	97
12	Chapter Twelve	114
13	Chapter Thirteen	126
14	Chapter Fourteen	184
15	Chapter Fifteen	197
16	Chapter Sixteen	223
17	Chapter Seventeen	237
18	Chapter Eighteen	264
19	Chapter Nineteen	284
20	Chapter Twenty	297
21	Chapter Twenty-One	306
22	Chapter Twenty-Two	339
23	Chapter Twenty-Three	344
24	Chapter Twenty-Four	352
	Epilogue	355

ACKNOWLEDGMENTS

We would like to thank the international independent author community for so many things. Most importantly, for your friendship and support of Thomas as he established himself in his career as a young writer. Thomas spoke often of his friends around the world who shared his passion for creative storytelling, and he was so grateful to have each of you in his life. Thank you for giving him that sense of belonging.

To Derek Armstrong, Kylie Colter, Monica Corwin, Danielle Romero, Gwynn White, and so many others we've come to know through this tragedy, we truly do not have words to express our gratitude for how you rallied around our family in our darkest days. We love and appreciate each of you, and know that Thomas is so proud.

To the entire team at Mibl Art, especially Mark and Olivia, we can't thank you enough for bringing Thomas's design vision for his books to life. Your talents as designers are only exceeded by your compassion, patience and kindness as human beings. Thank you for being who you are.

Finally, we would like to acknowledge you, the reader. Every time you read Thomas's words and talk about his books with your family and friends, you contribute to keeping his legacy alive. We are eternally grateful for that.

Chapter One

It had been a messy break; not Brennan's worst of the night, but far from the best.

"Remember the acronym I taught you," Sam said, moving into position across the table. A long fluorescent light, lined on either side with ceramic billiard balls, illuminated the green felt surface and highlighted the crests and waves of his slightly curling hair.

"Think," he said, drawing the cue level with the table.

"Imagine." He emphasized this point by closing his eyes briefly and taking a deep breath.

"Take aim." The pool cue slid back and forth in his hands as he confirmed his chosen angle.

"Sh—"

"And shoot," Brennan supplied. Sam's cue connected awkwardly with the white ball, a hollow thwack that sounded as bad as the shot had been. Instead of a powerful stroke, he succeeded only in lightly scattering both stripes and solids. He scowled at the open table.

"You know I hate it when you do that," he said, passing the cue back to Brennan.

"A good player should be able to deal with all distractions."

"You sound like a golfer, not a pool player."

"That was my father," Brennan said distractedly. Despite his advice, he wasn't much better at ignoring outside influences when it came to pool. In a moment of silence, he took an easy straight-shot and sunk a solid in the corner. "We didn't make it to the back nine together very often," he said, "but it was a good place for him to meet clients."

"What did your father do?"

Brennan hedged. "He was a negotiator, of sorts. 'High-risk asset management,' he would call it."

Sam glanced around at their nearest neighbors. A couple men sat in a corner booth, smoke drifting lazily from a half-full ashtray; they were engaged in a quiet conversation. Another gentleman, leaning heavily on his elbows at the bar, picked through a small bowl of corn nuts. Half-undressed and looking for work, a sultry woman of the night gave Sam a nod and a smile that promised pleasurable things to come.

"Six months ago," he said, turning back to Brennan, "she would've been just my type."

"Six months ago, *she'd* have been the one getting between you and Bishop."

Sam grimaced. "Don't remind me. So your dad, asset management? Sounds like he was an accountant or something."

"Something like that. How are things with the two of you?"

"With Bishop? They're improving, I suppose. At least she's willing to speak to me again, ever since the hospital." He took a long sip from his beer before puffing up his chest. "Saving someone's life will do that."

"If I recall correctly, *she* saved *your* life."

"Details, details," he said. "It's the thought that counts. Probably too soon to tell, but I think things are on the mend."

Brennan doubted the chances of them ever getting back together. Noel was a strong and independent woman, and as far as Brennan could tell, Sam had shot his odds to hell the moment he'd decided she wasn't worth his complete devotion. Brennan wasn't about to turn on a friend, though, so he let Sam hold on to his delusion.

Something vibrated; Sam deftly placed his empty bottle on a tall table and pulled out his phone. He smiled briefly before starting to tap out a reply.

"Well speak of the devil," Brennan said, grinning as he drained the last of his own bottle. "How's Bishop?"

Sam finished whatever he was writing before looking up. "Huh? Oh, fine. She wants to know if I'm available tomorrow night," he said, a cocky smile tugging at his lips.

"Dinner and a movie?"

He scoffed. "I wish. More likely than not, she'll want to take me on for the new case."

Brennan grimaced. The prediction given months ago by Benjamin had proven to be true. Five bodies had dropped in the last ten and a half weeks, discovered every other Saturday morning like clockwork. The police had little information to work with, and the deadline for the next expected drop was fast approaching. If they didn't have a breakthrough in the next four days, somebody would be turning up cold come the weekend.

"But I can't," Sam continued with an air of regret. Sam McCarthy was a former detective himself, now in the business of private investigation. It was more lucrative, he set his own hours, and he was better than most at what he did. Unfortunately, his ego wouldn't fit in the overhead luggage space of a jumbo jet. "Already committed to another case. I'm on retainer for the next two days."

False.

Brennan frowned. For as long as he could remember, Brennan had been able to tell when people were telling him the truth and when they were lying through their teeth. As a kid, it had been a quiet feeling in the pit of his stomach. It was the kind of thing that most cops had to some degree, a "gut feeling" that had better-than-even odds of being right. Nowadays, though, it was a small voice that whispered in his skull, equally as unavoidable as a speeding bullet or morning wood.

He lined up another shot, but the target ball bounced off the edge of a pocket and rolled hopelessly behind the 8 ball. He scowled and reached for his bottle before remembering it was empty. His mind was too distracted to play now.

There was no cause he could think of to explain why his best friend would lie to him now. Still, he had to trust that it was for a good reason. If he called out his friends on every white lie, he'd find himself alone very quickly. Brennan mustered his best poker face. While nobody could lie to him, he himself had become very adept at the talent. It was the greatest lesson his father had ever taught him.

"Shouldn't you be tracking down a missing husband or something," Brennan asked, "instead of playing pool in a dingy bar?"

Sam finished another text and put away his phone. "You're absolutely right," he said, pushing himself away from the pillar. He grabbed his jacket from the back of his stool and donned it in one swift motion. It was the kind of move James Bond might have pulled after a long night of Texas hold 'em. He caught Brennan's eye. "I know you were joking, but I actually do need to go."

"What? You're leaving in the middle of our game?" Brennan demanded. Every ball was still on the table, with the exception of his one sunk solid.

"Sorry, partner. When the lady calls, I answer."

That was as close to an answer as Brennan was going to get. He knew that Sam wasn't working a case; maybe he was actually making progress with Bishop. "At least take your turn before you go," Brennan said, offering the pool cue.

Sam sighed, took the stick, and quickly lined up a shot. He looked like a prowling panther over the cue, all black leather and lean body. A stripe sunk smoothly into the pocket, and he was in position for a follow-up shot before the white ball had stopped moving.

Another pocketed ball.

And then another.

And another.

In the span of a minute, Sam not only cleared the table of any striped balls, but he had also pushed Brennan's solids into unfortunate positions against the walls. He was breathing calmly and wore only a hint of a smirk as he sized up the 8 ball. One fluid motion brought him down over the table. His face was a mask of concentration, his eyes focused entirely on the far pocket that was his goal. He breathed deep, and the cue moved in his hands as he exhaled.

A solid hit, and the game was over.

"God dammit," Sam swore as the white ball followed its black companion into the pocket. The two men at the corner table shook their heads and gave him a look of empathy; everyone who played pool eventually got stung by the 8 Ball Rule.

"Don't let Bishop hear you talking like that," Brennan said, pulling on his own light coat. It wasn't yet winter, but the wind was high and the temperature dropped steadily with each day. Odols, like the rest of Wisconsin, was famous for its half-year winter weather, and it seemed like this season was gearing up to be the coldest on record. He pushed open the bar door and was met with a gust of wind that wiped away the scent of beer and cigarettes.

Brennan accompanied Sam to the shuttle station. The shuttle loops ringed Odols in two massive concentric circles; moving like precise cogs in a fine-tuned machine, the shuttles ran a continuous circuit that provided transportation for the majority of the city's public commuters.

"Give my regards to Greg," Sam said, tipping an imaginary hat toward Brennan as he took a seat.

"I'll let him know," Brennan promised. His friend nodded and watched until he was out of sight.

He took quick steps down the tunnel stairs that led to his own platform. It amazed him how quickly the atmosphere could change, even for a brief moment between shuttle stations. The platform behind him had been busy, even at night, and the city sounds were a constant background noise. However, the moment he entered the connecting tunnel, all of that commotion was replaced by dull yellow lights and outdated event posters lining a mostly deserted corridor of concrete and neglected dampness. It was the kind of place that mothers warned their children about, a seedy location that begged for muggers and worse to take up residence.

A large pile of mangy fur coats and worn leather had made its home on several pieces of flattened cardboard. Only the slight movement from shallow breaths revealed that there was a person under all of those recycled animals. Brennan moved closer, but was almost instantly repulsed by a pungent odor emanating from the raggedy man.

"Sir," he said, nudging one torn-up boot with his shoe. "You can't sleep here."

Red-rimmed eyes peered out from a fold in the fur. The voice that came from the chapped gray lips was soft and raspy. "Nowhere else *to* sleep."

Brennan lifted his shirt just enough to let his badge show in the dim lighting. The man wrapped in throwaway coats sat up a little straighter, or perhaps a little more defensively, as if expecting trouble. "You can't stay here tonight, though. This is a public transit center."

"It's cold out there, officer," he said. "Too cold for the likes of me to just be huddling out in the open."

He had a point, of course; the streets weren't as bad as he said now, but they would be a death trap for anybody living from curb to curb at night during winter. Unfortunately, the tunnel wasn't much better; the long, narrow space would just become a wind funnel for the frigid air blowing through the city.

Brennan noticed the sheen of sweat on the man's brow, the agitated way he looked from one end of the tunnel to the other, and the insistent scratching at his own arm beneath the fur coat. He knew the signs all too well from watching his nephew.

"Are you on the patch?" he asked.

The man became more agitated. "Never touched the stuff."

False.

In the weeks following the demise of Leviathan's patch-dealing operation, dozens of knock-offs had hit the streets. Without their signature product on the market, enterprising dealers catered to the pumped-up patch addicts, each with their own home-brewed blend. The result was a plague of symptoms caused by improper dosages and impurities in the base ingredients. As bad as Leviathan's Chamalla had been, the aftermath of its absence was even worse.

This man needed help, and not the kind that came from passing strangers' pocket change.

"There's a church nearby, not too far from here. St. Agabus. You know it?" From beneath the matted clothes came a dazed look and incredulous eyes. "I'll need a confirmation on that," Brennan said. A shallow nod, mouth slightly agape. "Good," he continued. "I'm going to pass through here again in ten minutes, and I expect you to be gone by then, you understand? Go to St. Agabus's. They can get you a hot meal and a warm bed."

Still confused, the man at least had enough sense to start gathering his meager belongings. Brennan had no intention of returning, but it was a white lie worth telling if it got this forsaken man off the cold streets for a night. He watched until the man had collected himself and left the tunnel before continuing to his station. He climbed the flight of stairs at the other end of the passage and came out to the shuttle platform, which was covered overhead by a wide strip of clear glass.

The shuttle he'd intended to take was already gone, but another would be along within ten minutes. He pulled out his phone and pressed the first number on speed-dial. A young man's voice answered on the third ring.

"Uncle Arty?"

"Hey, Greg, just calling to give you a heads-up that I'm coming home." He looked down at his watch and added a half-hour for the commute. "I'll be there by eight o'clock or so."

"That's good, I'll see you soon." His words sounded oddly slurred over the phone. "Want me to put a cold one on ice for when you get here?" *A "cold one"? Ahh, that's it,* Brennan thought. His nephew must have snuck a little something out of his liquor cabinet.

"As long as it's a Coke," Brennan said. The three beers earlier hadn't done much for him, considering his size, but they'd succeeded in making him a little drowsy. Likewise, the caffeine wouldn't do much to wake him up, but at least he wouldn't crash the instant he sat down on the couch.

"Will do. See you soon," Greg repeated.

Brennan ended the call and leaned back against the bench, his eyes lifted upward toward the hazy night sky. The city was too bright for any stargazing, but he liked to imagine that he could see them, suspended high above like tiny snowflakes on cold black pavement. Low and heavy and full, the moon still outshone any light of man, and it looked larger than usual tonight. Brennan's head lolled as he stared up at it, but the reverie was broken as his shuttle pulled loudly into the station.

Feeling good and at one with the universe, Brennan stepped onto the shuttle and sat heavily in one of its lightly padded seats. The window was cool to the touch and felt good against his skin. Maybe he was more buzzed than he cared to admit, but the shuttle ride would give him time to clear his head before he got back to the apartment. They were deep into autumn, and leaves weren't the only things falling in the city of Odols.

He had a serial killer to catch.

Chapter Two

Alex Brüding calmly listened to the voices of her neighbors.

It had nothing to do with thin walls or shouting matches. To anyone else, the building was perfectly quiet. The doors were basically slabs of honeycombed reinforced steel, and the soundproofed walls were second only to those of an anechoic chamber in Minneapolis. That absolute ability to close off the outside world was one of the very reasons she lived in the most expensive apartment complex in the city.

However, nothing on this earth could stop her from listening in on the private thoughts of those around her. It was a sixth sense of sorts, but one that seemed more real than the other five put together. It hadn't always been a gift to her. When she was just a girl, Alex had thought she'd been cursed with madness, hearing voices that nobody else could. Now, though, she had accepted and embraced who she was. Without effort, she stared up at the raised ceiling of her bedroom and sifted through the cacophony of resentful grumblings, distrustful suspicions, and lusty daydreams.

This last collection fascinated her the most. She herself had been the focus of wandering eyes more than once, and knowing the intimate thoughts that accompanied them did wonders for her self-esteem. More than that, every casual flirt or lingering touch she observed carried extra meaning, given the proper context. Knowledge was power, and she intended to amass as much power for herself as she could.

Satisfied that she had caught up with her neighbors' generally mundane lives, she rose from the queen-sized bed and set about preparing herself for the evening. While her neighbors might have been winding down from the day, her night was just getting started.

She had been ready for the past half hour, ever since she'd texted her date for the evening. A silky cherry-red chemise clung intriguingly to her chest while hanging just long enough to give teasing glimpses of her thighs. At just over five-nine, she had plenty of leg to work with, and she could look down on most people when wearing heels.

Alex frowned at her strawberry hair, which was slightly mussed from lying on the bed. She took a fine-toothed comb to it, drawing out the slender strands until she was satisfied. She considered adding lipstick, but settled on a clear, flavored gloss instead. Knuckles rapped lightly against the steel door, and Alex glided out of her bedroom and down the hallway. She passed the bathroom, guest room, kitchen, and living room before reaching the door, and her lover's hand was raised to knock again when she opened it.

"Hi there," he said, his lips spreading in a vulpine smile. The red curls of his hair stood out sharply against his black clothes. *You look fantastic*, she heard him rehearse in his head. A moment later, his mouth caught up to his brain.

"Thank you, Sam," she said, smiling at the compliment. "You're always such a sweetie." She stood in the doorframe another moment, letting his eyes drink in all that they could, before stepping aside and waving him in.

"Sorry I'm late," he explained, walking as far as the kitchen before turning to face her. "I was having drinks with a friend and—"

Alex cut him off as she planted her lips upon his. They were still cold from being outside and tasted like cheap beer, but she didn't care. His body, too, was cold, but she would soon fix that. Sam's brain was still processing the comment about his friend, but she pushed away the name and the thought from her mind. It was background noise that she didn't need to hear right now. A second later, she felt his primal urges rise to the surface, and she found herself pushed up against the wall.

"I needed this," she sighed, moving to work the leather jacket from his shoulders.

"What kind of gentleman would I be to keep my lady waiting any longer?"

He thinks he's terribly clever, doesn't he? She pushed him away, down the hallway toward her room. "Has anyone ever told you that you talk too much?"

Chapter Three

True to his word, Greg had left a Coke in the freezer.

Unfortunately, the timing had made it so the bottle was fully frozen by the time Brennan was able to recover it. "Hey, Greg," he called out, putting the plastic bottle on the counter to thaw.

"Yo," came the dignified response from, of all places, the bathroom.

"I can see you're busy." Brennan opened the bottom right cupboard, one which wasn't casually accessible, to see which of his bottles had been pilfered by his underage nephew. If Greg throwing up in the toilet was the worst of Brennan's concerns, he could count himself a lucky man.

Oddly, though, nothing seemed out of place. Two dozen bottles of locally brewed beer were still in their unopened box. The bottles of Stoli and Belvedere, both gifts from Sam, still had a fine layer of dust coating their unbroken seals, and the Captain, usually mixed with Coke, was more or less in line with the volume he remembered.

"I thought you didn't want any of the hard stuff," Greg said from behind, stepping out of the bathroom. Brown hair threatened to sweep down over his eyes, more representative of a much-needed haircut than any particular fashion choice. He wiped his mouth with one hand, and he shivered in spite of the long-sleeved shirt and sweatpants he was wearing.

Brennan's knees popped as he rose to his feet. "Just making sure you didn't get into my stash."

"You have a stash?"

"Like you didn't already know," he said. He raised a skeptical eyebrow and looked pointedly at his nephew's sweaty brow and wobbling stance. "But you haven't touched any of these, so what's up? Are you getting sick?" He reached forward to feel Greg's forehead, but the younger man retreated.

"I'm fine," he said. "You know how it is when the temperature starts to drop. It's probably just a flu or something, and I'm the first to catch it."

False.

Brennan grunted noncommittally. His nephew was a recovering addict. Chamalla copycats had flooded the streets at half the price. Brennan was rarely home to keep watch over him. It didn't take an enormous effort to connect the dots, and he knew an easy way to confirm his suspicions.

"Sam mentioned he might be catching something, too," Brennan said, rubbing his chin. "He said his body was burning up; he could barely stand to keep his jacket on, even when we were outside." The words followed each other like ducklings in a row, the lie coalescing as easily as dew drops on a cool morning.

"I feel the same thing," Greg said. He was rubbing at his arm, same as he had been coming out of the bathroom.

"You should get out of that long-sleeved shirt, then, and put something lighter on."

Greg shook his head. "No, no, that wouldn't be a good idea." His eyes darted up; they were bloodshot, with a hint of dark bags starting to form beneath the heavy lids. "It's still cold out, you know. I don't want to catch something worse by being exposed like that."

Brennan sighed. "All right, look, here's the deal. I know you're using, and I know you're hurting from it right now." He extended a hand. "Let me help you."

Greg continued to shake, but it seemed beyond his control. He nodded jerkily and moved to sit down on the couch. Brennan sat next to him and rolled up Greg's right sleeve; the skin was clear, except for an extremely faded square-shaped scar that was only really visible because he knew where to look. When Leviathan had been active, their Chamalla patches had produced hallucinations and a strong addiction to the drug, but some other ingredients had been responsible for slowly burning away at the skin of the application zone.

Hesitantly, Brennan moved on to the other sleeve. Three-quarters of the way up, the shirt material peeled rather than rolled away from the skin, and he had to force his stomach not to rebel. The skin all around the patch was like an open sore, oozing clear pus and blood even as the patch pumped something black and toxic into Greg's system. Brennan started to lift the patch away, but Greg yelped out in pain; Brennan had to hold his arm to keep him from recoiling away entirely.

"I can't get it off!" Greg sobbed. "That's what I was trying to do in the bathroom, before you got home. This thing, it's—it's bad, real bad."

"What the hell were you thinking?" Brennan was more exasperated than angry. Clean for just over three months, somehow his nephew had fallen off the wagon, this time with an even worse concoction flowing through his veins.

"It's going to sound stupid," he mumbled, looking anywhere else but Brennan's eyes.

"You can trust me. Whatever it is, I won't get mad. I just want to help."

"It's like—" He stopped to rub at his eyes and wipe across his nose with his free hand. "I just wanted to feel it again, you know?"

"Feel what again?"

"The fever dreams," Greg said wistfully. "I felt like I could do anything, because I could see *everything*. The past, the future…it's hard to explain. Did you ever wish you had a superpower as a child?"

Brennan shook his head. If he were honest with himself, he might admit that he already *did* have a superpower. But these days, it was beginning to feel more like a curse than a blessing.

"To have that kind of sureness about something," Greg continued, "is so liberating. And I can do some good with it, too! I helped find Detective Bishop, right? You couldn't have solved it without me!"

That was exactly the problem. While Bishop had been grateful for the rescue attempt, just exactly *how* Brennan had learned of her location was still suspect. He had reported it as an anonymous tip, but he knew Sam suspected something, his outward nature notwithstanding. It seemed everyone was playing it close to the vest these days.

"So you were thinking…what? You'd get the visions again if you relapsed into patches?"

"Relapsed," Greg scoffed. "You make it sound like I did it for the fix."

"Didn't you?" Brennan asked. He gingerly lifted a bit more of the patch, exposing more afflicted skin in the process. His nephew inhaled sharply. "I wouldn't blame you if that's the case, but I need to know."

"No, Uncle Arty." To his credit, Greg looked him straight in the eye as he answered. "I only wanted to be special again, to have visions like I did before. Without that, I don't want the patches."

Truth.

Brennan grunted. "Here, hold this up," he said, passing the lifted side of the patch to Greg. He went to the kitchen and soaked a washcloth under warm water, then returned to the couch. "You said 'patches,' plural. Where did you apply the others?" he asked, pinching the raised patch between his fingers again.

Greg reached to the hem of his shirt. "Mostly on my chest and—" He cut off in a howl of pain as Brennan ripped the remainder of the patch from his arm and quickly pressed the damp cloth against the open wound. Greg swore a steady stream of expletives as Brennan went to toss the toxic patch in the trash.

"Just like ripping off a Band-Aid," he said, cleaning his hands thoroughly in the sink. His fingertips just barely started to tingle where they'd brushed the patch. "I want to get you in to see a doctor tomorrow, too, and have him look at that arm."

"Whatever."

He shut off the tap and dried his hands. "Greg, listen to me. Maybe the patches were responsible for what you saw, but maybe they weren't."

"You think people are just *born* special?"

Brennan couldn't reveal his own power. Not yet, at any rate. He had already told Greg about his past experience as a Sleeper, and his nephew had taken it surprisingly well. He could count the number of confidants privy to that secret on a single hand, and those others had all been Sleepers themselves. But the gap between being a Sleeper and being…well, something else, was still too big to bridge. Sleepers were generally accepted as boogeymen in Odols, walking the fine line between covert operatives and figures from folklore. He had been one of them, too, a long time ago. As far as Brennan knew, he was the only person who possessed a talent above and beyond a Sleeper's standard set of skills.

Until Greg, that is.

"I think you might have a gift," he said. He carefully kept excitement from creeping into his voice. "It's not unheard of, after all. They have all those shows now about superhuman strength, endurance, telepathy—"

"Yeah, but all of those people are fakes. It's scripted, everyone knows that."

"Really? The psychic boy wonder is now arguing against the existence of psychics?"

That got a grudging smile out of his nephew. "I'm not—No, I'm not saying that they don't exist, necessarily. But what are the odds, really, that *I'm* one of them?"

If it's genetic, the chances are far greater than you think. "Anything's possible," Brennan said with a shrug. "How is your arm looking?"

Greg peeked under the washcloth; his face paled a few shades. "It's, uh, not pretty."

"Do you feel *anything* from the patch?"

"Nothing good. Next to Chamalla, this stuff is shit."

"Eloquent," Brennan said dryly. "Watch that mouth of yours."

"But you curse all the time!"

"Yes. Yes I do. I also hunt down killers and spend more nights awake than not." *I also used to stalk the sleeping minds of nightmarish criminals. I was a hero—and a monster.* "How much do you really want to be like me?"

Greg swallowed hard and looked away. His nephew didn't know all of the details of his past work, but nobody on the street had anything good to say about Sleepers. If Odols was a city of legends, Sleepers were the demons who hunted in the shadows.

"I'm going to bed," Greg said. He moved quickly to the bathroom and shut the door behind him, leaving Brennan alone with his thoughts. And his phone. He felt the lure of sleep tugging on him, but he had to make a couple calls first.

First, he dialed the precinct, with an extension code to the basement. It rang eight times before he hung up. Apparently, Wally didn't believe in keeping voicemail. His apartment was less than a block away—practically across the street. But if Wally wasn't picking up, he wasn't in the office.

Probably sleeping, like a normal person, he thought, scrolling down through his contacts list.

The second number also went unanswered, but he didn't expect his doctor to be in this late at night. However, she at least believed in voicemail, and he left a message to schedule an appointment for the next morning for Greg.

He could hear the water stop flowing as Greg finished brushing his teeth; it wouldn't be long before his nephew reemerged to go to sleep on the pullout sofa bed. Brennan didn't need an awkward, pre-sleep conversation about his boogeyman past. He nearly had his bedroom door closed when Greg appeared, his face peeking out from the bathroom.

"Uncle Arty?"

"Yeah?"

"I love you," Greg said, looking slightly uncomfortable. "God, that sounds corny. But you're all I've got now, you know?"

Brennan smiled. Despite the upbringing he'd had and the dangerous road that he occasionally walked, his nephew was still a caring young man. "Love you too, kid," he said. "Get some sleep."

Chapter Four

Arthur Brennan.

Alex woke with a start. Her whole body shivered with fear, though she had no rational reason to explain it. Despite the absence of clothes, she wasn't cold; far from it, she felt far too warm from the heavy bedspread and the snoring man beside her, whose body was a living radiator. Her legs were tangled in the silk sheets, and she struggled silently against them until she could free herself from the bed.

The air was deliciously cool against her skin. She stretched with both her arms and her mind. She touched dozens of people, their minds humming as they dreamed. Sleeping was a dull activity for most, as far as Alex was concerned. Their dreams never reached anything close to exhilarating, and she wondered sometimes if she was the only person who was truly *alive*, truly aware of how precious her time was. Her father certainly didn't, but he had good reason to disregard time.

No, it wasn't the cold that had awoken her. She tried to calm herself, to make the goose bumps on her arms disappear, but whatever had disturbed her sleep was still affecting her on some level. She walked to the closet and wrapped a long white bathrobe around herself.

Every light was off, but she didn't need them to get around her apartment. Eyes wide open, she pretended that she was a mountain lion, a predator perfectly at ease with the dark. After all, what woman *didn't* secretly wish to be a cougar one day?

Alex glanced at the kitchen clock; it was just past two in the morning, and the building was absolutely dead. The white robe swished around her legs as she walked out the front door. She was in the middle of a long hallway which continued for a long while in both directions. She continued to probe, but everybody on her floor was sound asleep. Her footsteps made no noise on the padded carpeting on her way to the elevator. The doors slid open with minimal creaking, and the usual ping that sounded the elevator's arrival was subdued at night, so it would likely go unnoticed. But now which way to go?

A pressure weighed on the top of her head like an oncoming migraine. She lifted her chin toward the ceiling, and the weight shifted to her forehead. *Up it is.* Alex pushed the button for the top floor, just to be sure.

She leaned against the metal handholds as the elevator ascended. Almost immediately, the pressure on her skull doubled in intensity, and pretty soon she was white-knuckling the railing.

Arthur Brennan.

She heard the voice more clearly now, and she trembled as its familiar aura touched her mind. It was definitely the same thought that had woken her, though she had no idea what it meant. More so, though, she was disturbed by the person the thought was originating from.

As a young girl, she had accepted that every thought carries emotions, and every emotion radiates a color of some kind. Pleasant thoughts, ones of compassion and love, were royal blue. Violet or purple often accompanied envious thoughts, which were almost always tinged with a little greedy green as well.

The thought that carried that name, Arthur Brennan, was coated with deep, blood red dripping in black malice.

It was utterly fascinating. *Something new*, she thought. The residents of Harcour Towers had always been greedy and self-absorbed, and those attributes rarely amounted to much thinking. It took someone with a real degree of passion and fury, not to mention a heaping amount of brainpower, for Alex to hear them from so far away.

Through trial and error, she determined that the voice was coming from the sixteenth floor. She didn't dare leave the elevator, not now at least. The last thing she needed was to confront a nigh-homicidal maniac with attachment issues. There was little variation in the brainwave activity; whoever it was, they were single-mindedly *obsessed* with Arthur Brennan.

"Whoever the hell that is," she muttered, jabbing the door closure button repeatedly. The psychic pressure was too much, and it was getting to her. The boring humdrum background noise of a thousand plebeians thinking common thoughts? No problem. But this madness was something else, something she couldn't handle right now with little sleep and no coffee.

If Sam stirred at the noise made by her return to the apartment, Alex never saw it; he was still sound asleep when she crawled back under the covers and curled up against his comforting warmth. With a dozen floors between her and the belligerent thought, her mind was much quieter, and she embraced sleep as tightly as a familiar lover.

ϕ ϕ ϕ

"Rise and shine, sleepyhead," said Sam, a subjective millisecond later, as he tore open the wall-length curtains.

There he goes again, she thought, *thinking he's clever*. Blinded by the sudden light, she tracked his thoughts.

Sensory thoughts, like a lot of other things, went completely unnoticed by normal people. The brain processed too much information in any given day to assign much importance to one sense, so most people took it for granted that they had an audiovisual suite come standard with their bodies. But each one of those impulses from the eyes, every decibel picked up by the ears, even the slightest sense of touch on the hairs of their hands, was translated into a thought the brain could understand. Background noise. And what they could see, Alex could see.

In a large enough group, she could see and hear everything. For all intents and purposes, she could *be* everywhere.

Blind and startled, she borrowed on his thoughts. She saw herself on the bed, through his eyes, and reversed the angle in her head. She flung a pillow across the room that caught Sam flatly across the face. She heard his surprise even as she primed and launched a follow-up strike. They didn't do any harm to him, but it was the thought that counted. She thrashed her way out from under the covers and promptly pulled the curtains together again.

"Glad to see you're in a good mood today," he said. Even after being hit with pillows lightly coated in drool, he had a grin on his face, one that was too infectious to resist for long.

"I'm—" The memory of several hours ago came to the fore. A nighttime walk prompted by an angry voice cursing the name of a stranger. She filed it away for later. "I'm fantastic, actually," Alex said, adopting a smile of her own. "But no morning before coffee."

"Morning comes whether you like it or not." He was wearing only a pair of boxers as he embraced her. His body wasn't as warm as it had seemed under the covers, but she still indulged him in a brief hug.

"But it stays out there," she said, gesturing toward the window, "unless you let it in. No morning before coffee," she repeated.

Sam sighed. "I can take a hint. I'll get us a couple cups from the lobby—" Alex made a face at that suggestion. "—I mean, from anywhere *but* the lobby. Who would even suggest lobby coffee? An idiot, that's who."

"I knew you'd understand," Alex said. She patted him lightly on the cheek and moved to the closet as

Sam started pulling on yesterday's clothes. "There's a coffeehouse I know that uses the best imported beans you've ever tasted."

"And where is that, exactly?"

"Oh, just two blocks that way," she said, gesturing vaguely toward the window.

"Okay, great, we can go there on the way to the shuttle station."

"I'm actually feeling a little gross from last night and thought I'd take a shower. You don't mind buying them and bringing them back here, do you?"

Sam stared incredulously at her with his coppery eyes. She knew what he was thinking, and her mouth curled slightly in anticipation. "You want me to walk two blocks to fetch you a cup of coffee?" he asked.

"If you wouldn't mind," she said, beaming back at him. She clasped her hands and just barely pouted with her lower lip, making the perfect image of a desperate girl pleading for a small favor. That, and she was still fantastically naked. "I'll make it up to you, I promise." She had to stop herself from grinning as his thoughts raced to what that promise could hold.

He ran a hand through his short, curly hair. "All right, I can do that," he relented. He grabbed his jacket and pecked Alex on the cheek as he headed out of the room. "Be back before you know it," he called. The door closed loudly behind him.

Alex strolled casually into the bathroom and turned on the shower. She waited until the steam started to fog up the mirror before stepping into the spray of hot water.

"Ohhh yes," she moaned. The water cascaded onto her back and flowed in rivulets down her legs as she combed her fingers through her hair. Her skin was turning red from the heat, which someone weaker might have described as scalding, but she didn't mind. Sex was good on any day of the week, but the shower afterward? It was heavenly.

Five minutes into the shower, she heard her phone go off in the other room. She let it ring out, content to remain in soapy bliss. Anyone who was calling this early in the morning—actually, she didn't know what time it was, but anyone who called at *any* time in the morning was generally nobody she wanted to talk to. Besides, no morning before coffee. She had to keep to her own rule.

The phone rang for a second time, though, and the list of people who had her number was fairly short. Add persistence at an annoying time of day and Alex felt certain she knew who was calling, as well as the fact that she would do well to answer.

She turned off the water and dried herself as quickly as she could. Her feet still made marks of condensation on the floor as she retrieved her phone from the bedroom. She dialed back, and a man picked up on the first ring.

"Alexis," he said without preamble. "I thought you were coming over for breakfast today."

"Yeah, I still am. Why? What time is it?" she asked even as she checked the clock. Quarter past eleven. "Shit, Dad, I must have overslept."

"Another one of your men?" he asked. It didn't sound like a question, and she didn't dignify it with a response. "It's too late now, breakfast is over."

"I can still make it for lunch." Her father didn't answer, which she took as an invitation to continue. "I'll be there in half an hour. How does that sound?"

"Great," he said, "see you in twenty."

Alex sighed as her father hung up. Brüding family meals were battlefields, and every conversation was a potential landmine. The best she could do was survive. But that also meant that morning was coming before coffee, something that displeased her greatly. She dialed Sam's number.

"Hey," he answered. "Did you know that café was actually five blocks—?"

"Yeah, sorry. About that—I'm actually going to need a rain check on that. My dad just called and I'm late for lunch."

"Oh, okay. Well I already paid for the coffee…" he said, his voice trailing off.

"Lucky you," Alex said. She shrugged on a dress shirt as she nestled the phone between her ear and shoulder. "Looks like you get double caffeinated today."

"You're seriously not going to join me?" It didn't take a mind-reader to hear his disappointment.

"I really can't, babe. Dad's a hard case."

"All right, I get it. Go," he said, "have family time."

"Thanks, I knew you'd understand." She bit her lip as she slipped on a pair of low-heeled shoes. "And I can still make good on my promise tonight," she said softly, letting that statement make its way to the more primitive parts of Sam's brain.

"I'll call you tonight when I'm free." The excitement in his voice was palpable.

"Ciao, lover boy."

Chapter Five

The Odols Police Department was an ugly, squat building of gray stone and red brick.

It was located less than a hundred steps from Brennan's apartment. Its proximity was a double-edged sword. It was close enough that severe weather could largely be ignored, as he'd only be exposed to it for a few seconds. However, by the same token, the city could be shut down and he would still be expected to walk to work.

Today, though, the weather was unseasonably warm, one last hurrah of summer before the city was plunged into half a year of heavy snow and harsh winds. Brennan's phone buzzed just as he pushed his way through the glass double-door entrance.

"Detective Brennan, just returning all your missed calls. What's up?" It was Wally, the resident pathologist for OPD.

"I'm walking into the station now," Brennan said. "I thought I'd drop by and get another once-over of the body before you give her over to the family."

"You have some kind of fetish I should be warned about? This is the fifth time in three days that you've visited her."

"Shut it. I just need to catch this guy, and she's our best lead at the moment. Hey, I'm heading down the stairs, I'll see you in a few."

He ended the call. The only staircase which led to the basement was located in the back of the building, close to an emergency exit that opened into an alleyway. The hallway was bleached white, like the rest of the building, and framed photos of past police chiefs at formal functions hung from the walls. He turned the corner and stepped quickly down the flight of stairs, the beats of his feet on metal echoing hollowly in the empty chamber.

The pathologist was there to meet him at the bottom. At five-and-a-quarter feet tall, he was not an imposing figure. His dark head was cleanly shaven, except for a thin stripe of hair that ran down the middle to the nape of his neck. He wore a thermal shirt and khakis, and small studs pierced the lobes of his ears.

"Hey, Detective," he said, offering his hand. The long sleeve of his shirt rode up, and a hint of black ink was visible on the skin beneath.

"Wally," Brennan said enthusiastically. "I didn't know you had tattoos!"

"Just a few."

"It's surprising to see you without your lab coat on."

"I'm a real person outside the morgue? Huh. This is a startling revelation." Wally looped a clean white apron around his neck and cinched it at the waist. "Besides, that's only for practical purposes, not a fashion statement. Sanitation, for one thing." He handed an identical apron to the detective. "Plus, it's colder than Bishop down here," he added with a grin.

Brennan grunted. His old partner had been given a commendation for excellent fieldwork and bravery in the line of duty following the botched rescue attempt at the hospital. Brennan and Sam had attempted to save her from a violent drug lord and had found themselves in need of rescuing. Shortly thereafter, a promotion had lifted her from detective to lieutenant, and she was now effectively in charge of the homicide division. His boss. He hadn't realized that he wasn't the only one feeling the distance that her promotion created.

"Yeah, well, I'm sure she has a lot on her plate," he said, pulling on a pair of neoprene gloves. "Having to handle these cases as her first assignment on the job *can't* be good for her morale."

"Let's make this quick," Wally suggested. "The funeral home arranged to pick up the body at noon, so you have about fifteen minutes."

The morgue was a medium-sized, rectangular room that took up a third of the station's basement. Wally hadn't been lying when he said it was cold down there. Even without the air conditioning on, it was easily ten degrees cooler than the lobby upstairs. Square hatches with empty metal slabs inside lined one wall; against another wall was a cleaning station. Three raised tables stood in the center of the room, and one of them was occupied.

"Kelsi Woodill," Wally said. "Twenty-one years old, nursing student at Odols University. She was last seen leaving from a party on campus, and her body was discovered the next morning by the roommate, Sara Portoso." Wally sounded bored as he spoke, and he probably was; he'd said all of this before, and it was only Brennan's commitment to ritual that made him recite it now. He circled the table. "Lividity puts the time of death somewhere between midnight and two o'clock. Midnight going into Saturday, just like the others."

"So she was surrounded by other people all night?"

"If it was a good party, sure."

"Did her roommate hear or see anything suspicious?"

"What do I look like, a witness?" He gestured to the table. "All I know is what the body tells me while it's on the slab. No signs of sexual assault or other trauma. Single fatal stab wound to the back. It severed the spinal column and she bled out quickly; with sensation to her lower half cut off, I doubt she felt anything. It's a peaceful way to go, if you think about it. No suffering."

Kelsi Woodill's hair hung limply from her pale scalp. She had a gymnast's build, short but powerful, and she would have been attractive in life. Less than a year and she would have been out in the working world, a full adult. Whatever Wally might suggest, she had met a violent end, and she'd been robbed of her life.

"But why was she killed?" Brennan asked.

Wally shrugged. "Why were any of them killed? It seems that our killer has nothing in common with any of the victims. The only real link between any of them is the cause of death."

Brennan rubbed at his chin. "I'm going to have to speak with her roommate."

"I didn't think you were working this case."

"Not officially, no," he said. "But Kelsi Woodill is our fifth victim, and we are no closer to finding the killer than we were three months ago. Even if Bishop doesn't realize it, we kind of need all hands on deck with this one."

"Fine, all right. I'll give you Sara Portoso's contact information, but I need something from you as well."

"What is it?"

"A favor," he said. He stared up at Brennan with intense, dark eyes. "I don't know what I could need, or when, but you'll owe me one."

Brennan appraised the man with new eyes. "Absolutely. A favor for a friend, I can do that."

Wally smiled, but still hesitated. "Lieutenant Bishop was very clear in keeping you away from these murders...I could lose my job."

"This won't get back to the lieutenant," Brennan promised solemnly. "It'll stay between you and me."

The pathologist breathed out a sigh of relief. "Okay, good," he said. "Come with me."

They tossed the gloves as they left the room, and Brennan was grateful to be away from the too-pale corpse of the young woman. It was still cool in the hall, but not nearly as cold as in the morgue. He followed Wally down the hallway until he ducked through a door on the left.

"My office," Wally explained. It was a small room, less than two cubicles' worth of space pushed together, and the antiseptic smell of the morgue wafted in the air. Wally retrieved a manila folder from his desk and thumbed quickly through the pages within. "Ah, here it is," he declared, pulling out a single sheet. It was the incident report that had been filed with the discovery of Kelsi Woodill's body. In the witness section, under her name and address, was Sara Portoso's phone number. Brennan took a few seconds to add it to his own contact list, then handed the sheet back to Wally, who replaced it and the folder back on the desk.

"There," Wally said, sighing again. "It's like you were never even here."

Brennan raised an eyebrow. "I wasn't. You were down here alone, waiting for the funeral director to arrive."

Wally opened and closed his mouth. "Exactly."

"You're doing the right thing," Brennan assured him. "When this is all over, we can grab a drink and discuss that favor."

Chapter Six

IT WAS JUST after noon when Alex's taxi arrived outside *Chez Brüding*.

She shoved several bills at the driver and got out, smoothing out any phantom wrinkles in her clothes as she approached the family house. Perched on a grassy knoll, the wide veranda gave an impressive view of Odols and the surrounding countryside. She could just see the peaks of the mountains to the south piercing through the clouds. The house itself was a remnant of the early-century housing bubble, and her father had bought it at just the opportune time.

This house, and also the next closest dozen houses. Once those had been demolished, the Brüdings were left with a rather expansive yard.

She knocked loudly and quickly checked her clothes one more time as she waited. The butler, a servant by the name of Kern, opened the door a moment later. He was an elderly man who rarely spoke, and he was silent even as he ushered her to the dining room. His one good eye twinkled with kindness as she thanked him and took a seat at the table.

It was a long table in an even longer room, and it was set for a gathering of more than a dozen people, despite the fact that her parents had lived here alone for many years. Portraits hung from the walls, including several photos of Alex from her teenage years. Everything was as it had been since her childhood; she'd never even changed her room since college, despite her increasingly more frequent trips back home.

"You're here," came a voice, amplified by the room's natural acoustics. James Brüding, the dark-haired, fair-skinned patriarch of the family, emerged from the warmly lit library that served as his study. He was tall enough to play basketball and moved with a grace that was uncommon for his apparent age, and very uncommon for his true age.

"I'm glad to see you," he said, embracing his daughter. His voice was warmer now than it had been on the phone, and she let herself fold into his arms. "Sorry for how I was on the phone earlier, it was a rough morning."

"It's fine, Dad," she murmured. "I forgive you."

A few seconds later, he broke the hug and held her at arm's length. "Your hair," he said. "You've done something to it."

Alex grinned. "More like I *haven't* done something to it. I decided to forgo the dye this time."

It looks nice, James thought, smiling down at her. He knew about her power as surely as she knew about his; it made for interesting conversations, her talking and him thinking.

"Thank you," she said. "I'm still considering a change, but we'll see."

Shall we eat?

Alex nodded, and she took a seat next to her father at one end of the table. Kern, ever silent, carried out two trays laden with fruit slices and sandwich wedges and set them down before retreating to the kitchen. A moment later, he returned with a silver carafe. Ice clinked as Kern poured a glass of spring water for each of them.

James lifted his glass, and Alex mirrored him. "To family," he toasted.

"To family." Their glasses connected with a chime that was swallowed quickly in the silence of the grand room. Alex nibbled on one half of a sandwich and watched herself through her father's eyes. She looked good; beautiful, even, with the sunlight silhouetting her. There were lines in her face, though, that were unfamiliar and unwanted. Not for the first time, she envied her father's power. She was grateful that he couldn't hear *her* thoughts at that moment. James Brüding had not raised his daughter to be weak, and jealousy made all men—and women—weak.

"What's on your mind?" her father asked aloud.

Alex stopped channeling his thoughts and looked with her own eyes. He was watching her closely. Her father had always had an intense curiosity about him, an acute awareness of and interest in everything around him. He could tell something was bothering her without being psychic.

"It's this guy I'm seeing," she said.

"Is he giving you a hard time?"

She shook her head. "No, nothing like that. He's actually really sweet. We met a few weeks ago, and he has been nothing but a gentleman to me. But in spite of all that…there's no connection. I don't feel anything for him."

"You just met him," he said. "Give it time to develop."

Alex frowned. "I've *given* it time," she groaned. "How long does it take for humans to develop feelings for each other?"

James glanced around the room, but it seemed that Kern had made himself scarce. Alex's father looked at her steadily, and she could sense him carefully arranging and protecting his thoughts. "I can't promise that it will ever happen," he said. "When your mother and I first met, we butted heads all the time. There wasn't a single thing we could agree on. One day, something just clicked, and everything fell into place."

"Yes, but you two are *normal*!" Alex protested. She sat back in her chair with her arms crossed. She didn't meet his eyes when she spoke. "What happens if I never know love? What kind of person doesn't *love*?"

I love you, her father replied. *I've always known exactly the kind of person you are, and I know the woman you'll grow into. And we love you.*

We, she thought. He'd said "we." It was as good a subject as any, just so long as the focus wasn't on herself. "How is she?" Alex asked.

James's eyes crinkled slightly, but otherwise he showed no reaction to the change in conversation. "Your mother is doing fine. She has good days and bad days," he said, reaching for a sandwich wedge. He briefly held it in his hands, considering it, before tearing it roughly down the middle. "Today is a bad day."

"Can I see her?"

Her father hemmed and hawed momentarily. "I don't think that would be such a good idea. She's been in a lot of pain recently, and the doctor just increased the dosage of her medication."

"She's going to get better, though, right? It comes and goes."

"We can always hope." It didn't sound like her father was holding on to much hope. "Meanwhile, I have a new drug under development that shows promise. Trial testing starts in a month, and if those results are favorable, we should be able to go ahead with human test subjects by year's end."

Alex sipped quietly at her drink. She and her father both knew that her mother wouldn't survive to see Christmas at the rate she was going. "Is there any way to accelerate the process?"

"Not legally," he said simply.

There was no sense in hiding it; everyone in the market was culpable of *some* wrongdoing, and Alex would have known about it regardless. She reconciled it with the fact that he was producing medicine that saved people. If that meant going through backchannels to bypass red tape, she fully supported him.

"When we were still a separate entity," he continued, "it would have just been a matter of depositing the right amount into the right people's bank accounts." His expression soured, and he bit violently into the other half of his sandwich. "Now that we're merged with SymbioTech, though…No, there's too much oversight, too much risk involved."

"So you work for them now?"

"They would never phrase it that way. Significant downsizing from my own company, and all of their executives are now *our* executives."

"If it's such a raw deal, why did you agree to sell to them?"

James sighed. "If it were up to me, we wouldn't have. But the board of trustees decides what's best for the company, and with the direction the market was moving, SymbioTech seemed the way to go. We couldn't beat them, so we joined them."

"At least you live to fight another day," Alex said, giving a false smile. "And now you get to use *their* resources to get what you want."

Her father smirked. "That is one over-simplified, naively optimistic way of looking at it." *Thank you.* She could feel the royal blue feel-good emotions that accompanied the thought, and she felt truly happy for the first time all day.

"Speaking of work," she prompted.

"I've been working out of the home office today," he said, gesturing to the library.

"Ah, I see."

"But if you need to go for some reason, by all means, don't let me keep you."

Alex frowned as he said that. She thought the monthly visits had been enough, but the emotions carried in her father's words indicated that he missed her far more than he let on. *Whenever I leave, he's only left with* her.

"I'm sorry, Dad," she said. "Something came up recently that I really do need to attend to."

James nodded. "Of course, I understand. I do hope you get to visit us again soon." He leaned in to kiss her on both cheeks, and then brought her in for another hug.

"I'll be back as soon as I can," she promised.

I love you.

"Love you too, Dad." Alex slowly disengaged from her father and started walking toward the front door. As she left, James returned to his study and closed its two doors behind him. The family photos stared down at Alex as she made her way to the foyer. At some point, Kern had appeared just a step ahead of her, and he accompanied her the rest of the way.

"I took the liberty of calling a taxi for you," Kern informed her.

She looked out the door to where a gray-and-yellow car waited in the roundabout driveway, its engine purring while it idled. "Kern," she said, suddenly rounding on him. "Do you think you could tell the driver to wait a few more minutes? There's somebody I forgot to visit."

Kern's one good eye twinkled approvingly as he nodded. "Of course, Miss Alexis."

"Just Alex," she corrected. Alex left him and proceeded down one of the first-floor hallways. The hardwood floor had been worn down over the years by many passing feet. She took care to avoid the floorboards that creaked, keeping mostly up against the wall. She flinched as one board groaned loudly in protest beneath her foot; she could have sworn it was one of the more solid ones when she was growing up. Her father didn't suddenly appear, and she tiptoed the rest of the way to the solid oak door of her mother's bedroom. She knocked softly on the door and, hearing no reply, quietly let herself in.

When her mother was gripped with illness, her father made all the necessary arrangements for her to live on the ground floor of their home. An old parlor room, once home to poker chips and billiard tables, had been retrofitted into her new chambers, complete with an easily accessible personal bathroom. The floor-to-ceiling windows looked out over the city to the south and green pastures to the west, and they were tinted at such an angle that the setting sun would not disturb her sleep.

Stephanie Brüding was a shadow of her former self. She lay prostrate in her bed, her head propped up by a multitude of pillows. Her face was blank and expressionless, and her eyes stared vacantly toward the windows. If she heard Alex enter the room, she gave no indication of it.

"Mom?" Alex called. No response. She walked closer to the bed and raised her voice. "Mom, it's me, Alex."

A flicker of movement, and then Stephanie's head turned toward her daughter. Alex felt a pang in her chest. There was no recognition in those eyes, only a mild interest in the new person in the room.

"It's Alex," she repeated, moving to sit on the edge of the bed. From the doorway, she could have pretended that her mother was the same as she'd remembered from her childhood. Up close, she could see the effects of the disease on her mother's body. She had lost a lot of weight, an unhealthy amount, and her cheekbones and jaw stood out prominently. Her eyes were sunken and watery, and her skin had aged prematurely. Gray was now the dominant color of what was left of her hair.

Alex swallowed her misgivings and reached out to one of Stephanie's gnarled, bony hands. It was clammy, but she smiled into her mother's eyes. "It's so nice to see you," she said, her lie dripping with warmth. She wanted to see her, but never like this. It was the old Stephanie that she wished were here right now.

Stephanie's face broke out into a smile. "Oh, you too, sweetie," she said. "Yes, it's very nice to see you."

Alex seriously doubted that her mother knew who she was anymore, but she nodded. "It's a beautiful day outside. Would you like to see it?"

Her mother fussed with her blanket. "Oh, I don't know. I'm *so* tired today, perhaps another time."

"Okay," Alex said, patting her hand. She didn't know what else to do, so she just rubbed the leathery skin of her mother's hand as they stared outside. Her taxi was waiting for her, but she knew that these moments were limited; a few months from now, her father would be a widower.

"Now that is love," said a voice from the doorway. She looked up, startled, only to see Kern standing in the doorway. He had a stupid grin on his face, one that somehow made him seem younger and older at the same time.

Kern, you sly dog, she thought. *So you* did *hear Father at lunch.* He was wrong, though. Alex wasn't doing this out of love for her mother, only pity and a sense of obligation. She returned his smile, though, since that was what he was expecting, and then turned back to her mother. "Mom," she said, leaning in toward that withered face. "Kern is going to keep you company now."

Her head bobbed, possibly in agreement. Alex didn't dare make contact with her mother's mind.

"Thank you," Alex said to Kern. She stood and offered her mother one last smile, but Stephanie's attention was elsewhere. She followed her gaze, which landed somewhere on the wall *between* two windows. "I'll be back when I can," she murmured.

"Your company is always a pleasure," Kern said.

I bet, she thought, *with my mother like that.* Even her small amount of time with the woman had been unnerving, and Alex made her way back to the foyer, completely disregarding the creaking of the floorboards beneath her hastened steps.

She had bigger things to worry about, though. There was still the matter of the mysterious tenant and his vendetta against whoever Arthur Brennan was. With that much psychic energy being thrown around, Alex knew she wouldn't sleep well until the issue was resolved. Even a dozen floors away, she could hear his fury.

But what exactly am I going to do? As she climbed into the taxi, the answer wasn't abundantly clear. She was the furthest a person could be from a sympathetic grief counselor, and she surely wasn't about to up and move from *her* apartment building. A mounting migraine threatened to rear its ugly head as she felt the stress building up. She swore inwardly as the cab pulled away from the house.

And she still hadn't had any coffee.

Chapter Seven

The address Wally had given for Sara Portoso's apartment led to a building that was significantly nicer than the one Brennan lived in now.

It was a hulking beast of a complex half a dozen stories tall that took up the size of half a city block. Brick walls inlaid with columns of concrete, with steel-and-concrete balconies for every apartment that looked out on the street below. The lobby, basically a waiting room for the elevators, was visible through the glass of the windows and front door. Equally visible was the security camera that stared back at him.

He tried the handle to the door, but it refused to budge. An electronic scanner of some kind was wired to the door; only tenants with swipe cards would be able to enter the building. As far as campus living went, Kelsi Woodill had been living in a fortress. Her fourth-floor room would have been all but inaccessible to a stranger. Her body had been discovered inside the apartment in her very room, so presumably she had returned home safely. If someone had accompanied her, the security camera would have seen, and the police would have had a suspect.

Brennan looked at the camera again. Ordinarily, he would have held his silver shield up to the glass and had whoever was watching buzz him in. He wasn't here in any official capacity, though; Bishop had specifically stonewalled him from getting involved in the case. He wasn't sure why. But if it somehow got back to her that he was here, he didn't know what kind of trouble she would stir.

"You're tying my hands here, Bishop," he growled.

"Excuse me?"

Brennan turned and saw a young man with a confused look on his face. He was supporting a large brown bag of groceries in one arm and held a small white card in the other, no thicker than a quarter. "Sorry," Brennan said, "just talking to myself."

The young man huffed and shifted the bag's weight. "I just need to get through," he said. Brennan stepped back and let the college kid swipe the key card.

"Here, let me get that for you," Brennan offered, opening the door.

The kid held the bag in both hands and nodded his thanks.

Piggybacking, Brennan thought. *Is this how the killer got in?* A flash caught his eye; a sliver of light had glinted off the glossy black casing of the security camera. *No, he would have still been seen entering the building.* Grocery-boy pressed the button for the elevator, but Brennan ignored him and took to the staircase on the left.

During his years as a Sleeper, Brennan had learned to put up with two types of pain: psychic trauma and physical debilitation. When he'd lost his wife to the same Sleepers he'd once served with, he had been exposed to emotional pain of the highest magnitude. Now, as his body was starting to show the wear and tear of his years, he put himself through a new kind of pain that kicked his ass every day: cardio.

Nothing made the body weak faster than a desk job and donuts, and that was exactly what Brennan had been subjecting himself to for the past few years. The past three months of running were now paying dividends as he climbed four flights of stairs without breathing hard at the top.

He emerged from the stairwell into a fairly short hallway. Ensconced lights hung from the walls and the tile floor had recently been cleaned. No cameras in the hall, which was unfortunate; it might have given them a view of the killer. There were only four rooms in view before the hall turned sharply to the left, but Brennan didn't need to look far; Kelsi Woodill had died behind the door closest to the stairs.

He walked up to apartment 402 and knocked on the door. A moment later, a young woman answered. She was brunette, relatively short, and looked more mature than her years. She wore a sweatshirt that was a few sizes too large, though it still curved amply over her chest.

"Can I help you?" she asked.

"Sara Portoso?"

"Yes?"

He showed her his shield. "Detective Brennan. I'm with Odols Homicide, do you mind if I come in?"

"Of course." Sara gulped. "I mean, no, I don't mind," she said, standing aside to let him in. "I already spoke to the other detectives, I told them everything I know."

"I understand. I'm just following up, making sure we didn't miss anything." He looked around the apartment as he spoke. Unlike one dead pharmacist he once knew, everything they owned seemed average, ordinary, perfectly within a college student's budget. "You didn't happen to notice anything missing from the apartment, did you?"

Sara shook her head. "No, nothing of mine is missing. I don't know exactly what all Kelsi had—" She choked back a sob when she said her roommate's name. "I'm pretty sure everything is here, though."

Brennan placed a comforting hand on her shoulder. "You didn't hear or see anything strange on Friday night?"

"I'm not much of a partier," she said. "I was already in bed and asleep by the time she came home. I knocked on her door in the morning to wake her up, since we were supposed to study for midterms together. She didn't respond, so I opened the door and...found her." Sara sniffled and wiped at her eyes. "Oh God...there was so much blood," she said in a horrified whisper.

That story was consistent with what Wally had told him at the station. The killer had been swift and silent, so effectively so that Sara couldn't hear the murder happening through the thin wall that separated their rooms.

"Do you mind if I take a look around her room?" Brennan asked. Sara didn't say anything, but she waved a hand toward the other bedroom. It had two yellow strips of "Do Not Cross" police tape across the door, and a question suddenly occurred to him. "Are you still *living* here?"

Sara sniffled again and raised one dark eyebrow at him. "Of course not. I came by to pick up a few things; the school is paying for a hotel room until everything is moved out of her room and the carpet is replaced." She wrapped her arms around herself as if she were cold. "Even still, I think I'm going to find a new place. It doesn't feel right to stay here after what happened."

Brennan nodded absently. He was more amazed that he happened to intercept Sara at the right time; it had completely slipped his mind that she might not have been here at all, in which case the trip would have been for nothing.

He made his way to Kelsi's room and opened the door. The room smelled like a crisp autumn breeze, sharply at odds with the metallic scent of blood that he had expected. A wooden frame was all that was left of Kelsi's bed; the comforter, pillows, sheets, and even the mattress had all been soaked through with blood. A dark red, almost brown stain marred the carpet directly beneath and next to the bed.

That's Kelsi's lifeblood, Brennan thought. *All that's left of it, dried to practically nothing.*

There was a small jewelry box on a dresser. Inside, he found a dozen different pairs of earrings and several matching bracelets. Some of the pieces were fitted with valuable gemstones, and one even had a few diamonds. *Not the sort of thing you'd leave behind during a burglary,* Brennan thought.

Nothing else in the room was speaking to him. Whatever had caused her murder, money apparently wasn't a motive for the killer. Wally had disqualified sexual assault as a motive, too, during his autopsy.

Brennan closed the door behind him and rejoined Sara in the modest living room. As he passed the kitchen, he glanced out the sliding glass door that led to the balcony. It looked like Sara had collected herself, though her eyes were still slightly rimmed with red. "Why don't we get some fresh air?" Brennan suggested, tilting his head toward the balcony.

She nodded and led the way, and the chilly air made her shiver as they stepped outside. Wordlessly, Brennan shrugged out of his jacket and draped it over her sweatshirt. Sara mumbled her thanks. Brennan inhaled deeply, and he heard her copy him as she took in a brisk breath. *Good*, he thought. The air would do her good.

Brennan took the opportunity to look around, particularly straight down toward the street four stories below. The balcony looked out over an alleyway; at night, it would be empty of everything except dumpsters and telephone poles. It was a long way down—or a long way *up*. There were balconies all the way down, and it wouldn't take much more than a modest length of rope to climb up to the next level. But to climb four floors, murder someone, and then scale back down the building, all without being detected? The strength and dexterity they'd need would be phenomenal.

A few minutes passed before Brennan realized the silence had turned awkward. Sara glanced anxiously at him before sliding the heavy jacket from her shoulders. "Thanks again," she said. "I should really be getting the rest of my stuff."

"Of course," Brennan said. They started walking toward the front door. "Is there anything I can help you carry downstairs?"

"Oh, no, it's fine. I've got it."

"You've been very helpful, Sara. I'm sorry for your loss."

She sniffled, and Brennan feared the tears might start flowing again. But she simply gave him a small smile and closed the door behind him. Brennan contemplated the elevator at the end of the hall. *That way be quitters,* he thought.

He sighed, then turned and took the stairs.

Chapter Eight

ALEX ARRIVED BACK at her apartment just as the sun was beginning to set.

It would have been sooner, but she'd had an essential stop to make. She took a heavenly sip from her cup of java and sighed in bliss. Coffee was just the thing she needed after visiting her mother. She paid the taxi driver and stared up at her apartment complex. A behemoth of a building, it held its ground in the very center of Odols. And somewhere far above, there was a strange man with one serious grudge.

And if I don't make him stop, I'm never going to get any sleep.

She felt a buzz in the air the moment she stepped into the building. Something, or someone, was different than usual. She searched intangibly with her mind, touching upon the thoughts of everyone in the lobby.

If I work through the night, I can get the project done by—

—wonder if the pool is open—

—isn't my job to watch a bunch of spoiled—

—I can sense you, you know.

Alex was startled back into herself, and she quickly walled away all of the others. Still, though, she felt the buzzing sensation as she walked stiffly to the elevator. *What was that?* Nobody had ever been aware of her psychic presence before, not even a whiff. Now, somebody was here that knew about her? *Impossible.*

She kept her guard up even as the doors closed, leaving her alone in the rising metal box. A deep breath, and she started to mull it over. Another person with powers? It made sense, actually. Her father was ever-young, or as close as could be, and she was a mind-reader. She would be ignorant to believe that she and her father were unique in their gifts. Surely there were others.

The thought chilled her. Ghost stories from her childhood came unbidden to her mind. Sleepers, they were called. They were monsters that invaded the dreams of naughty children. It was a tale that mothers made up to scare their kids into behaving. But what if it wasn't?

Were these Sleepers just other gifted people? Could so many have the same power? Her father was the closest relation she had, yet their gifts were nothing alike.

More importantly, Alex wondered who had sensed her in the lobby. It was entirely possible that she had wandered right past the man she was looking for, the angry tenant from the sixteenth floor. If that was the case, he was very psychically powerful *and* held a death wish for someone, a volatile combination.

The elevator dinged loudly and opened onto her floor. Alex walked quickly down the hall and fumbled with her key while opening the door to her apartment. *It's the coffee making me jittery,* she assured herself.

Once she was inside, however, she felt another pressure on her mind.

Arthur Brennan.

It was the same kind of red sensation she had felt in the dead of night, a strong psychic presence coming from above her. She hadn't felt it in the lobby, though, which made her think it was the angry tenant.

But if he's still upstairs, she thought, *then who did I encounter in the lobby?*

"Oh shit," she swore to the empty apartment. "There are two of them." One roaring red presence of violence and one buzzing mind of polite curiosity. "In fact, if I didn't know any better, I'd say lobby-guy was bemused."

Alex shook her head and opened a cabinet, pulling down a bottle from the top shelf. She helped herself to a generous glass of a sweet red wine. She lifted the glass to her lips and paused. "Talking to myself," she said into her wine. "First sign of insanity. I'll drink to that." She toasted an imaginary guest, stared at the open space with heavy eyes, and then gulped down half the glass in one go.

Her mother had gone crazy. Little things at first, small signs of forgetfulness, but it had gradually evolved to where she no longer recognized faces or places. "I wonder if she was like me, once," Alex said bitterly. She gently swirled the wine before taking another sip. The alcohol did its work over the next couple minutes as she finished her glass and poured another.

Getting drunk just as she was on the verge of being discovered had not been her plan, but she slowly realized that she wouldn't be able to concentrate on anything, not even sleep, while her mind was active with the thoughts of the enraged man. Thus reasoned, she drank a good amount of the second glass.

"And who the hell is Arthur Brennan?"

Her curtains didn't answer.

She knew it wasn't a good idea, but the wine had put her in a good mood, and Alex pulled out her phone. Her thumb swiped down through her list of contacts until she reached the S category: Sam was the first in the grouping. He picked up on the third ring.

"Hey, what's up?"

He didn't address her by name. Even with her thoughts muddled, Alex knew he was with somebody. "I'm here by myself and wondering what you're doing," she replied. Her words sounded thick, but she preferred to think they came off as sultry over the phone. She heard him inhale sharply.

"Ah, really not the best time," he said.

Alex heard typing in the background. She also knew that Sam was not a one-woman kind of guy. "Are you on a dating site right now?" she asked, feigning anger.

"Are you drunk right now?"

"Hey, who's accusing who?" There was a pregnant pause. "Whom. Who's accusing whom?"

Sam chuckled into the receiver. "I wouldn't have corrected you on that, I have no idea how those are used. But I guess that answers my question."

"Can I expect you later tonight?"

"Might need a rain check on that one."

Alex had no feelings for the man, but she still found herself disappointed. The wine was setting her on fire in other ways, and she hadn't expected to be turned down.

"Fine," she said. "But be warned, I might rain check your rain check."

"Life is fraught with risks," Sam said, and the call ended.

She looked at her phone for a full minute, and when he didn't call back she tossed it onto the leather sofa. "Screw him," she muttered before she started giggling to herself. "That's what I was *trying* to do."

Arthur Brennan.

"Yeah, yeah, I hear you," she said, raising her glass to the ceiling. She brought it to her lips and finished it off, and the voice died down to a whisper. She couldn't stop the thoughts from coming, but she could drown them as they arrived. The clock told her it was far too early to sleep, but the alcohol coursing through her system said otherwise. Napping sounded like an excellent idea.

As she flopped down onto her bed, Alex knew instantly that she'd made the right call.

Chapter Nine

"Who was that?" Brennan asked.

Sam shut off his phone and set it on the desk. "Nobody with anything urgent."

Truth.

They were back at Brennan's apartment, presumably just hanging out again. In truth, Brennan had asked Sam to watch over Greg after his doctor's appointment, which his friend had agreed to easily. It was that kind of loyalty that made Brennan continue to value his friendship. It was precisely that kind of loyalty which blindsided him as well.

At some point in the day, he and Greg had decided that Brennan *needed* an online dating profile.

"I'm really not comfortable with this," he said, even as Sam continued to type away on his laptop. Greg sat on the couch with a smug grin on his face, nursing a mug of hot chocolate that had far too few tiny marshmallows.

"Yeah, well, that's why we didn't ask you," Sam said, offering Brennan his cheeriest smile. "We knew you'd be a big spoilsport about it."

"I have a serial killer to catch."

"Whose murders you're officially not supposed to be investigating," Sam noted. Brennan raised an eyebrow. "Hey, I have contacts, I know these things."

"Wally," Brennan concluded.

"I plead the fifth."

"Uh-huh. Well I guess I don't owe him one anymore."

"Oh, no," Sam said. A look of dread crossed his face. "You owe Wallace a favor?"

"Yeah, why?"

Sam shuddered visibly. "Man, I'm glad I'm not you. You do *not* want to owe that dude a favor." A heavy frown descended upon Brennan's brow, but before he could ask anything more, Sam finished typing with a keystroke of definite finality. "Voilà."

Brennan turned the laptop so he could see it. "CopAFeel dot US?"

"Where lonely detectives meet lonelier crime enthusiasts."

"This can't be a real site."

"As real as you or me, partner. And this is just the tip of the iceberg. You wouldn't believe how many niche dating sites are out there."

"I'm married."

"You *were* married," Sam said, not unkindly. "I'm sorry about what happened to Mara, but that was years ago. Either you can continue to live in the past, or you can give love another chance."

"We think it's time you got on the market again," Greg chimed in.

"Mara wouldn't want you to be forever alone on her behalf," Sam reasoned.

And there it was, the ultimate argument for living after a loss. If he dated someone else, if he removed the gold ring that had encircled his finger for many years, would Brennan be desecrating the memory of his dead wife—or fulfilling her final wishes for him?

It couldn't hurt to meet new people.

He chewed on the inside of his cheek as he looked back at the website. It had bold, simple colors and pictures of couples holding hands chained together with handcuffs. "Is this...a bondage site?"

"What?" Sam spun the screen toward him. "No, man, not like that. It's to sell the whole cop-loving theme. These are women who are attracted to men that do the things we do."

"The things that *we* do? Are you on here, Sam?"

His friend rubbed at the back of his head. "In the past, yes. Now it's purely for research, for you!" He made a few quick clicks, and a woman's portrait came up. "How about this one? She's a single widow, like yourself, and loves kids." He nodded toward the couch.

"Hey!" Greg objected. "I'm a full-on adult."

"An adult with no job and whom still lives at home? You're a kid." Sam looked briefly puzzled with himself. "*Who* still lives at home? Dammit, I don't know."

Greg didn't bother to argue, choosing instead to sip quietly from his cocoa.

"I feel like this is all a bit sudden," Brennan said, taking the laptop back and closing it. "Besides, CopAFeel seems more like a website for quickies rather than fostering relationships."

Sam placed a hand on his shoulder. "Baby steps, kemosabe. You need to crawl before you can walk."

"I thought I was already up to baby stepping. Now I need to crawl?"

"I'm mixing metaphors here, give me a break."

"As long as you're my ever-faithful sidekick, Tonto, then I think I can allow that." Brennan grinned, but Sam just shook his head and pulled on his jacket.

"All right, give me everything you have on the serial killer case," Sam said.

Brennan was caught off guard. "I thought you didn't have any time to work on the case. What happened to being on retainer for two days?"

Sam touched the tip of his nose. "That's why you collect up-front, in cash," he said. "I finished early, and I could always use extra cash from the department."

"I can't pay you," Brennan reminded him. "Officially, I'm not on the case."

Sam waved his hand. "I'll dig something up and convince Bishop to commission my services...and then commission my *services*," he added, wiggling his eyebrows suggestively.

"She's still going to wonder how you got involved with the case to begin with."

"Wallace," Sam said instantly. "He technically did tell me, unprompted, to keep you away from the case. He opened the door for me to be involved. I'll just say he piqued my interest."

"Perfect. I don't have it all down right now, but I'll send you a file later tonight."

"Sounds good." Sam slapped him on the back. "I'll talk to you soon. See you later, Greg!"

Greg waved as the apartment door shut behind Sam. Brennan contemplated the closed laptop and looked at his nephew on the couch. "You really think this is a good idea?"

"He's good at his job, right? Seems like the police could use his help as much as yours."

"Not that," Brennan said. "I meant the online dating. I haven't been with anyone else since your aunt died."

Something shifted about the way Greg held himself, because a moment later he was as serious as Brennan had ever seen him. "This is exactly what Sam and I were talking about. You need to stop thinking about your life in relation to hers. It doesn't mean you can't remember her, but honoring her memory and holding on to a ghost are two separate things."

Brennan stared at him for a long minute. "You're entirely too mature for your age."

Greg laughed. "I'm just a kid, remember?"

"That's something I've been meaning to talk to you about," Brennan said. "Have you given any thought about college? Or a job?"

"I thought you were cool with me staying here."

"I am, of course. But you don't want to be that guy who sleeps on a sofa his entire life. You're missing out on crucial experience by being cooped up in here all day." He crossed his arms and leaned against the counter. "What if you want to bring a girl back to your place? Because you sure as hell aren't doing it on the couch."

Greg remained silent.

"*Or my bed*," Brennan added, and a smile cracked across Greg's lips. "What I'm saying is that you're almost nineteen and still don't have any solid goals. You need to have *action* in life to make it meaningful."

"So with your sex life on hold," Greg said, "how meaningful has your personal life been recently?"

It was Brennan's turn to hold his silence.

"I'll make you a deal, Uncle Arty. If you agree to expand your dating life, I will agree to start looking around for a job."

Brennan frowned. "This isn't really a negotiation."

"No, it's not. This is me forcing you to do something for your own good," Greg said pointedly.

"Touché," Brennan said. "All right, it's a deal."

Greg grinned. "Excellent. I'll start in the morning." He hid his mouth behind a hand as he yawned widely. "Wow, what time is it?"

"Not late enough for you to be tired yet," Brennan said.

"Maybe it's the drugs the good doctor gave me to fight the patch. I've been feeling out of it *all* day."

"Hold on, so that means that your scheme with Sam to get me into dating was just a side effect? That all of your advice was just the drugs talking?"

The largest grin spread across Greg's face. "A deal's a deal," he said merrily.

Brennan wiped a hand against his mouth. "Yeah, I suppose so. Go on, get ready for bed, then." He collected his laptop and retreated to his room as Greg made his way to the bathroom. He sighed gratefully as he sat down on the king-sized bed. After a long day of hoofing it around town and being blindsided by a dating plot, it felt good to just relax and let himself melt into the pillows.

But I can't relax yet, he thought. He pulled up a writing app and quickly typed up all of the salient notes he'd picked up on his visit to Kelsi Woodill's apartment. There admittedly wasn't much to report. "Cast a wider net and see what you pull in," Brennan mumbled, speaking his final message to Sam aloud. If anyone could find something the police hadn't, it would be Sam. He sent the notes and message and nearly closed the laptop when the other open tab caught his eye.

He clicked through, and CopAFeel asserted itself on the screen. The widow's green eyes stared at him through the screen. Clara Thompson. She had lost someone, too, just like he had. But there she was, putting herself out there. What if she was struck with tragedy again? Wasn't she worried about being exposed like that?

Why is she more courageous than me?

PATIENT DARKNESS

Brennan opened the chat box and composed a message.

Chapter Ten

Alex swore violently as soon as she regained consciousness.

She was roused from her wine-dreams by the incessant pounding of a jackhammer inside her skull. The blouse she had passed out in was soaked through with sweat, and the sheets beneath her legs felt equally damp. Thankfully, she had had the good sense of mind to set her wineglass on the nightstand before surrendering her body to its drunken slumber. The last thing she needed was to replace wine-stained bedsheets. Fuzzy and buzzing, her mind communicated slowly with the rest of her body.

She swung her legs over the edge of the bed and sat up. Her tongue felt wooden in her mouth, and there was a lingering scent of wine on her breath. Her fingers were stiff, and she fumbled with the buttons of her top.

Next came the bra, then the rest of her clothes. She shivered as the cold air cozied up against her smooth, clammy skin. It didn't carry the same feeling of comfort as it had the other night. Alex needed a shower, the hotter the better.

She stood immobile for several minutes beneath the intense spray. The tension residing in her shoulders trickled away, knots unfolding beneath the steady stream of water. Once the thin veneer of sweat had been wiped away, the warmth spread through her limbs in earnest. Memories of what had happened the night before came back to her in bits and pieces. Almost at the same time, she felt a now-familiar presence pressing against the fringes of her consciousness.

Arthur Brennan.

You're fucking kidding me. Alex resisted the urge to slam her head against the tiled wall. Unwilling to leave the shower just yet, she reached out with her mind. She touched a dozen different dreaming people before she found someone who was awake. Judging by the dull and inactive brain, she figured it was a man. He was watching the television, or rather, mindlessly staring at the screen while something played in the background. She suspected he was neither awake nor asleep, but in some transitory stage. *I just need you to look at the clock,* she thought.

Seemingly by pure coincidence, the man lolled his head and looked toward the kitchen. Three thirty in the morning.

Back in her shower, Alex sighed. It was early, too early to be awake, but her early slumber meant she'd captured a full night's amount of sleep. Even if she went back to bed now, she knew she wouldn't find rest.

"What's a girl to do?" she pondered. She turned off the water and stepped out of the shower. Steam clouded the mirror and hung in the air like fog over the moors. Alex wondered at her internal narrator. It wasn't often that she compared her bathroom to the Scottish highlands.

The cloying, humid air escaped from the room as she opened the door, and her body tingled all over as colder air rushed to meet her. It felt right this time without her coating of feverish sweat, and she was reluctant to leave that feeling even as she started pulling on clean clothes. She wormed her way into a snug pair of dark jeans, then slipped on a gray t-shirt over her bra. She checked herself in the mirror and added a leather jacket to the ensemble.

Alex emerged from her room as silent as a mouse, walking on the balls of her feet in heavily padded socks. She never wore shoes in her apartment, and only rarely so in the building as a whole. She stopped in the kitchen, confirmed the time, and grabbed a short, sharp blade from a wooden block full of knives meant for chopping, slicing, dicing, and whatever other motions were involved in cooking. She didn't even know why she grabbed it, only that it felt good in the grip of her hand.

What am I going to do, kill him? It seemed a bit much to kill a stranger for keeping her from sleeping at night. If she gave in to those urges regularly, her building would be almost entirely devoid of tenants. Still, she held the knife.

She padded softly and swiftly down the hall to the elevator, which opened at her touch with a mercifully quiet ping. It was a relatively short ride to the sixteenth floor, and the psychic pressure she'd felt before was dramatically reduced in strength. Either the stranger had gone to sleep, which would make her job all that much easier, or else her resistance to the mental assault was simply improving.

Win-win, she thought as the elevator doors opened. The hallways were identical to those of her own floor, and Alex relied on the pressure on her skull to guide her. She turned left and walked slowly, and the pressure mounted gradually with each passing step. Alex watched the room numbers as she moved. Sixteen-oh-eight. Sixteen-ten. Sixteen-twelve. Sixteen-fourteen.

She paused. Two steps back toward room sixteen-twelve, and she felt certain that she had reached her destination. The psychic pressure peaked as she pressed her ear to the door; nothing could be heard from the other side.

Like hers, this door required a key. Alex cursed herself for leaving her lock picking kit in her room. She wasn't an expert by any means, but it was an idle hobby that had turned into an occasionally useful talent. She bit her lip as she surveyed the door. Even if she could pick the lock, was there another layer of security beyond it? It seemed unlikely.

It won't take more than two minutes to get the kit and come back, she reasoned. She hardly took a step before the door to room sixteen-twelve opened inward, and Alex jumped back in surprise.

A man appeared from the darkness. He was short, with a wreath of white hair that made him look like a wizened Renaissance monk. His clothes were rumpled, yet still spoke of expensive origins. Dark glasses concealed his eyes, and he ventured forth with a slender cane half a step ahead of his feet.

Alex held her breath. This was not the kind of man she had been expecting. She remembered the heavy weight in her hand. Had she been about to murder an old, blind man just so she could get some sleep? *Yes, he's blind.* She suddenly had an image of two men standing stock still in front of a T-Rex. *Hold your breath and don't move. He can't see you.*

"But I can hear you," the old man said. His lips moved as soon as she had completed her thought, as if taking his turn during the course of a normal conversation.

Alex didn't respond, nor did she so much as twitch a muscle. It was impossible for him to hear her.

"Up here," he said. He tapped his wrinkled dome for emphasis. His dark glasses were locked on her exact position. "You speak quite loudly with your thoughts. It is a wonder that anyone can sleep at night with you lurking around."

He spoke in a stilted manner as if he were taking deliberate care to ignore contractions, or perhaps was unaware of them altogether. Was he toying with her? What kind of game was this? Alex had been lured by the most psychically violent thoughts she had ever heard, those of a veritable madman, yet this geezer was as calm and collected as if—

As if he expected me to be here.

And then, the impossible. A smile cracked across the old man's leathery lips. "Please, do come inside. I know why you are here."

She shook her head and took a step in retreat.

"You have nothing to fear," he chided. "I sensed your confusion the moment you stepped inside the building. Yours is a powerful gift, and not the first of its kind that I have witnessed."

Alex's composure cracked, and she cleared her throat. "When I stepped inside the building?"

He seemed delighted to hear her speak. "Yes, that is right. You reached out to me in the lobby."

Ahh, so you're the one. She immediately reined in her probe and imagined a stone wall between her mind and the outside world. He had been the one to speak to her with his thoughts. Somehow, he had sensed her in his mind when no one else had. She couldn't allow him to hear any more of her thoughts.

His head tilted curiously, as if he could feel the retreating tide of her psychic probe. "There is no sense in hiding who we are from each other." He leaned heavily on his cane, one hand resting on top of the other. "My name is Benjamin. What might you be called?"

She considered lying. This man, Benjamin, was a stranger. More importantly, he was a stranger who knew what she was. The knife was still in her hand, hidden behind her back. He was slow, old, and weak. It would take less than a second to end it all here. Yet something stayed her hand.

She wasn't a murderer. Even if it was in her best interests, even if it protected her from being exposed as her father had always feared would happen, Alex couldn't strike down a blind, unarmed man.

What am I thinking? Of course I can. Her hand tightened around the knife's grip. It was her or him. She realized that it was no longer a petty case of losing a little peace and quiet. This was for her own protection, the preservation of *her* own life.

"That would be ill-advised," Benjamin rasped. In the span of a moment, he had assumed a defensive stance. The cane, no longer supporting him, was held like a staff between both hands. Blind or not, he apparently had some way of sensing her movements. Even the slightest muscle contraction from gripping the knife hadn't escaped his gaze.

Alex dropped the knife. "I apologize," she said, adopting Benjamin's speech pattern. She had read somewhere that mimicry was the easiest way to build a rapport with someone new. It had served her well so far in life, allowing her to blend easily with normal people. "You may call me Stephanie."

"Stephanie," he echoed. He said the name again and frowned, but the staff became a cane once more and pleasant features quickly returned to his face. "It is a pleasure to make your acquaintance, Reader."

"Excuse me?"

"You are a Reader," Benjamin stated calmly. "I am a Pathfinder."

Alex dropped the copycat speech pattern. "No idea what you're talking about, but you're not who I was looking for." She turned to leave.

"If you leave now, you may never find peace. I know what torments you, and I know what will set you free."

"You do?"

Benjamin pointed into his room with the cane. "Come inside and I will explain everything."

"You don't know what my questions are."

"You do not know which questions are worth asking."

Alex looked toward the dark doorway with apprehension. She knew that the source of burning, naked hatred for Arthur Brennan lay somewhere in that darkness. "Fine," she said. "Take me inside. I want to speak with whoever is in there."

Benjamin nodded. "He would like very much to be heard."

The old man turned sharply and walked back into the room, seemingly without need of his cane. Alex followed him, though she groped the wall until her hand found a light switch. It made sense that the room hadn't been lit before; a blind man had no need for lights. But what of the other man?

Inside the apartment, the furniture was identical to her own, though everything was arranged in a rather simpler layout. Glass end tables were pushed against walls or other furniture so that nothing stood out as an island, nothing directly in the way of a blind man's meanderings. It gave the apartment a greater sense of openness. Without the lights on, it might have easily been a gaping cave shrouded in shadows.

Two for two describing normal rooms with creepy imagery. Imagination, thy name is overactive.

"In here," Benjamin said. He stood outside the bedroom at the end of the hall and waited expectantly. Alex opened the door with the same enthusiasm that one might have while unveiling a basket full of cobras. The interior was surprisingly underwhelming.

It was dark inside, but not pitch black. A sliver was parted between the curtains, through which the light of the center city seeped in. A bed, smaller than hers, was pushed against the far wall and lay directly in the path of incoming light. Reclined on the bed was a man of average height and unimpressive features, and if not for the tubes connected to his arms he might have been resting peacefully. He was still at rest, but it looked more like the kind of repose that was reserved for coma patients and those near death.

"He's Fractured," Alex said aloud. She immediately retreated behind the stone wall of her mental defenses. Fractured minds were hopeless to cure, far beyond the reach of modern medicine. She suddenly understood why the psychic shouting had been so singularly driven by one powerful emotion—the bedridden figure was, quite literally, a madman. He would obsess about this one fixed idea until the end of his days.

"It is a terrible fate," Benjamin said. "I would not wish this upon my worst enemy, nor even upon the person responsible for doing this."

"Arthur Brennan?"

"You are familiar with him?"

Alex shook her head. "No, but it's kind of hard to keep *him*"—she looked toward the bed—"from broadcasting it, and I'm the only one receiving." She rubbed at her temples. "I didn't realize someone could transmit thoughts like that."

Benjamin frowned. "You have already done this yourself," he said, his tone perplexed.

"You're wrong. I read minds—when I want to, and even when I don't—but nothing more." She walked to the window and peered out through the crack in the curtains. "So who is Arthur Brennan?"

"A Sleeper. A detective. The one I hold responsible for this man's current state of mind."

Alex still had her eyebrow raised from the first in the list. "A Sleeper? They don't exist."

"If we do not exist," Benjamin said quietly, "then how do you explain my being here? How is it that I can sense your presence in my thoughts? Do you truly think that you and your father are alone in your gifts?"

She lowered her eyebrow and slipped on a neutral mask. "I don't know what you're talking about."

"The man who did this carries a badge and a gun and pretends to uphold the law. However, he has hunted more men and women around the world as a Sleeper than he has ever caught for the police. He is a ruthless thug, no better than his father."

Alex watched him carefully for a long minute. "This man," she said, pointing to the bed. "Who is he to you?"

"Henry. He was my grandson. He *is* my grandson," he amended. His voice sounded thick with remorse. "In his mind, Arthur Brennan holds me responsible for the death of his wife, and he chose to abandon our mission because of it. Henry was tasked with bringing Brennan in for debriefing."

"Debriefing?"

"Yes. Despite peaceful intentions, an altercation occurred, one which left my grandson without any sense of reality."

"You said you wouldn't wish this upon your worst enemy *or* Arthur Brennan. After what happened, this man isn't your number one enemy?"

His gaze landed heavily upon her. "No," he said simply.

"Okay," Alex said. "This cop thinks you killed his wife, and you think he Fractured your grandson. Henry here clearly holds a grudge; it's the only damn thing he's been thinking since you got here. But what kind of life is this for him? Why is he holding on? Why are *you* holding on to him?"

"He will not find rest in the next world until he makes peace with this one."

Alex rolled her eyes. "Right, because that isn't cryptic and twisted."

"I beg your pardon?"

"You seriously think that getting revenge will put his soul at ease?"

Benjamin shook his head. "I do not seek vengeance upon Arthur Brennan."

It was Alex's turn to be confused. "I'm sorry? I obviously didn't hear you right, it sounded like you *don't* want to murder the man who killed your grandson."

"Henry is not dead, nor do I wish death upon anyone, Miss Brüding." Alex shivered as he said that. She had never given him her last name. Hell, she'd even given him a false first name. "The Great Spirit would not suffer those who needlessly cause harm to others. I suspect Arthur Brennan will receive his just desserts in the next life. No, I do not intend to hasten his departure from this earth. In fact, he is essential for stemming the tide of death that washes over this city."

Alex stared at him openly, mouth slightly agape. "So...you need his *help*?"

"Put simply, yes."

She gripped her jacket closer to herself as chills ran down her spine. Before her stood a man who, despite blindness and age, was clearly more dangerous than most men alive. He felt personally begrudged by one of his Sleepers—which in itself said a lot about him, if he considered the Sleepers to be "his"—and yet he needed this cop to be a temporary ally against...what, exactly?

"The tide of death," Alex said. "What are you talking about?"

"We are being targeted."

"Sleepers?"

Benjamin waved a hand. "Sleepers initially, yes, but the target list has since expanded." He took off his dark glasses and met Alex's eyes. His were milky white, all except for a thin ring of gold that circled where his pupils once were. It must have been a trick of the light, but they looked like they glowed faintly.

"Expanded to who?" *To whom*, she corrected mentally. *Damn you, Sam.*

"Anyone with a power," Benjamin said somberly.

She let those words sink in for a moment. "There can't be that many of you, that many of us. Until now, I was under the impression that my father and I were unique in Odols."

"You were wrong. I do not intend to be rude, but I must be blunt in telling you that time is of the essence. We are all in danger, and none of us will be safe until this serial killer is brought to justice."

"So let the police handle it, that's their job," Alex said. "I can look after myself. I don't want to be involved in any of this."

Benjamin bristled at her words. "You are already a part of this," he said harshly. "There is nothing connecting the murders that can be traced by the *police*." The last word was filled with no small amount of scorn. "Arthur Brennan, as crude an instrument as he might be, is the only tool at our disposal. Point him in the right direction, and he will lead the police to our hunter."

"Why me?"

"Because he is utterly incapable of reason. Brennan will never accept my word. He holds his lies too close to his heart."

"And when this is over," Alex said, "do you plan on killing him?"

"I fail to see how that is any of your concern." His eerily glowing eyes bored holes in her.

Alex's gaze shifted away to the bed. "Henry? What is his part in all of this?"

Benjamin regarded his ailing grandson with pity. "He is as much a part of this as you or I. Until the serial killer is caught and Brennan himself is brought to justice for his actions, my grandson remains."

"You don't think it's cruel to keep him alive like this?" she asked, gesturing to the life support equipment piled around his bed.

"Killing is a mortal sin," Benjamin said. His eyes met hers, and they carried a different kind of intensity this time. "Death leaves a mark on the soul, one which cannot be washed away and which remains in place until it is our time to be judged. Mine is sullied without a doubt, but my actions have always been for the greater good. I am confident in my decisions." He placed a spotted, wrinkled hand on Henry's shoulder. "If I took the life of my own blood, I couldn't—I would never be able to live with myself."

"It could be a kindness to your grandson," Alex suggested.

Benjamin refused to acknowledge what she said. "Will you speak with Arthur Brennan?"

If the old man before her was right, Brennan was her best chance at remaining alive. Without his help, a serial killer would remain at large. Someday—perhaps not today or tomorrow, but at some time in the future—that murderer would track her down for what she was. Alex didn't know what she was getting involved in, but somebody was hunting people with powers, and she was a pragmatic survivor to the end.

"Fine," she said eventually. "I'll talk to him. Any idea where he lives?"

Chapter Eleven

Brennan woke early, just as the murky black of night was giving way to a wan gray morning.

He rubbed the sleep from his eyes and picked his laptop up off the floor. It turned itself on at his touch, and he navigated to his email. He frowned at the results and refreshed the page again to be sure. No new messages.

It was odd, but he had butterflies in his stomach ever since he had sent a private message to Clara Thompson. He hadn't approved of the idea of online dating, yet now he was refreshing his inbox like a lovesick teenager.

I need to see a shrink. He closed the laptop again and rose from bed. It was cold out from beneath the blankets, and he quickly covered himself with heavier clothes. He heard the distinct sound of dry cereal being poured into a bowl and headed for the kitchen.

"I sent a message to a prospective date," Brennan announced.

Greg looked unimpressed. "Congratulations."

"Remember that agreement we reached last night? The one where I meet beautiful women in exchange for you finding a job?"

"Oh, right." His nephew sighed, pouring milk into the bowl. "Yeah, I'll get right on that."

In spite of the wording, it didn't sound like sarcasm. "Good," Brennan said. "Hey, I've got to run."

"Did Sam get back to you with something?"

"No, not yet. But I realized last night that I've been looking at this case all wrong."

Greg shoved a spoonful of cereal into his mouth. "Oh yeah? How so?"

"I'm looking for a serial killer, someone who seemingly knew all of these disparate victims, or at least had a purpose for tracking them."

"Sounds reasonable."

"It does, but that's not going to work here. The victims have nothing linking them, no common acquaintances or even tangible locations they visited."

"What about *intangible* locations?" Greg suggested. Brennan gave him an even look. "What?

You used to track people before, right? As a Sleeper? Maybe they have something mentally in common."

"No," Brennan said. "I can't do that right now, it's too exposed."

"Too exposed to who?" Greg's question was met with pointed silence. "Fine. So what *are* you looking for, dear uncle?" he asked with fake cheer.

"When I went to Kelsi Woodill's apartment, her roommate was there moving out some of her things."

"You think she did it?"

Brennan shook his head. "No motive, and she looked pretty disturbed by the whole thing. Besides, she has even less of a connection to the other victims than our phantom suspect. No, she didn't do it. But while I was there, I noticed that her apartment is on the fourth floor and has a balcony overlooking an alley."

"Point of entrance?" Greg guessed.

"Exactly. There are no security cameras covering the alley, and the girls never felt a need to lock their balcony door. Who would even be able to reach that balcony?"

"Someone who can fly?" he suggested. "But that still doesn't explain why she was targeted."

"That doesn't matter right now," Brennan said. "Remember, I'm not looking for the *why* of it just yet. It's not a matter of who knew all the victims, but rather *how* they were all reached. My question before wasn't rhetorical. Who could actually reach that balcony?"

Greg stirred the milk in his bowl. "Maintenance workers? They have cherry pickers, right? One of those could reach the fourth floor."

"Someone would have heard or seen something that big."

"What are you thinking?"

"The killer most likely climbed up, scaling each balcony until he reached the fourth floor, which suggests a considerable amount of strength."

"So you're looking for a massive man with bulging thews? That should be a fun arrest."

"Nah, too much muscle can be inhibiting, especially when he's looking to climb straight up four stories. It's all about your muscle-to-weight ratio; a big guy with thick, veiny arms is going to be a lot heavier than someone with a medium build and a lot of lean muscle. Judging by how the roommate heard nothing and nobody happened to walk by in the street as all of this happened, I'm confident our killer was fast as well as strong."

Greg frowned at his uncle. "How does this help— Hey, where are you going?"

Brennan grinned as he grabbed his jacket. "Fast, strong, and clearly dealing with anger management problems? I'm going boxing."

PATIENT DARKNESS

ф ф ф

THE CLOSEST OFFICIAL boxing arena was a dive of a gym in southwestern Odols, owned by a man named Cassius. Upon entering, Brennan was met with a wave of sound from clanging weights, thumping punches, and grunting men. While his ears dealt with the noise, his nose was likewise assaulted by the scent of talcum powder, disinfectant, and body odor. Lots of body odor.

Cassius's place was born out of an abandoned warehouse, refitted to accommodate the dozens of men who were testing the limits of how much muscle could be amassed before their skin tore open. Some of the men gave a new meaning to the term "ripped."

A large raised platform dominated the center of the room, a regulation-sized arena for boxers to square off against each other. Two women were sparring at the moment, though it was difficult to make out their faces in any greater detail; they bobbed and weaved too quickly to be seen, each reacting to the other's jabs.

Brennan was half a dozen steps inside when a man approached him. He wore a plain white tank top that stretched perilously across his pecs and left his gigantic arms out on full display. His dark skin strained to contain the bulging muscles beneath. He moved with the casual arrogance of someone who worked out regularly and could likely hold their own in a fight.

"Cassius Clay?" Brennan asked.

"You're looking at him."

"Detective Brennan, OPD Homicide," he said, flashing his badge. "I have to say, you look shorter in person. And a lot more alive."

Cassius's eyes narrowed. "I'm guessing you don't have many friends, Detective."

"With a winning personality like mine? You'd be surprised."

"Doubtful." He crossed his arms, casually displaying the tools he used to pummel opponents in the boxing ring. "What do you want?"

"I need to ask you a few questions about someone who might be a regular here."

"Why?"

"You hear about the murders happening all over town?"

"Of course," Cassius said. Brennan let his words sink in for a moment, and some of the arrogance fled his face. "Oh. Oh, damn."

"Exactly."

"You think one of my guys would have done this?" His arms flexed slightly thicker as he tensed up.

"That's why I'm here."

Cassius motioned for Brennan to follow him, and they started walking through the gym, presumably to the office in the back. "It's terrible to hear about those poor people, just a damn shame."

"The faster we can bring this guy to justice, the better."

"Do you have a name?"

Brennan rubbed at his neck. "Not yet," he hedged. "But we're narrowing it down."

"Narrowing it down," Cassius grunted. "What makes you think I can help?"

"We're looking for someone strong, limber, and quick. Most likely male," Brennan said, eyeing the female boxers. "But we don't know enough to be sure."

Cassius waved an arm out the office window. "Take a look around, Detective. Every one of my members matches your description. Some have history with the law, but they've been on the right side since they joined up here. I run a clean business."

His tone was defensive, but Brennan knew he was telling the truth. Despite his imposing physique, Cassius was just a man who didn't want trouble. Maybe he took the preventative route, becoming so big that nobody would dare cross him. In a way, it was the same tactic Brennan used, though he resembled a solid tree more than a bulldozer on steroids.

"So none of them would be capable of killing?"

Cassius scratched at his nose. "A few of them are capable, sure, but they've reformed. If I hear they're causing trouble, they're out of here, no exceptions. They have a problem, they come here to work it out. Besides, everyone keeps each other in check, so I haven't had any problems."

Brennan frowned. "How many ex-cons come here?"

"Look, Detective, I know you look down on people like us. Before you ask, yes, I served time. I'm a changed man," he said. "We all are. Everyone out there right now is looking to make a fresh start, or simply escaping to somewhere they belong. You don't have to be a criminal to feel like an outsider. Here, they can be among friends."

"Friends?"

"People less likely to kill them," he amended. "My point being, they aren't criminals anymore."

"What about non-convicts?"

"Fewer of those around here. I'm sorry I can't be more helpful."

"No, it's—thank you," Brennan said. He held out his hand and shared grips with Cassius. It was an effort to keep his disappointment from showing. "You just vouched for a couple dozen men. Narrowing down the list of suspects is extremely helpful."

Cassius nodded. "You know the way out."

Brennan left the office and glanced around the gym. He met a few pairs of eyes from some very large men, but they were curious stares, not threatening. He tried not to breathe too deeply as the smell of body odor wafted through the warm, stale air. The boxing square was empty, but the rest of the gym still buzzed with activity. His steps were inaudible over the din. He very nearly reached the door when he felt a large, fat hand tap on his shoulder.

He turned to see a short woman of strong stature. Blonde strands of hair were matted to her sweaty forehead and her face was flushed. She breathed heavily, as if she had just been sprinting, and her pale skin was pulled taut across her high cheekbones. Brennan realized that what he had thought was a meaty fist was actually her almost child-like hand inside a red padded boxing glove.

"Lieutenant," he said in surprise.

"Brennan." She nodded stiffly, her eyebrows frowning severely. "What are you doing here?"

He hesitated. Bishop had given him a direct order to stay away from the case, and now she had caught him red-handed working a lead. "Looking for a new place to work out," he lied quickly.

"Uh-huh. And you're waving your badge around to make a fashion statement?"

"I thought there might be a discount for law enforcement. What are *you* doing here?"

"Is there something wrong with where I blow off steam?"

Brennan eyed the hardened criminals—ex-criminals—that were paying attention to their conversation. "Not at all. This is a lovely place."

"All right, smartass, you don't *have* to be here, you know."

"I was just on my way out."

She caught his arm as he turned. "Hey, Brennan, hold on. Father Dylan told me that a homeless man came to him looking for shelter a couple nights ago."

"Yeah, so?"

"He said *you* sent him." Bishop's eyes shined as she spoke. "He told Father Dylan he'd been sent there by an enormous freak; I couldn't think of anybody else that fits that description."

Brennan had completely forgotten about the man he'd evicted from the tunnel in uptown. He was even more surprised to hear that his advice had been heeded after all. "Good," he said. "One more vagrant off the streets."

"Brennan! I know you didn't do it out of duty." Her voice softened. "You actually believed the Church could help him."

"Whatever helps you sleep at night," he said. His allegiance to a higher power had been lost a long time ago. If there was an actual Him up there, Brennan would be His last choice for a messenger.

"He'd like you to come by when you can."

"The homeless guy?"

"Father Dylan."

"Oh, right. I'm kind of in the middle of something right now."

Bishop placed a padded fist on her hip. A scowl chased away the slight look of admiration from her face. "What would that be?" she asked harshly.

Oh, shit.

He felt his phone vibrate in his pocket and was struck with inspiration. "It's, um, kind of embarrassing."

"Try me."

"Well, um—" Brennan made a show of looking nervous, wringing his hands and forcing some mumbling. "See, Sam and Greg set me up with an online dating profile. And it, uh, got a match."

Bishop's eyebrows reached for the ceiling. "Oh? You're doing online dating now?"

"*I'm* not, it was their idea." He realized sounding defensive only made him seem guiltier. "Anyway, I have to get back to the apartment."

"Have you set a date yet?"

"We're not getting married."

Bishop grinned. "You idiot. I meant an actual *date*. Get together, have food, make love."

"On the first date? That seems quick."

"You're so naïve, Brennan," she said, shaking her head.

"I'm heading home to shower. You should get one, too," he added. "You smell awful."

She punched him playfully on the arm. It hurt a little. "You try being fresh after juking and jabbing for the better part of an hour."

"I am always fresh," he said, earning another smile from Bishop.

"Straight out of the hood. And you wonder why you've been single for so long. All right, I'm going to let you get out of here, but one more thing." Bishop rose up on her toes, and Brennan inclined his head to hear her whisper. "If I catch you sniffing around this case again," she said, her voice deadly soft in his ear, "I am placing you on suspension. I don't know what you're doing here and I don't want to know. It ends now. Nod if you understand me."

His chin dipped shallowly.

"Good," Bishop said, resting back on her heels. She had switched from friend to lieutenant and back again in less than a minute. "Go on, get ready for your date."

Brennan watched as she walked away. He was too stunned to move. His partnership with Detective Bishop had been a relatively short one, ending when she received her office and the promotion it signified, but he thought they had developed a fairly good rapport in that time. She'd been hard as nails, true, but not without a measure of kindness. *Lieutenant* Bishop, on the other hand, was an entirely new woman.

Or maybe the same woman with new trappings of power, Brennan thought sullenly.

"Hey, I'm glad I caught you!" A loud voice drew Brennan from his thoughts. It was Cassius. He walked up level with Brennan and followed his gaze at Bishop's retreating form. "She's one hell of a fighter, that one. You two have history?"

Brennan grunted. "Not the romantic kind."

"Shame. No big loss, though. You're not her type."

"You've known me all of five minutes and suddenly you're Mister Insightful?"

Cassius shrugged his enormous shoulders. "I call it like I see it."

"You were excited to catch me?" Brennan prompted.

"Right. I got to thinking about what you said, and one of my regulars hasn't shown up in a couple weeks. Big guy, mostly kept to himself. He had tats on his arms, but not the kind you get from doing time or running with gangbangers."

"You didn't notice when one of your regulars went missing?"

"Hey, someone comes in every couple of days, maybe once a week, you don't pay too much attention." He scratched his chin thoughtfully. "Been almost two weeks now since I've seen him, though."

"Does this big guy have a name?"

"Johnny Appleseed."

Brennan gave him a level look.

"What? That's the name he gave, and he paid in cash. I didn't ask any further."

"Who runs a clean business but deals in cash?" He ignored Cassius's scowl and sighed. "I'm not here to shut you down, just looking for our killer. Do you have a photo of Johnny? I can't look around the city for a bruiser with ink, not unless I'm looking for a fight."

Cassius chuckled. "I don't have a photo, but I think I know where you can find him."

"Home address?"

"Hah, if only. No, there was a pub he used to talk about. It was called The Tap, or something like that. He talked about it like it was his second home."

"And you're fine with just turning in your friend?"

"If he's a murderer, he ain't my friend. But as a business owner, I have to worry if one of my clients isn't going to be around next month. If you find him there, let me know, one way or the other."

In spite of himself, Brennan found himself liking Cassius. He was a straightforward enough guy who didn't tolerate nonsense in his gym. He clasped hands with him again before stepping out into the cool, relatively fresh air of the open city street.

Brennan pulled his phone out and checked his inbox. He felt a tingle in his stomach as he read through the new message. Clara Thompson had responded to him through CopAFeel. She was delighted to hear from him and invited him to have dinner tonight.

I'll be damned, it actually worked. His stomach butterflies beat their wings a little more forcefully. It had *worked*. The last date he had been on was with his wife, Mara, who—

He shook his head. His left fist clenched, and he felt the band of metal that still wrapped around one finger. It had been years since she was lost to him, but Brennan still wore the ring in her honor. It was his only tie to her now, the most enduring remnant of his departed wife.

The phone's screen powered down from inactivity as Brennan's mind raced. Technically, now his lie to Bishop was a perfect truth; he just hadn't known it at the time. If he tracked down The Tap now, though, she would almost certainly find out and have his badge. Besides, he didn't know how long it might take, and now he had plans for the evening. It was still early afternoon, but the sun was setting earlier with each passing day. He had enough time to make it up to St. Agabus's, though, to speak with Father Dylan. That would gain him brownie points with Bishop and possibly get her off his back for a while.

Brennan made a quick call. "Sam, you're still on retainer, right?"

"For the next thirty hours, I'm all yours. What do you need?"

"Two things. I need you to look for a bar, tentatively named The Tap. I just got a source that says one of his usual clients has gone underground, and that's where we're most likely to find him."

"Sure thing," Sam said, repeating the name at half-speed as he wrote it down. "And the second thing?"

The heat rose in Brennan's cheeks. "I need you to recommend a good place for dinner for two. Not too formal, but somewhere nice."

Sam oohed over the phone. "You got a date?"

"Don't sound so surprised!"

"I know a few places, partner, let me make some calls. Do you know what time tonight?"

"Make it for eight o'clock."

"You got it."

Brennan hung up and started walking to the nearest shuttle station heading north.

Chapter Twelve

ALEX SENSED THE men's ill intentions from a block away.

She ordered the taxi to wait and got out, holding a heavy silver briefcase in one gloved hand. In the other, she held a small cube of plastic and wiring. She could only hope the palm-sized block of explosives wouldn't be necessary. The wind pushed at her back as she approached the building where she was meeting her client. It was a large structure of sheet metal and concrete, a broad warehouse with large windows lining the upper sections of the outer wall. There was a certain air to the neighborhood, a general miasma of seediness that gave off a sickly feeling. It had attitude, the kind that subconsciously steered away normal, well-adjusted people from casually strolling through.

Alex didn't fall into that category. She felt over a dozen sets of eyes watching her from alleyways and catwalks, accompanied by gray sensations of detached wariness. If they were shocked that their employer was a woman, it didn't show in their emotions. She could appreciate that kind of professionalism. Her father had good sense when it came to choosing his employees.

The men she was meeting with were responsible for helping her father find test subjects for his medical research. Alex knew that their work was largely illegal, and she doubted that many—if any—of the recipients of his serum had been volunteers. Still, they were a means to an end in finding a cure for her mother, and her father kept a discretionary fund solely for their payroll. Alex was convinced that they could be hired for an afternoon of relatively mundane target practice.

"That's far enough, Ms. Brüding." She looked up and saw a bald man standing on an upper level of the warehouse's fire escape. He spoke with a patient voice, if not an entirely respectful one. "Mr. Brüding didn't mention any new assignment. To what do we owe the pleasure of your visit?"

Alex met his eyes confidently. "I have some business to discuss with you, Heinrich. Perhaps we could speak inside?"

Heinrich nodded to his men on either side, and their postures instantly relaxed. "Of course, Ms.

Brüding. Open the gate," he called to someone inside. The corrugated metal door to the warehouse floor slid on rollers, allowing Alex to enter with briefcase in hand. It closed again once she was inside, and two more men took up positions beside her.

The interior was sparse. Two large, foldable tables had been pushed together in the center of the room, surrounded by half a dozen cheap chairs. Additional guards milled about by the doors and windows, and every one of them wore a mask of feigned disinterest on their faces. Still, their eyes tracked her movement as she approached the metal table.

Heinrich came down to greet her, his footsteps heavy and loud on the iron steps. He gestured to a pair of empty chairs, and they both took their seats. Alex noted with satisfaction that even though the room was full of men, the guards kept far enough away that their conversation would be relatively private.

"Thank you," she said, placing the briefcase on the table. "I appreciate you meeting with me."

"I normally work with your father." Heinrich's accent was more pronounced now that she could hear him up close.

"This is my own business. I need you to stage a hit on someone."

He rubbed his jaw. "A job like this takes proper time to plan."

Alex shared her plan with him, and Heinrich's frown deepened when she got to the part about keeping the target alive.

"I work *with* your father," Heinrich repeated. "My men and I are not his toys, and we are certainly not yours. Your father hires us, but we are not his employees, and our price is not cheap." His speech was measured, his vocabulary carefully chosen, both products of intense education in English as a second language.

Alex rapped her knuckles meaningfully against the briefcase. "I came prepared."

Heinrich looked doubtful. Alex reached for the man's thoughts, but they proved elusive. *Either he's an empty-headed dimwit with excellent diction, or else...*She scanned the other men within reach. In each mind she touched, she encountered a brick wall. It was not a case of not being able to enter their thoughts, but rather that each one was actively engrossed in imagining a solid brick wall, endless in length and height.

These were her father's men, despite what Heinrich said. *Did he train them...to resist me?* Aside from her father and now Benjamin, nobody knew of her telepathy. She could still access the sensory inputs of Heinrich's men, but that was the limit. Beyond that, she was as helpless as a common person.

She had never felt so vulnerable.

Heinrich regarded her with a shrewd expression. "You want to hire Leviathan for this job? That is fine. But I wonder what Mr. Brüding would think of his daughter co-opting his resources."

"Bullshit," Alex said. She had been caught off guard by the mercenaries' mental defenses, but she was well-prepared for Heinrich's attempt at blackmail. "Your men and your guns are, as you say, not his toys. You don't care who hires you so long as you get paid."

"Correct." Heinrich's lips spread in the hungry grin of a shark. "But James Brüding would care very much to know why his own daughter is enlisting our services. His pockets are much deeper than yours, and I like money."

"I have included an additional five thousand for your discretion," she said, pushing the briefcase toward Heinrich.

"Double it."

"You exaggerate your importance," she said coldly.

"Yet you still come to me for help. Double it or no deal."

Alex sighed, playing up her role as the naïve, blindsided girl. She knew walking in to the meeting that Heinrich would try something like this, and she came prepared. Still, she had to act the part. With a show of reluctance, she reached into her jacket and pulled out a stack of hundred-dollar bills. "This makes ten thousand," she said, placing the money next to the briefcase. "But you will follow my instructions to the letter. No deviation."

Heinrich reached across the table, placing a large, meaty hand on top of the briefcase. "*Ja*, of course," he said, pulling the money toward him. Alex felt his gaze turn critical, a swirl of hazel curiosity emerging from his thought patterns. "Who is this man you want us to shoot?"

"A homicide detective from OPD, Arthur Brennan."

"Arthur Brennan," Heinrich repeated flatly. He had stopped thumbing through the bound stack of bills. "This is the same man who shut down our operations here three months ago?"

For the second time since entering the warehouse, Alex found herself uncertain. She had never heard of Arthur Brennan until a few days ago, and now it seemed that he had already had dealings with Leviathan. Her father would almost certainly have known about this.

If these men know how to resist me, he must *have trained them to do so. How much is he actually hiding from me?* Alex hadn't believed it possible to conceal anything from her probing mind, but that certainty was being unraveled by the second.

"Whatever your history with the man," Alex said, recovering her voice, "I expect that you will honor our agreement. He is *not* to be killed."

"Absolutely."

"Or seriously injured."

Heinrich scowled. His frown deepened when he opened the briefcase and looked inside. "This is not the amount we agreed upon."

"You'll get the other half when the assignment is complete. This is a token of good faith," she said, gesturing to the money he held. "Deviate from our deal and you will break that faith."

"Your father taught you well," Heinrich stated bitterly. "The detective will not be killed during this operation." He extended his bear paw of a hand and shook Alex's; his enveloped hers as easily as a clam concealing its pearl. Somehow, Alex felt that Heinrich had gained more from their meeting than just a lump sum of money.

As she left the warehouse, distinctly aware of the eyes silently watching her retreat, Alex replayed the exact words from her exchange with Heinrich. His training apparently prevented her from accessing his thoughts, but she hadn't missed the fact that his parting statement had been carefully crafted to allow for an opportunistic loophole. If he harmed Arthur Brennan *after* Alex delivered the second part of their payment, then Heinrich could fulfill his end of the arrangement *and* enact his revenge.

If Heinrich kills Brennan before he can find this serial killer, I'm a dead woman.

She would just need to find a way to keep the good detective alive past tonight.

ϕ ϕ ϕ

THE TAXI ARRIVED at her apartment with just a couple hours to spare until sundown. She quickly shed the formal dress suit she had worn to her meeting with Heinrich and pulled on an outfit consisting mainly of form-fitting leather and black wool. Alex took a moment to admire herself in the mirror before climbing back into the waiting cab.

"You do know that the meter is continuously running, yes?" the driver asked.

"That won't be a problem," Alex said. She passed him a handful of bills, each one of which could cover an hour of massage therapy. "One more stop to make, and then I want you to wipe today's trip from your travel log."

"It will look suspicious," he countered, "if it looks like I did not have any passengers this afternoon."

She handed him another bill. "Tell your boss that you took the afternoon off to celebrate your anniversary with your wife."

"How did you know?"

"I'm psychic," she said glibly. The driver looked at her for a moment before laughing.

"Whatever you say, lady."

It was a peaceful drive, or at least as peaceful as it could have been, given the circumstances. Compared to the rest of her day, which had started so long ago with her early morning chat with Benjamin, the whiplash from weaving through inner city traffic was sublime. For some idiotic reason, Arthur Brennan had to live in the heart of the city, and across from OPD headquarters, no less. It was actually not too far from her own apartment, but the necessary evil of rush hour traffic was something she ordinarily only endured for her father. If her own life were not at risk, she would have been home now sipping from one of Sam's bottles of Pinot Noir and relaxing into the positively adequate physical comfort of his arms.

Alex frowned. Even now, while imagining her ideal stress-free scenario, she was incapable of dredging up some form of emotion. All of those things felt good, yes, but they lacked the actual sentiment of enjoyment that she knew she should be experiencing.

A sudden lane shift caused Alex to jostle around in the backseat.

Damn you, Brennan.

"Did you say something?" The cabbie looked in the rearview mirror at her.

"What?"

He waved a hand. "Sorry, I thought I heard something."

Keep your attention on the road, she thought bitterly.

"I swear, there it is again," he said, looking around doubtfully. "Maybe I am hearing someone's music? Yes, that must be it."

Alex stared in disbelief at the back of her driver's head. He had reacted, both times, in perfect sync with her thoughts. She reached out tentatively with her psychic probe, but there was nothing unusual about him. He was human. Average. Ordinary. Dull. *Not like me.*

The driver rolled down his window and stuck his ear out. "Now I know I'm not imagining it," he said. "It was clear as day in my head."

"It's an old song," Alex stammered, covering for herself. She said a few of the lyrics aloud.

"*Hot* like me! That is what I must have heard," the driver concluded, chuckling quietly.

With a deep breath, Alex forced herself to look out the window. Her eyes glazed over, and she felt the pounding pain of a migraine coming on. She opened her purse and unscrewed the prescription bottle inside; she tossed back three white pills and swallowed hard, silently willing the medicine to work quickly. She was dangerously aware of the private thoughts of all those around her, their collective psychic presence threatening to crowd her out of her own mind.

What was it that Benjamin said in his apartment? That I had called out to him with my thoughts? Alex puzzled over it as the taxi took another turn. It was consistent with her observations, and it would explain the odd phenomenon that had just occurred with the driver. She had been in charge of her power for so long that it was jarring to imagine that the connection might work both ways.

Alex turned her attention to the driver. His bald spot gleamed with a thin layer of sweat, and she could see in the rearview mirror that his eyes were still darting around nervously. He was driving toward Arthur Brennan's apartment, but Alex sensed that he was on the verge of a nervous breakdown. She reached out again, enveloping his mind with her awareness and holding it there. A minute passed, then another, until she felt a kind of bond form between their thoughts. She was not in control of his mind, per se, but she held it in her grasp like a small hamster; his own thoughts squirmed around, unable to comprehend this new power that had taken over.

I am imagining all of this, she thought, transferring the idea through the link. She was careful to copy his sentence structure and to keep her tone neutral. It was experimental, but probably the best she would be able to do until she better understood her own power. Alex pushed the tune of the old song into his head for good measure.

Thirty seconds later, Alex saw the change taking place. His eyes strayed from the road less often, and his dome lost its sheen as his heartbeat dropped to a steady rhythm. He bobbed his head slightly from side to side. "I know you like me," he sang quietly. He was terribly off-key, but the music brought Alex peace. "I know you do."

She sighed happily as she leaned against the window and receded from his mind. *So he was right,* she realized, thinking of Benjamin. There was more to her power than she had ever known, and in less than a day she had gained a rudimentary understanding of how to use it. Alex had always prided herself on being a fast learner. She smiled smugly all the way to Brennan's apartment.

Chapter Thirteen

The cathedral stood proudly against the colorful backdrop of the setting sun.

St. Agabus's was one of the oldest buildings in Odols, having been originally founded alongside the rest of the town during colonial times. Its original purpose had been to convert natives to Christianity and provide traditional services for the frontier settlers. As the country expanded and time passed, it underwent several reconstructions until it became the enormous monument that it was today.

Stained-glass windows soared thirty feet high between thick columns of weather-hardened stone. There were wings off to either side of the main great hall, resembling a giant cross as seen from the air. The pair of staggeringly large wooden doors that completed the building's entranceway looked like they could withstand a heavy siege from bloodthirsty orcs; Noah could have used them as rafts and still have accomplished his mission.

He could have even saved the unicorns, Brennan thought as he looked up at the overzealous craftsmanship. He made use of a smaller set of doors that were carved like a mouse hole from the larger pair. Inside were several statues, all of the same young woman. Her face was fair, and a hooded robe concealed much of her hair and figure. In the cupped hands of each statue was a shallow pool of water. Brennan walked past them and into the great hall.

Two columns of pews lined each side of the carpeted central procession walkway, and the rows extended all the way from the entrance to the altar. Thousands of people could fit without ever touching elbows. High above, Brennan saw the crucial arches that held everything together, as well as endless decorative embellishments that served no function.

The cathedral was mostly empty, as it was a Thursday evening, but a few dedicated worshippers still kneeled with their eyes closed and hands clasped. Brennan walked quietly down the aisle. Even though he had abandoned the faith many years ago, his time around Bishop had rekindled a healthy respect for those who at least believed in something. He felt it would be wrong to intrude any more on their privacy than was necessary.

His feet carried him off to the side, beyond the altar and into one of the wings of the cathedral where the more private chambers were located. He passed the kitchen where the Eucharist was prepared, then turned into Father Dylan's office. It was the only one that had a door to it, a privilege of being the most senior priest.

Brennan knocked on the door as he pushed it open, and Father Dylan looked up from the papers on his desk. He was a small man, roughly sixty years in age and as active as anyone within the community. His hair had long since gone gray and thin, but his eyes were clear and alert. A toothy smile breached his lips as recognition raised his thick eyebrows. "Arthur," he said. "Please, come, sit down."

The old priest's enthusiasm made it easy for Brennan to return his smile. "Thank you, Father."

"How are you?" The last time he had seen Father Dylan, he was burying his sister. Before that, their last face-to-face interaction was when Brennan had been just a boy, still doe-eyed and attending mass with his parents. Still, Father Dylan spoke warmly, with the kind of casual familiarity that all old priests seemed to possess.

"Good," Brennan said automatically. "How has the church been? Bishop tells me good things."

"Noel is a good Christian, and her presence here is a blessing to all of us. You didn't come here to ask about my congregation, though. Noel gave you my message?"

Brennan nodded. "The homeless guy. How is he?"

"*Harold* is doing fine. He told me what you did for him. I'm impressed and touched that you thought to send him here," Father Dylan said. "I have been reaching out to the local community to help him find work, and meanwhile he has been sleeping on one of our cots downstairs."

"In the crypt?"

"Heavens, no. We have extra chambers for visiting bishops and priests, as well as temporary quarters for the less fortunate."

"I just wanted him out of the tunnel before a uni came by and threw him in a cell."

"I'm sure that was the reason." Father Dylan's eyes twinkled, and he leaned forward confidentially. "You have a good heart, Arthur. There is no shame in letting it show."

You don't know everything I've done. Brennan shifted uncomfortably in his seat. "I'm not the man everyone thinks I am."

"What you did for Harold was the act of a good man. It is obvious that Noel sees the same quality in you, or you would not have won her respect. Why do you not see it in yourself?"

"Modesty is a virtue."

"That was not a rhetorical question, my son. Tell me, really, why you feel so undeserving of our praise."

"We don't have to sit in those screened boxes to speak confidentially, do we?"

Father Dylan spread his hands. "Anonymity would be pointless now, don't you think?"

"Fair enough." Brennan's throat felt dry. "I guess my story starts with my father."

"Your father?"

"He was *not* a good man. He brought a lot of pain to those he disagreed with, and passive misery to everyone around him. I was young, and I didn't recognize what he truly was until it was too late."

"What did he do for a living?"

"As a job? He was a financial consultant. But that was just a front for his real position within the mafia."

Father Dylan's eyes widened, but he said nothing.

"For years, he was taking money in exchange for information. One day, he was the one calling the shots. Like I said, I was too young to realize then what my father had become."

"Perhaps he was making the best of a bad situation."

"You weren't there," Brennan said darkly. "He became distant, but we pretended not to notice anything because the bills were getting paid and Maddy and I were going to private school. We attended mass every Sunday like a normal family. It was actually kind of…nice." His face darkened. "Except for when *he* was home."

"I remember him," Father Dylan said. His eyes gained a faraway look. "Joseph was always polite, courteous, a quiet man. It is hard to imagine him as you describe. Did he ever raise his hand against you?"

Brennan shook his head. "He was a hard ass, a liar, and a murderer. But he never struck us." He stared hard out the window. "The best thing I can say about him is that he wasn't a wife beater."

Father Dylan stared silently until Brennan finally met his eyes. "It can be easy to find fault in others, especially when we ourselves are feeling guilty."

"I don't feel guilty about anything."

"Oh? Perhaps you misunderstood the meaning of confession." Father Dylan leaned back in his seat. "God helps those who help themselves, Arthur."

"I don't believe in him anymore."

"Children often lose faith in their parents as they get older."

"I wasn't referring to my dad."

"Neither was I." Father Dylan smiled faintly and clasped his hands over his stomach, the perfect picture of patience.

Brennan sighed. "You know how the government has the witness protection program?"

"I am familiar with it."

"That's what happened to my father."

Father Dylan nodded sympathetically. "That explains his sudden disappearance from our congregation. Still, I don't understand why you would feel guilty. His leaving was not at all your fault—"

"He didn't turn state's evidence," Brennan interrupted.

"I don't understand."

"I told you, I realized what a monster my father had become, and I couldn't live under the same roof as him anymore."

"So...*you* gave the police what they needed to know to arrest your father?"

Brennan swallowed hard. "Not exactly." He had kept the truth buried for so long, a secret locked away in a vault in his mind. The memory still held a great deal of pain, and it was not a freshly scabbed injury anymore; this was a scar upon his soul, an irreversible act that had the opposite effect from what he had wanted. To reopen that wound would be to reveal a part of himself that he had secreted away for decades.

"I gave information to another boss, another crime outfit. They killed him."

"Oh, Arthur…why did you not go to the authorities?"

"They would have seized everything! It would have left my mother and sister and me without a home, without any way to survive." His voice was raw with emotion as he spoke. "And beyond anything else…I wanted him *gone*. Not in prison, not on the run. Gone from this world and from our lives, so that he couldn't hurt any of us again."

"Arthur." Father Dylan's voice was soft, his gentle prompt pulling Brennan from his confession. "We don't have to talk about this if you are not ready. I didn't mean to push."

Brennan felt something warm trickle down over his cheek. He brushed at it, and the sleeve came away damp. His eyes had moistened without him realizing. "He's dead, and I'm not sure I did the right thing," he said quietly.

Calm contemplation crept into the silence that followed. Brennan willed his eyes to dry as he stared resolutely out the window. Skyscrapers cast long shadows on the busy streets. In the distance, a fire engine started to wail. The city carried on, heedless of his inner turmoil.

"There are few moments in my life," Father Dylan began, "where I can say I truly believe I did the right thing. Oh, many times I *felt* that what I did was just, but in the end those actions were the result of petty needs. Lust in the form of love. Greed masquerading as ambition. Vengeance under the guise of justice. When I search within myself, these moments are the source of my greatest shame."

"Do you practice small speeches like this?" Brennan asked. "This isn't the best pep talk I've heard."

Father Dylan gave a small smile. "You are a good man, Arthur. I know it, even if you do not. Your actions were misguided, but I believe your motives were pure."

"Good intentions…I hear the road to hell is paved with those."

"You truly believe you are destined for Hell?" Father Dylan asked mildly. Brennan remained silent. "You brought pain to your mother. To your sister. You will always live with this, and it will try to harden your heart. Do not let it. There is nothing that cannot be overcome by love, but you must be willing to let it in. When a stone is thrown in your path, be like the river and move around it."

Brennan raised a skeptical eyebrow. "For a Catholic priest, that sure had a lot of Buddhist undertones." He was rewarded with another enigmatic smile.

"I am a man of faith," Father Dylan stated simply. "My faith is twofold, in both God and His creations. I believe in my fellow man; I *believe* that if you live harmoniously with others and improve the world around you when you can, then you can't be too far from God's plan. I can't ask for more than that."

"So if a good man goes down a dark path…?"

"He can be redeemed." Father Dylan looked amused as he spoke. "The Bible is an object lesson in the power of redemption. All humans were redeemed for their sins when a good man allowed himself to be nailed to a cross; you would be an arrogant fool to think of yourself as an exception to this. Whatever dark deeds you have done in your past, you can be absolved of them."

"Bishop has been keeping me away from the case," Brennan said suddenly.

"Noel?"

"She isn't stonewalling me for no reason." He wiped a hand across his tired eyes and pinched the bridge of his nose. He stood quickly. "I don't know why I didn't see it earlier. Sorry, Father, but I need to go."

Father Dylan rose from his seat. "Is everything all right?"

"Just peachy," he replied gruffly. "But I just realized that Bishop is making one of those judgment errors we were just talking about. I've been working in the shadows because she's holding me back. Now it's about time I found out why."

"She must have her reasons."

"Sure she does. Like she realized her boyfriend is cheating on her and that I knew about it?" Brennan frowned as Father Dylan's jaw dropped slightly. "Yeah. I keep a lot of secrets, and not all of them are mine. But her personal grudge is throwing a monkey wrench into this investigation, and there isn't much time."

"The serial killer on the news?"

Brennan nodded. "Someone else is going to die in about thirty hours unless we stop him." He watched the blood drain from Father Dylan's face.

"I will speak to Noel for you."

"Thank you, Father, but I don't think—"

He cut him off with a wave of his hand. "Arthur, trust me. I know her. I can help her see reason." His pale blue eyes held something fierce in them.

Brennan thanked him again, this time with sincerity. He felt a vibration, and he pulled his phone from his pocket. It was Sam. "Excuse me, Father."

"Of course."

"Sam," he said as he walked into the hall. "What's up?"

"The Regent, eight fifteen tonight."

"What?"

"Your dinner reservations. And do *not* ask what I had to do to book a table for you on such short notice."

"What did you have to do?"

"You nonconformist, you." Brennan could hear the grin in Sam's voice. "Where are you now? Back at your place?"

"On my way there now. Did you find out any more about The Tap?"

"I figured the date took more immediate precedence."

"Seriously?"

"Don't worry, partner, I work quickly. I'll have something for you by the time you return from dinner. Scout's honor."

"You're not a scout," Brennan reminded him.

"As far as you know."

"Nor do you have honor."

"Now that's just mean. Wear something nice tonight, and when the server comes to take your drinks, order a Cabernet Sauvignon or some sort of red blend."

"Isn't this all a bit much for a first date? I would have gone for something simpler."

"Brennan," he said sharply. "It's not about what you want. Cater to *her* interests. Sheesh, a few years off the dating scene and you've gone completely senile. All right, just *show up* and I'll take care of the rest."

He considered saying a few choice words to his friend, but he was about to get on the shuttle, and he still needed to send the dinner details to Clara. "Fine," Brennan said. "And…thanks. Let me know what you can find out about The Tap. It's our only lead at the moment."

There was a pause before Sam spoke. "Have you brought Noel in on it?"

"You know I can't. She has been keeping me on ice for this entire case, and it isn't helping anyone." He overrode Sam as he began to protest. "I just spoke with her priest, Father Dylan. He has agreed to talk to her about it, all right? But we have just over a day left and I can't afford to spend any more time on the bench."

"I don't like the idea of keeping this from her," Sam said. "It could be even worse for you if she finds out you kept her in the dark."

Despite the cool air, Brennan suddenly felt heat flush his face. His voice was hoarse as he thought back to their night of playing pool. When Sam had left him, he had lied about going to meet up with Bishop. "I think we all have our secrets to keep," Brennan said. He was being purposefully cryptic, and he hoped Sam understood enough to let the issue rest for now.

Another pause. "I think we should talk about what happened at the hospital," Sam said eventually, his voice equally subdued. "You still haven't told me a lot of things, actually, and I feel I have a right to know."

Dread sunk its claws into Brennan's back, and he stood stiffly as he boarded the shuttle that would take him home. He had never told Sam about his past as a Sleeper. He had never told *anyone* about his particular power, the one not even other Sleepers possessed. The entire rescue operation three months ago had hinged upon him implicitly trusting that Greg could find Bishop by using one of the patches laced with hallucinogenic Chamalla. If he revealed who he was and what he could really do, Brennan had no clue how Sam would react. He was his best friend, but even the strongest of friendships had their limits.

"I'm on the shuttle now," he said, his voice low. "We can talk about this after we catch our serial killer."

He heard Sam sigh heavily. "Right. I'll find The Tap and send you an email tonight." Some of the familiar joviality crept back into his voice. "Good luck on your date tonight, lady killer."

ϕ ϕ ϕ

"It really shouldn't be this hard of a decision." Greg was looking on in amusement as Brennan held up two different ties in front of the mirror. "The red one," Greg said wearily, drawing out the syllables as if Brennan were hard of hearing—or particularly slow.

"Red?" Brennan held it up again, unconvinced. "Isn't that too aggressive of a color?"

"Come on, the blue doesn't even go well with your suit—which, by the way, is probably too dressy for a first date."

Brennan shrugged and looped the red tie around his popped-up collar. "If I show up in a golf shirt and jeans, I won't even be allowed into The Regent."

Greg let out a low whistle. "That place is a little outside of your price range."

"Said the unemployed high school graduate."

"Touché."

Brennan pulled on the tail of the tie, tightening it until it formed a knot over the hollow of his neck. It hung just left of center, and Brennan fiddled with it for a few seconds before releasing a sigh of resignation. He started the process over again. "It's all about making a good first impression," he said. "The restaurant staff will be expecting me to dress a certain way. *Clara* will, too."

"Are we addressing her on a first name basis already?"

"*We* aren't doing anything. I'm going on a date thanks to you—"

"You're welcome."

"—And you will be scouring the Internet for jobs. I don't care if it takes all night. I want you to have something lined up by tomorrow, even if that just means walking into the corner store and asking for an application."

Greg wiped a hand over his face, causing Brennan to smile faintly. It was a ghost of the very same gesture Brennan made when he was frustrated. "Look, Uncle Arty, I wasn't totally acting in good faith when I made that deal. I mean, I never actually expected you to go on a date with this woman. Or any woman anytime soon, in fact."

Brennan paused in his tie adjustment. His eyes, gazing into the mirror, fell to the ring that still encircled his finger. A long minute passed before he spoke, and his voice broke slightly as he did. "It was a surprise for me as well," he said. "Your aunt was the love of my life, and I don't think anybody can replace her in my heart. But you and Sam are right; I can't keep living in the past."

He was unsure of when it had started, but Brennan found himself slowly turning his wedding ring with his free hand. The silk tie hung in a loose noose around his neck. He felt Greg staring at him from behind, and he quickly dropped his hands. "Sorry," he said. "I haven't talked about Mara with many people ever since her death."

"It's fine," Greg said compassionately. "I didn't mean to bring it up—"

"You didn't, I'm just being—"

"—It was stupid of me to—"

"—You don't want to hear about any of that."

The two of them broke off simultaneously and stared at each other. After a moment, Greg let out a nervous chuckle. "Can we go back to deciding the color of your tie?" he asked.

Brennan smiled wanly. "I'll keep the red. Thanks."

A long exhale escaped Greg's lips. "So you're going to order the steak and lobster? With an extra bottle of champagne?"

"I'm looking to relax for once," Brennan said. "Not take out a mortgage just to pay for dinner."

"Can you get a mortgage on a rented apartment?"

"Fair point."

"On that note, we should really consider getting a bigger place." Greg blushed as Brennan turned to affix him with raised eyes. He rubbed self-consciously at the bandage that covered his patch burn. "Sleeping on your pullout couch is nice and all, and I really appreciate you taking me in after…well, *after*. But maybe we could get one of those new Scottages they're building."

"Scottages?"

"The guy who is building them is named Scott. Last name, probably. And I'm assuming they look like cottages."

"Huh. Where are they being built?"

Greg shrugged. "Somewhere outside the city."

"Outside the city? You do know that I'm a cop, right? I work right across the street," Brennan said, stressing the last few words.

"Oh. Well if you need someone to housesit for you, I'm your man. I'll even give you a discount, since you're family."

"So you want me to pay for the rent of a luxury cottage in the picturesque countryside *and* pay you to live there in my stead?" He shook his head. "There must be some lingering toxins from the patch that are addling your brain."

"Hey," Greg protested. "When my housesitting business takes off, just remember that you could have been in on the ground floor."

Satisfied with the knot of his tie, Brennan walked over toward the couch. "What do you think?"

"You're trying too hard," Greg stated simply. "But I'm sure she will appreciate the gesture. Shouldn't you be leaving soon?"

Brennan checked his phone. He had a scant half hour to meet Clara at The Regent, and he wanted to be early so that she would not be waiting when she arrived. "Yeah, I need to go. Do you remember what you need to do tonight?"

"Search for a job and make myself scarce sometime around ten o'clock," Greg recited without enthusiasm.

"Make yourself scarce? Why would you do that?"

"Look, Uncle Arty, I know not many people would consider you to be fun or charming. I mean, *really* few people."

"Hey!"

Greg went on undeterred. "Have you considered that this night might not end when the bill is paid? That this woman—Clara—might for whatever reason want to come back to your place?"

Brennan stood still and stared uncomprehendingly at his nephew. After a moment, he released a breath he hadn't realized he had been holding. "I didn't—" He caught himself starting a lie designed to deceive even himself. "Actually, Sam suggested something along those lines."

"At least someone is looking at this date with some sense. There's nothing less sexy than bringing a date home to your nephew—witty and handsome as he is—passed out on the sofa." Greg leaned back onto the armrest with an enormous grin on his face.

Brennan felt immensely uncomfortable discussing sex with his nephew, especially with regards to his own potential plans for the evening. "I'm leaving now," he said abruptly. He grabbed his jacket off the back of a tall chair near the island bar that separated the kitchen from the living room.

"Give some thought to that Scottage plan," Greg reminded him with a wink.

"We'll see," Brennan called back, closing the door firmly behind him. He practically glided down the stairs to the ground floor, spurred on by an internal clock that warned him of the impending arrival deadline.

Cold air met him as he pushed open the door to the street. Living in midtown, he was relatively close to all of the high-end restaurants Odols had to offer, and The Regent was one of the classiest. It was located a half dozen city blocks away from his apartment, though, and hailing a taxi at this hour would be slower than going on foot.

Brennan jogged at a brisk pace, and the air was cool enough that sweat was prevented from beading along his forehead. It felt good to be moving at this speed after months—*years*—of mostly walking and sitting. For the second time this week, he was thankful for the new workout regime that was whipping his body into better shape than it had seen in years. Still, the sudden exertion was forcing his breath to come with some difficulty, and his lungs worked overtime to provide oxygen to his legs.

He arrived in front of The Regent with two minutes to spare.

The Regent was one of the ritziest places in Odols. The ground floor was a fine cuisine restaurant, and their kitchen boasted some of the most renowned chefs in the country. Towering over the restaurant was the rest of The Regent—a soaring luxury hotel that cast shadows on every building surrounding it. A monolithic structure of glass and steel, it offered its guests the best view of Odols—provided they could afford the exorbitant nightly costs of staying.

A reed-thin man in a midnight blue restaurant uniform stepped forward, presumably to turn away the strange, panting man who had suddenly appeared in their valet lane. Brennan held up a hand to stall him, allowing himself to catch a few more breaths. His eyes passed over the other guests entering the restaurant, scanning their faces for any familiar features.

The uniformed attendant hovered nearby; a small metal clip on his breast pocket read *Terry*. Brennan felt Terry's eyes pass over his suit and tie, obviously taking in the fact that he was not a vagabond here to cause trouble. "Is everything quite all right, sir?"

"Yeah, fine. I'm looking for someone, though. You may have seen her? Tall, brunette, about the same age as me?"

Terry cleared his throat and peered purposefully around Brennan's shoulder.

"Arthur?"

He turned to find the source of the mature, feminine voice. The profile photo he had seen online did not do her justice. Clara Thompson was taller than average, with the top of her head just barely reaching Brennan's nose. Her leaf-green eyes were rimmed with laugh lines, and the soft curve of her smile seemed comfortable on her lips. Soft highlights on either side framed her face. Beneath her long white trench coat, she wore a knee-length dress whose color approached the blackest of purples. It shimmered under the evening lights of the city. Her eyes were wide with curiosity.

"Arthur Brennan?" she repeated, taking a step closer to him.

He smiled warmly and willed the butterflies in his stomach to disappear. "Yes, hi. Clara?" He bridged the distance between them.

Her lips parted to show a set of gleaming white teeth. The creases around her eyes found their familiar places. "Hi, it's nice to meet you," she said. Clara moved in and they exchanged a quick hug. Brennan could smell a light, flowery scent that wafted gently from her silken hair.

The two parted and regarded each other silently for a brief moment. Terry took the opportunity to reinsert himself into the situation. "I'll get the door for you two."

Brennan hovered his hand a half inch above the small of Clara's back as he ushered her to go first. She offered a polite smile and stepped forward into the subdued lighting of the restaurant's foyer. A young woman with perfect posture gave them a cheery smile from behind her podium.

"The name of your reservation, sir?"

"Brennan, Arthur Brennan," he replied in his best Bond impersonation.

Somehow, she managed not to roll her eyes, maintaining her professional cheer without even blinking. "Brennan," she said, repeating the name several times as she made a show of checking and rechecking the list of reservations. "I'm sorry, sir, but your name does not appear to be here."

Clara gave Brennan a worried look, and a thought occurred to him. "Try another name. Sam McCarthy, he's a friend of mine. He set up the reservation."

With an almost inaudible sigh of skepticism, the hostess looked again, this time further down the list. Her lips parted slightly in surprise. "Sam McCarthy, eight fifteen reservation for two." She glanced up at the two of them with a false smile plastered on her face. "We are ready for you now. Follow me, please."

There was an inner set of doors that were opened by other attendants. Inside, the restaurant was alive with the buzz of hundreds of hushed conversations. The hostess ushered Brennan and Clara through the restaurant, past several open tables, until Brennan worried that she was leading them to an undesirable table close to the restrooms. This was not the case, however, as they turned and arrived at a cozy square table situated in one of the corners of the restaurant.

Unlike the other tables, which had somber black tablecloths, theirs was draped in a fine white fabric and already held several flickering candles. It was partially enclosed, with carefully sculpted wood beams and thick blocks of glass that obscured easy observation from others in the restaurant. The walls around the table were hidden by a gauzy curtain, behind which water trickled with a quiet murmur. It was backlit as well, giving a calming blue aura to the area around the table.

"This is beyond cool," Clara whispered.

They took their seats on the single rounded bench and sat roughly ninety degrees apart. The hostess gave them a more genuine smile this time. "You two have a wonderful meal!"

"Thank you," Brennan said to her back as she turned and started to glide away.

Clara looked at the empty tabletop and gave a cough of laughter. "I think she forgot to give us our menus."

Brennan grinned. "I think you're right."

"We'll get them when our server comes, I guess." She looked at him with dancing excitement in her eyes. "So, Arthur, tell me something interesting about yourself."

"Something interesting about myself? Like what?"

"I don't know. Anything. What do you like to do in your spare time?"

"I like to read," he said. "And I have a good friend that I play pool with sometimes."

"I love a man who loves books," Clara said enthusiastically. "I wish I had more time for reading. My grandparents had a place in New Hampshire that we would visit every year, once in the summer and once around Christmas. They had a big, old wooden house down by the edge of the lake, with a screened-in back porch that looked out over the water." Her smile widened as she thought back to her childhood. "My favorite place in their house was a bay window on the second floor. It was as wide as I am long, and there was a deep ledge where I could sit and read as the sun rose in the morning."

Clara was a talkative person, Brennan noticed, but he also realized that he liked hearing the sound of her voice. "That must have been nice," he said.

Her excited eyes turned wistful as she met his gaze. "It was. But now I'm busy working with patients and trying to get a book published and, obviously, dating, and—" Clara puffed a sigh of frustration. "Life," she said bluntly. "It catches up to all of us, doesn't it?"

"That it does," Brennan said, laughing.

A large man with dark brown skin and a gleaming head came by the table with two flutes of champagne held in his wide hands. The white fabric of his chef's apron was pristine, almost glowing in the accented lighting of their secluded table. "Good evening, folks," he said, white teeth shining as he placed the glasses down in front of them. Brennan rose to his feet, and he and the chef exchanged grips. "Chef Ray, pleased to meet you."

"Arthur Brennan. And this is Clara Thompson," he said, and Clara quickly rose to shake hands with the chef.

"You have a great friend, Arthur," Chef Ray said. "And any friend of Sam's is a friend of mine."

A sense of pride battled with the shock Brennan felt. People either loved or hated Sam, and the latter group seemed more and more prevalent these days, so it was good to see that not all of his bridges had been burned.

"I don't know if Sam had a chance to explain what's going to happen here," Chef Ray continued, "but I'm going to prepare a multi-course meal for you, paired with several wines, and hopefully we're all going to have a great evening!" He clapped his hands together and beamed at the two of them.

"That sounds amazing," Clara said, awe evident in her voice.

Brennan nodded. "I can't wait," he told Chef Ray.

"Excellent! First, do either of you have any food allergies?"

They both shook their heads.

"And how do you like your meat cooked?"

"Medium rare," Clara responded.

"Medium well."

Chef Ray bowed his head slightly and raised his hands. "Perfect. Well enjoy yourselves tonight, and I'll bring out the first course shortly."

"Thank you," Brennan said.

Clara waited until the chef had left before leaning in to whisper. "Arthur…thank you. I promise I can pay for my half, or at least for the wine. But if I'm being completely honest, I don't usually spend so much when eating out, especially not for a single meal. I hope I am not seeming cheap, but would you mind if we kept things simple from here on out?" A long moment passed, and color rose in Clara's cheeks. "I'm sorry, that's implying a second date. I'm being silly, I—"

"No, not at all," Brennan said quickly. A grin made its way onto his face, in spite of his best efforts. "I'm relieved, actually."

"You are?"

"Yes!" He laughed and slid slightly closer to her. "It has been a long time since I last saw anyone, and I want you to enjoy tonight."

"You'll have to give my thanks to your friend for setting this up."

Brennan laughed. "I definitely will. Though I gave him a hard time earlier today, and I think him saddling me with a seven-course meal is his way of getting back while still looking out for me. Next time, I'll make a home-cooked meal for us."

Clara's eyes shined as she looked into his. "Perfectly fine with me," she said. She lifted her glass and took a gulp of champagne. "You cook?"

"I make ingredients interact with appliances and produce slightly more edible things," Brennan said, eliciting a laugh from Clara.

"Mmm, impressive. I'm afraid to admit that I have more of a green thumb than a culinary hand."

"Where do you garden, in a city like this?"

Clara laughed again, a fantastic sound to Brennan's ears. She moved her handbag and sidled a little closer to him. "Like I said, I don't have much recreational time. When I was in college, I helped out with tending to the gardens for academic credit, and before that I was always running around in my mother's flowers in the backyard." Clara shook her head, still smiling. "She always hated when I did that."

"Why is that?"

"I think she was afraid I would step on one of her precious flowers. She would import bulbs and seeds from all across Europe and create the most beautiful natural arrangements with them. I realized at some point that I could win her affection by planting instead of playing, and I was surprisingly good at it." She shrugged. "I guess it stuck."

A woman with dirty blonde hair appeared with two fresh glasses and a bottle of white wine, as a younger man followed behind with a basket of bread. Chef Ray came out at that moment and delivered two lightly steaming bowls to the table.

"To start you off tonight, we have a French onion soup with gruyère cheese and caramelized onions, served in a brandy broth."

"Sounds delicious," Brennan said.

Clara moved her empty champagne flute to the side and picked up the other glass. After a polite sip, she sighed appreciatively. "That is *really* good."

Brennan drank a mouthful and squelched the scowl that came to his lips. His late wife had been a fan of white wines, but Brennan had never developed a liking for them.

"So," Clara said after a second sip, "what is it like to be a detective? You must see a lot of exciting things."

"That's one word for it," he said.

"How would you describe your job?"

"There are moments of excitement, sure, but those are surrounded by a lot of paperwork. Mostly, it is stressful. It's a pretty unforgiving job, and there are a lot of opportunities to get yourself shot."

"See? Excitement!"

Brennan smiled at her tongue-in-cheek humor. "After it happens once, it's not a process you're eager to repeat."

"So has it happened to you?"

"Getting shot?" Brennan thought about the botched rescue mission he and Sam had staged a few months ago. In their attempt to save Bishop, she had in turn become *their* salvation, taking out a ruthless drug lord in the process. "A couple times."

"When was the most recent?"

"You seem very interested in this topic," he joked.

"I work with victims of trauma," Clara said. "I can imagine very few things that would be more scarring, psychologically and physically, than a bullet wound. It sounds like that would be an awful experience, but your job sounds so much more exhilarating."

Brennan became intensely aware of how closely they were sitting. Over the course of the conversation and with the help of some wine, their hands were now just barely overlapping on the bench space between them. He let his fingertips brush against the edge of Clara's hand and wander over the smooth skin. They delicately traced the outline of her fingers before intertwining with them. He took another sip of the Riesling, this time not caring about the taste.

"This is nice," Clara said softly. She edged a bit closer, and her breath intermingled with his.

"I almost died," Brennan blurted out. The words fell out of his mouth before he could realize what he was saying. "A couple months ago."

Clara's hand tensed up, and her head moved fractionally backward. Her eyebrows knitted together in consternation. "What happened?"

"We were solving the homicide of a pharmacist named Nettle. The kid was barely out of college, with no prior arrests to his name. He would never have been a blip on anyone's radar if he had kept his nose clean." Brennan sighed heavily and took a big sip of wine.

"I'm guessing he didn't do that."

He shook his head. "Nettle became a middleman provider for a drug lord, and when he tried to increase his share of the profits, things turned violent."

"I think I read about that in the paper."

"What didn't make the headlines was that our coordinated strike on two possible locations for their storage depots went belly up. We lost half a dozen men, and my partner, Bishop, was taken hostage. It took us hours just to track her down, and thankfully she was still alive then."

"That's awful! Why didn't they kill her as well?" Brennan gave Clara a sharp look, and she held up a placating hand. "Don't get me wrong, I am glad they didn't, for your sake. But why keep her alive?"

Brennan shrugged. "Any number of reasons. I think they just recognized her face from poking around the pharmacy, and then again when she showed up at the warehouse. I was jumped, too, but they only saw me once before the hospital."

"The hospital?" she asked in alarm.

"Oh, no, not for me. Well, yes, I needed a hospital *afterwards*. What I mean is that we tracked down the location where they were holding her and, well, we staged a rescue."

Clara smiled in relief, and admiration shone from her eyes. "How did you know to find her there?"

Brennan stopped midway through another bite into his breadstick. It had been Greg who had found her, with a patch on his arm and the detached voice boardwalk psychics used while gazing into crystal balls. Except *his* vision had been real, against all doubts, and it was a startling revelation which Brennan had withheld even from Sam.

His best friend had joined him in the rescue op, without question, yet he was never made aware of the truth. It was that act that made Brennan realize now how fiercely loyal Sam could be. But the fact that Greg could be exposed—as either a patch addict or as a "freak" with a power like Brennan's—meant that he couldn't reveal the truth of how they found Bishop.

"We received an anonymous tip," he lied easily. "The caller said they had seen a woman matching Bishop's description being taken into the abandoned hospital uptown."

"Wow, that was lucky."

"Tell me about it."

Clara smiled lightly as she held out her glass to be filled again. "So you and a SWAT team busted in and saved her?" Heat flushed in his cheeks as Brennan recalled that night; Clara spotted the blush, and her wine hand dipped in response. "Don't tell me you went in there *alone*!"

"No, of course not. That would have been stupid." He poured until her glass was full. "I brought a friend."

She eyed him sternly. "Let me get this straight. You and your pal took on a violent drug lord, on his home turf, to save the damsel in distress? Without any backup?"

"When you say it like that, it sounds a little absurd…"

"Where was the rest of the police force?" she demanded.

At home, because I couldn't easily tell them my nephew had a drug-induced hallucination that led us straight to Bishop.

"They were exhausted from the dual raids," Brennan explained, keeping to his cover story. "After Bishop's team got hit, we spent the rest of the evening hunting down possible leads without any success. When I got the call, it was the middle of the night and most of us were already asleep. Besides, my informant wasn't what you would call a credible source."

Clara tried frowning, but her habitual smile cracked through the disapproving mask. "That is so…incredible. I would *never* be able to do a job like yours, not in a million years."

"Thanks." He considered it for a moment. "Is that something you say thanks for? When someone tells you that your career is just a little too insane for them?"

"That isn't what I meant!" Clara took another mouthful of wine, and her eyes fluttered rapidly as she started feeling its effects. She set her glass down on the table and looked at Brennan directly. "You lead such an amazing life compared to most people. In comparison, mine is so ordinary and—"

"Safe?"

She laughed. "I was going to say boring, but safe works just as well."

"Is that why you were on CopAFeel? Are you a bit of an adrenaline junkie?" He didn't know where the huskiness in his voice came from, and it felt unnatural to him, but it was apparently working well on Clara. She leaned closer in response to his voice.

"You could say I'm attracted to danger," she whispered. Her gaze tracked all over his suit, and Brennan felt like she was undressing him with her eyes.

I thought Sam was the only person who actually did that. To women, not me, he added self-consciously, as if anyone could hear his thoughts anyway.

"I'm attracted to a dangerous man who can keep me safe," Clara continued. Her thumb was massaging his hand insistently. "Is that weird?"

"Not at all," Brennan said, leaning in. "I think that's basically every love story, ever."

Their mouths met, and Brennan tasted the wine on her lips and tongue. The taste was sweet and savory, and he was reluctant to part ways after a few seconds had passed. It was an unfamiliar feeling that he was experiencing. After several years of marriage and even more years of grieving widowerhood, Brennan was now emotionally attached to Clara in a way that would have seemed impossible just a few days ago. It was lust right now, he knew, but perhaps with time it could develop into something more meaningful.

That's crazy, the rational part of his mind argued. *I haven't even* known *about her for a full day.*

Clara's eyes were wide, her pupils dilated, and she wore a satisfied grin as she leaned back into her seat. The blue lighting from the backlit waterfall behind her did interesting things to her features. If she had been lovely outside the restaurant, now she looked absolutely beautiful. Certain parts of Brennan clamored for her attention, for her lips to rejoin his and venture onward from there, but just then the second course arrived.

Chef Ray and the blonde waitress each held a dish of something that smelled absolutely delicious, and the scent that now wafted toward Brennan was sublime. His mouth watered as he looked at the meal before him, and his excitement was mirrored in Clara's expression.

"All right, folks," Chef Ray said. "For the second course, I've prepared for you pan-fried calamari with hot cherry peppers, accompanied by a rouille sauce."

After thanks were given and Chef Ray left, Clara took a fork to her calamari without preamble. She moaned as she chewed the succulent seafood, and she washed it down with another small sip of wine. "This is delicious," she said. "Definitely worth the small mortgage it took to come here. What is it?"

Her last question was in response to the sudden grin that took over Brennan's face. "Nothing," he replied. "I just made a very similar comment to my nephew earlier this evening."

"Great minds think alike, I suppose. It sounds like you are fond of your nephew. You've mentioned him twice so far."

"Have I?" Brennan smiled at the observation. "We seem to be getting a little closer each day. There have been a few rough patches, but on the whole…yeah, he's a great kid."

"That's awesome," Clara said enthusiastically. "Really, it's impressive that you two can get along so well. I can't tell you how many cases I've seen where trauma happened within the family because parents and children couldn't find a way to communicate effectively."

"He trusts me, it's as simple as that."

Clara frowned. "What about you? Do you trust him in return?"

Brennan thought of the night they had rescued Bishop, the night in which he had willingly chosen to put Greg in danger because his nephew had promised he could help. He had trusted him that night, but was it just his sixth sense that had caused him to believe Greg's sincerity?

"It's complicated," Brennan said. "I like to think that I can trust him, but then I remember that I've had good reasons to be wary."

Just then, the waitress came back with two new glasses of wine, red this time. "This is a Scarecrow Cabernet Sauvignon," she said, placing the glasses on the table. "It's a medium-bodied blend with tastes of blackberry, plum, and dark chocolate."

They thanked her as she left the table. Brennan used the brief intrusion to change topics. "If you could do anything you wanted, without having to worry about money, what would you do?"

"Anything at all?"

"To your heart's content."

Clara used the time spent chewing another piece of fried squid to think of a response. "I think I would want to travel," she said. "There are a lot of places I haven't been to yet that I always dreamed of visiting when I got older. Now that I'm here, though, I have a job and a house and other obligations that I can't drop all of a sudden. It isn't even about the money, though that's a big factor. I have a *life* here. I would miss my friends and relatives."

"Do you come from a big family?"

"Oh, yeah. Huge. I have eight brothers and sisters, though they've moved all throughout the country by now. What about you?"

"My family is significantly smaller," Brennan said vaguely, sipping his wine. "It's basically just me and my nephew now."

Clara nodded and wisely dropped the subject, just as their third course arrived. Chef Ray was grinning from ear to ear as he delivered two plates that smelled like heaven. "For our final course tonight, we have a sliced filet mignon with Cipollini onions and wild mushrooms." He turned to address Brennan. "I just want to thank you so much for coming out here tonight, and if you ever need anything, you know who to call."

Brennan smiled easily; it was hard not to respond to the infectious enthusiasm of the chef's good nature. "Thank you," he said, feeling it deeply. "And Sam thanks you."

"Anytime, anytime. You two have a wonderful evening!"

Water trickled behind them as Brennan and Clara each took a bite of the filet mignon. They moaned in unison and snagged another slice each before the conversation resumed.

"So what would you do with unlimited time and resources?" she asked, rebounding the original question.

"Oddly enough, probably the exact opposite of you. I'd want to find somewhere quiet to settle down and relax."

"You don't suffer from wanderlust?"

"I think it is a fantastic word, but no, not really. I got a lot of that out of my system early on."

"Oh? Where have you travelled?"

Images flashed in his head, memories of his time as a Sleeper on international missions. He had never felt more alive than when he was running through the old medina in Rabat, silenced bullets whizzing past his head even as the call to prayer sounded out in the early morning. "I've been to Morocco a few times," he said vaguely, counting off with his fingers. "I toured around Europe once when I was in college, which was nice. And my father used to have business in Ontario, so I have had my fill of Canada as well."

"Wow," Clara said, shaking her head. "I feel like a broken record, but I am insanely jealous of your life. You didn't tell me what you *would* do with all that free time. What do you find relaxing?"

Brennan was starting to feel a little lightheaded as the wine worked its way through his system, and he could tell that Clara was experiencing a similar buzz. "I like to read," he said. "I find science fascinating, but I'd never have the patience to do any of it myself. Maybe I'd buy a remote mountain cabin and become an amateur astronomer."

Clara laughed and raised her glass in salute. "I would one hundred perfect support that dream. Percent," she corrected. "One hundred percent."

"All right, you've had enough," Brennan joked. His cheeks hurt from grinning so much.

"But the evening has only just begun," Clara said. Her eyes danced with suggestive promise, and she leaned in for another kiss. Brennan met her halfway, and he held the kiss for several long moments before breaking away. Clara's expression was a mix of hunger and uncertainty, and she spoke with the deliberate pace of questionable sobriety. "I like you, Arthur Brennan. You're clever, funny, and you care deeply for those who are close to you. There aren't many good men like you around these days."

Brennan swallowed hard. He heard his heartbeat reverberating in his skull. "I feel the same way about you," he managed, his throat suddenly dry. "I like you too."

Clara set down her wine glass and slid to be seated shoulder to shoulder with Brennan. Her breath mingled with his as they looked into each other's eyes. "Let me know if I am moving too quickly," she murmured, her lips brushing against his as she spoke.

"At this point, I think we can safely skip dessert, right?"

"Definitely. You can have a special dessert back at my place." Her lips pursed slightly in contemplation. "If you want to, that is."

Brennan felt drunk on her perfume and found himself lost in the moment. A niggling thought pulled at the far threads of his consciousness, but his mind was too foggy to pay it much attention. Breathlessly, he said, "I can't think of anything I want more right now. Don't your cheeks hurt yet?"

Already grinning, Clara's smile widened slightly more. "Not at all. You clearly need more practice at this happiness thing," she teased.

"I may need your help with that." He kissed her lightly.

"Don't worry, my fees are very reasonable." Clara stole another kiss before shifting her attention to the entrance of their secluded seating area. Brennan followed her eyes and saw the waitress standing patiently, her eyes skillfully neither focused on their embrace nor completely ignoring them.

"Can I interest you two in any dessert tonight?" she asked. Her eyes twinkled with amusement, but she was professional enough to keep her face from revealing anything more.

"I'm about to be stuffed," Clara said, and then her cheeks turned a deep crimson. "I mean, I'm about stuffed. With food." She sealed her lips before she could say anything more.

"Just the bill, please," Brennan said quickly.

Their waitress glanced at him sideways. "Your meal has already been paid for in full, sir. Is there anything else I can do for you?"

Sam.

"No, thank you. Everything was excellent."

"I will pass your compliments on to the kitchen," she promised. "I hope you two have a fantastic rest of the evening!" She collected some of their finished plates and left.

Brennan looked over at Clara. "The night doesn't have to end here, you know."

"Does that line ever work?"

"If you say yes, I'll be one for one."

Clara grinned. "I'm going to say no to the line, but yes to the offer."

"Really?"

"I already offered dessert back at my place, remember?" She grabbed her purse and slid out from the booth. "Enough foreplay. Are you coming tonight or not?"

He accepted her outstretched hand. "Plus one point for the pun," he said. He didn't know what was going on with this evening, except that his legs were carrying him out of the booth and through the restaurant as Clara guided him to the exit. His brain was working at half power as his heart pumped blood to more significant regions.

The conflicted feelings he had suffered earlier in the evening were waning, replaced instead by a deep yearning that could only be quieted in one way. He allowed himself to be drawn by Clara's confident grip on his hand into the cool nighttime air. At least an hour and a half had passed inside the restaurant, and as Clara wrapped her arm around the crook of his elbow, Brennan wondered if Greg had relocated to Sam's place or if he was still at home waiting for a text message.

To his surprise, though, Clara started to tug insistently in the opposite direction of Brennan's apartment. "Come on, my car is this way," she told him.

"We're going back to your house?"

"That plan still works for you, right?"

Brennan shook his head in an attempt to sober up. "No, yeah, that sounds great. But you aren't in any shape to drive right now." He realized he had jinxed himself when, not a minute later, he tripped on a perfectly level slab of sidewalk.

"You aren't doing much better yourself, sailor," Clara teased, slurring slightly. "Still haven't found your land legs, have you?" She fell victim to her own karma demons, though, and Brennan managed to catch her mid-fall as one stiletto heel caught on the stubborn lip of a sidewalk crack. She laughed it off and caught the look he was giving her. "At least I had an excuse, Mr. Can't-Walk-On-Even-Ground."

"Good to know that that tongue of yours isn't curbed by a bottle of wine."

Clara affixed him with a sultry gaze. "You would be surprised at the things my tongue can do when I'm drunk. Not that I'm drunk," she clarified. "And wow, I sounded slutty just then. I hope you aren't judging me right now. I really don't go out like this very often, and I think I had a little too much."

"Now that we're standing and moving around, I can feel the wine a lot more," Brennan said sympathetically. He felt a little buzzed, but it was a far cry from where Clara seemed to be at the moment. Clara led the two of them onto a smaller side street. "Maybe we should get a cab."

"That's probably a good idea," Clara said, nodding slightly as they continued onward. The street was empty and quiet, and the soft light of the streetlamps was calming. The breeze was slight and brought cool air with it, and it smelled like it might rain later in the night. A single black SUV rumbled down the street, and the trash can next to Brennan crumpled inward following the low cough of a silenced pistol.

"What the—?" Clara began to ask, just before the nearest parked car exploded.

A wave of heat and pressure knocked Brennan off his feet. His back hit the ground a split second before his skull cracked against the pavement, and he was seeing stars when he opened his eyes. The street erupted with noise all around them, but it sounded like he was hearing everything from underwater. His eardrums had been damaged, most likely. Brennan touched the back of his head, and his fingers came back with blood on them.

Come on, you need to get up!

With the voice in his head urging him on, Brennan lurched to his feet, then promptly dropped to one knee. His head pounded in agony; his left arm seared with pain and it refused to work properly. Thankfully, his vision was recovering, and he blinked away the dust and ash that threatened to blind him. Clara had ended up against the wall, her prone body facing away from him.

Brennan stumbled to her side and rolled her over. Her coat had several tears and was dirtied in the fall, but there were only a few minor cuts on her legs and arms. One thin line of blood crossed the ridge of her forehead, and it made the side of her face look much worse than it actually was. Brennan brought his ear close to her mouth and nose, and a small exhalation of warm air told him she was still breathing. It was shallow, but she was still alive.

You have to move, the small voice in his head insisted. *I can get you out of here.*

That was odd; the voice didn't usually talk so much, or in the first person. Brennan shook his head. Now wasn't the time to wonder about his apparent psychosis. There was a much more physical threat to his wellbeing in that moment. The SUV that had been passing by during the attack now idled in the middle of the street. Doors opened on either side, and men began to disembark, each one holding a semi-automatic rifle. Dark smoke billowed from the burning wreckage of the car they had just destroyed.

"All right, time to go," Brennan huffed, jostling Clara in an attempt to wake her up. Her eyelids fluttered slightly but remained closed. Brennan maneuvered his arms beneath her as well as he could and grunted as he heaved her over his shoulder into a fireman's hold. She didn't weigh much, in spite of her height, but his body was still dazed and weak from the blast. His knees wobbled as he took shaky steps into a nearby alley. With luck, Brennan figured the smoke would buy them a few seconds as they made their escape.

The wall directly to Brennan's left gained several new pockmarks as bullets embedded themselves in the brick.

Or not.

Brennan swore loudly as more bullets whizzed past his head like an angry swarm of hornets. He sorely wished he had his gun, but he had left it at home with the assumption that his date night *wouldn't* devolve into an ambush by unknown assailants.

Clara started to stir, and Brennan staggered behind a dumpster just as another staccato of gunfire erupted overhead. "What the hell is going on?" she demanded. Her voice echoed the fear that was apparent in her wide eyes. "Arthur…"

Brennan shushed her as politely as he could. It came out as a loud hiss, though, to be heard over the sound of their impending deaths. He looked around desperately for anything that could serve as a weapon. Unlike in the movies, spare metal bars weren't just casually lying around. He pulled out his cell phone to dial for the police, only to realize that the screen had been shattered. It refused to turn on. "We're being shot at," he told her. "Or more likely, *I* am."

"By who?"

"Don't know, and it really isn't the time to care about that. You need to get out of here as fast as you can and call the cops."

She looked in dismay at the broken phone in his hand. "My phone was in my purse," she said.

"Then you'll have to find someone who can lend you theirs." They both ducked down further as bullets smashed against the other side of the dumpster. Brennan recognized it as suppression fire, meant to keep them subdued until their attackers could come around the side and face them.

"What about you?" Clara asked. "I can't just leave you here!"

"Fine, we don't have time to argue." It would have been better for her to run for help while he held them off, but now the odds of survival were pretty even either way for both of them. Brennan repositioned himself so that he was facing the open path away from the gunmen. "On three, I'm going to push this dumpster out to block the alley. It's heavy, and they'll need to stop firing for a few seconds to move it out of the way."

"And then what will we do?"

"Run." He stared intently into her eyes for what was likely the last time. That last bit of insight he kept to himself, though. "On the count of three," he reminded her.

Gunfire hammered against the dumpster from just a few feet away.

"Three!" Brennan shouted. He threw his weight against the battered hunk of steel, and the dumpster groaned as it started to slide away from the wall. "Run!"

Clara took off down the alley, holding her heels in one hand. He hadn't told her to go barefoot, but it was faster than attempting to run on several inches of borrowed height.

Smart.

The dumpster continued its slow progress. One of the wheels broke free from its bearing, and that corner abruptly lurched to the ground. Steel grinded against concrete, and while it meant it was harder for Brennan to move it into position, it also meant that his assailants would have the same difficulties.

And Brennan was a larger and stronger man than most.

Finally, the dumpster smashed against the opposite wall of the alley. Slanted on a diagonal, it completely blocked any line of sight from the other side. Brennan coughed up dust as he accidentally inhaled the odor emanating from the dumpster, and then started off down the alley in pursuit of Clara. He turned a corner and saw her dress disappearing around another bend a hundred feet away. Adrenaline surged through his veins as Brennan raced to catch up with her.

They are jumping over the dumpster.

His steps faltered as a sudden realization bashed him over the head like a slugger with a baseball bat. The voice he was hearing wasn't the usual one that accompanied his power.

Finally, he gets it.

Now that he listened closely, he could hear the difference. It was so obvious that he wondered how he hadn't heard it before.

You were just shot at and nearly blown up, the other voice commented dryly. *More to the point, though, they are catching up to you.*

How are you in my head? Brennan demanded. In his experience, the only people with that kind of power were Sleepers, and even then only when the subject was asleep.

Is that really the most pressing issue? I can help you.

True, Brennan's power chimed in.

He turned the corner and found Clara panting against the wall beneath a broken streetlight. She cried out as he appeared, and Brennan held up his hands to show her he wasn't a threat. "Clara, are you all right?"

She nodded wearily, not speaking as she caught her breath.

You can help by calling the police, Brennan thought to the mystery voice.

Gunshots were fired in midtown; someone will surely have called them. You two need to find safety, though. They will reach you before the authorities can get here.

Brennan frowned at the imagery, but immediately took solace in the fact that he had an ally where there was none before. It was even more reassuring that his power had backed up her claim, just as it had validated Greg during the summer when he'd promised he could find Bishop.

He looked over at his companion, who was sucking in air with heaving breaths, and then glanced back at the alley they had just vacated. He knew it wasn't enough of a lead to ditch their pursuers. His body was just about ready to give out, and Clara was on her last legs.

Fine, he replied. *How the hell do we get out of here?*

They have made it past your barricade.

"Shut up and help me!" Brennan shouted.

Clara shrunk away, startled, and looked at him with searching eyes. "Who are you talking to, Arthur?"

Calm down, came the voice. *There is a sewer system that runs directly beneath where you are standing.*

You want me to drop ten feet into a river of shit?

Technically, a river of runoff from rain. If you want to wait a little longer, your friends can accommodate you with a slightly shorter fall. About six feet, by my estimate.

Brennan gulped and glanced at Clara, who was still waiting expectantly for a response. "We need to move," he told her.

"Already? I thought you blocked the way. Aren't we safe now?"

"Not yet," he said. He grabbed her arm and pulled her toward a nearby storm drain. "Help me lift this up."

"You've got to be kidding me."

"Come on, grab that side," Brennan ordered. He looped his fingers around the bars of one side and shivered as the cold, wet steel pressed against his skin.

"Arthur, I don't know about—"

"Hey! We do *not* have time for this right now!"

Jolted into action by his voice, Clara hurried to the other side and set an uneasy hand on the storm drain. "Ooh, it's cold!" she exclaimed, shivering at the touch.

"On three. Three!"

They heaved together, though Brennan knew he was basically pulling for both of them, and the metal grate lifted slowly out of its rectangular depression in the pavement. Brennan heard a quiet trickle of water coming from the stream below. He kept pulling on the storm drain until its momentum shifted and it slammed heavily against the concrete.

"Go, go, go!" he urged Clara.

She moved so her legs were dangling through the hole in the ground and gave Brennan one last desperate glance. With his nod, she gripped his right arm with both hands, and he gently lowered her as far as he could reach. She let go with a small yelp and fell the few remaining feet. Her foot slipped on the slimy stone below, and she collapsed into a shallow puddle of water.

Ten seconds.

Brennan quickly threaded his legs into the opening and propped himself up with his elbows on street level. His body wanted to let gravity do its work, but he forced his one good arm to reach out and grab the metal bars of the heavy storm drain. He flexed and brought it slowly to a standing position, where the slightest shift of its weight in either direction could send it crashing to the ground.

Five seconds!

Brennan let himself fall, his left arm flailing helplessly as he held on tight with the right. The storm drain fell back into its depression. Brennan felt, more than heard, the pop of his shoulder sliding out of place as his descent jerked to a halt, and his grip went slack. He fell like a rag doll to the ground and bit back a scream as he landed on the freshly dislocated shoulder.

"Are you okay?" Clara asked. She gingerly touched the arm he was cradling, and this time Brennan cried out in pain.

Be quiet, warned the anonymous witness. *Keep out of sight and don't make a sound. They are right on top of you.*

Brennan couldn't move much, but he managed to inch his body out of the direct view coming in through the storm drain. Clara seemed to understand what he was doing and helped keep pressure off his shoulder as he moved.

"Your head is bleeding," she whispered.

He simply nodded and made a shushing gesture, minus the finger to the lips. Clara mistook his pursed lips as a sign for a kiss and, despite the gray water and gunmen surrounding them, planted her lips upon his. Either way, it stopped her from talking.

Muffled voices shouted out to each other in the alley above; Brennan could only hear enough to recognize they were speaking in German. They sounded angry, though, that much was clear. None of them had heard the storm drain slam shut, or else they would have already been rappelling into the tunnel.

Clara broke off the kiss and sat with her back against the curved wall, seemingly no longer worried about dirtying her dress. She had a dazed, far-off look in her eyes, and she held her hand lightly against her stomach. Shock could be hard on people, especially those so unaccustomed to dangerous situations.

The angry German shouting devolved into errant grumbling as the gunmen started tearing apart the alley. Brennan heard trash cans crashing to the ground, and several doors were pounded by heavy fists. There was no trace of their prey.

Brennan slipped in and out of consciousness a few times, and he did not know how much time had passed before the gunmen disappeared for good. At one point, he simply opened his eyes and heard nothing but the water trickling past his head and Clara on the verge of hyperventilating.

With a Herculean effort and a groan of pain, Brennan wriggled himself into a sitting position. He looked down with clear eyes at the damage to his left arm. It was difficult to see in the dark, but he guessed it had been burned and bloodied in the car blast. It didn't hurt anymore, which he took to be a bad sign. His other arm, however, responded to every minor movement with a plethora of painful signals, which Brennan didn't find any more comforting.

"You're in pain," Clara said in a hollow voice. Her eyes were wide and fully devoted to him, but Brennan could see she had a thousand-mile stare.

"I think I dislocated it."

"Do you want me to pop it back into place?" she asked.

Brennan had done that exact thing once or twice, and the experience never got any less painful. Also, he had either done it himself or had a skilled partner to take care of it, and Clara was definitely not a trained Sleeper. "That sort of thing only works in the movies," he said, letting her down gently. "But thanks."

She nodded dully and resumed staring at the wall.

Are you still there? Brennan asked, directing the thought to the psychic Samaritan. He didn't get a response.

The presence of someone with that kind of power was puzzling as well. They should not have been able to get inside Brennan's head the way they had, especially when he was fully awake. Another thought occurred to him, and he briefly wondered if this was all some terrible nightmare. It would explain how a Sleeper had infiltrated his mind and—

And what, exactly? Helped you? How sinister of me, the voice replied suddenly. *Trust me, you are awake. This is real. Also, you should see a doctor.*

About the voices in my head?

That would be a good reason, though I was referring to your head wound. And that arm. There was a pause. *And that other arm.*

I'm a wreck, I get it, Brennan thought, surprising himself with how casually he was carrying on this nonverbal conversation. *Just one question: are you a Sleeper?*

No, came the immediate reply.

Who are you?

Brennan waited several long minutes without getting a reply. He looked over at Clara, who was making a strange lurching motion.

"We need to get to a hospital," Brennan said. "You need to get checked out as well."

"Sounds good," she croaked. Less than a second later, she turned her head and emptied the contents of her stomach onto the tunnel floor. Either the wine had finally caught up to her, exacerbated by all of the running around, or else she just realized how close they had been to death. She wiped at her mouth and held her head as she looked at Brennan. "Is this what it's always like?"

"Welcome to my life, baby. Exciting enough for you?"

Clara sighed and rose to her feet. "A little too exciting," she said. "Come on, let's get you to a doctor."

Chapter Fourteen

Friday morning held all the promise in the world as Alex Brüding rolled out of bed.

She felt better than she had in a long time, in spite of the long night. Arthur Brennan was a much more interesting man than she had first envisioned. From the moment she touched his mind, she knew he was a Sleeper; the architecture of his thoughts was so *similar* to that of Benjamin. It was one thing for her to be told who he was, and another thing entirely to experience that intimate contact for herself.

Beneath the excitement over finally finding somebody worthy of her interest, Alex felt a bubbling anger toward Heinrich that frothed like a steaming stew threatening to boil over. She had given explicit orders that the target was not to be harmed. Or had she?

Alex closed her eyes and looked within herself. In her youth, she had imagined her mind as a long series of filing cabinets, each one filled with folders that neatly contained all of her thoughts and memories in an orderly manner that allowed her to access them at will. Somewhere along the line, she had made the upgrade to a fully computerized system.

Now, she walked among massive computer hard drives. They weren't to scale or even technically accurate representations, but they served their purpose. Her memories pulsed like fine gemstones on the surface of each storage unit. She brought forth the memory of her rendezvous with Heinrich and replayed it.

The detective will not be killed during this operation.

Alex sighed loudly and walked into the kitchen. His methods were brutal and unorthodox, but Heinrich had stayed true to the letter of the agreement. She was honor-bound to pay him the remaining half of the money later this afternoon.

And without actually getting Brennan on the right path to catch this killer, she thought glumly. She opened a fresh bag of imported beans, bought late last night after her subterfuge with Brennan, and started the percolating process that would bring her up to one hundred percent.

When she'd been inside Brennan's mind, Alex had picked up more information about the murders. Tonight was the night. If she didn't take a more active role in the investigation, in Brennan's life personally, then somebody else would fall victim to the serial killer's rampage. Considering that she was among a minority of those in Odols with powers, there was a distinct possibility that *she* could be the next target.

"I could always change my name, leave the country, and never look back," she said to the cup slowly being filled with black gold. She chewed her lower lip. "Benjamin would never leave me in peace for deserting him, though. I would be just as hunted by his *Sleepers*," she said, imbuing the last word with disdain.

That was another concern she had to contend with. Now that she was on Benjamin's radar, Alex was unsure of what his motives would be. Her quiet and content life of luxury was compromised, and she found herself all too easily enticed by these secret bouts of espionage.

Her coffee finished percolating, and she poured some into a wide-mouthed mug. She sighed contently as she inhaled its earthy aroma. There were few things in the world more satisfying than her morning brew.

Serial killer hunting aside, today was going to be a busy one. Alex needed to have a long chat with her father over how they could treat her mother over her final few months. Her long days of suffering were inevitable; she at least deserved to feel the sun on her skin and get out of bed more than once every few weeks.

She was also obligated to pay off the remaining half of her debt to Heinrich, as well as find a way to keep her pet detective alive long enough to fulfill his purpose to Benjamin. If she held off on paying Heinrich, his men would be less likely to hunt for Brennan, waiting as they were for their cut of the payment.

That would put them on my trail, though, Alex thought, sipping from her mug. That was an unacceptable tradeoff. Heinrich's men would be hounds baying for her blood if she didn't deliver the cash before the day was out.

Alex took deliberate steps into the living room and opened the drawer of the coffee table. She retrieved a cheap cell phone from inside, one of several burner phones she had purchased that week, and inserted its battery pack. She gulped another mouthful of coffee while she waited for the phone to cycle through its startup sequence.

After a few moments of perfect silence, she realized something was terribly wrong.

She could no longer hear the voices in her head. To a normal, well-adjusted individual, the absence would have been noted as a welcome relief—but Alex had never considered herself one of those people. It occurred to her that she had heard nothing from their minds since her return to the apartment late last night. The ambient noise of her neighbors' thoughts to which she had grown so accustomed was gone, and she felt naked without her shroud of whispers. Alex closed her eyes and attempted to reach out as she always had, extending a psychic probe to touch upon their intimate thoughts.

Nothing happened.

Alex shivered involuntarily. "What the fuck?" She slammed her coffee down on the table and ran to her room. She threw on a more presentable outfit—jeans and a loose-fitting shirt—and stalked back toward the front door. After a moment's consideration, she grabbed the burner phone from the coffee table before leaving the apartment, letting the door slam unceremoniously behind her.

It was early in the day, and she heard a few disgruntled voices respond to the noise she made. She disregarded their petty concerns. Her body trembled with fury and fear as she jabbed the button for the elevator. Its doors opened lazily, and she stabbed the button for the sixteenth floor.

By the time she arrived in front of Benjamin's door, Alex had cooled from burning rage to simmering frustration. Still, her knuckles landed heavily on the thick wooden door, and the booming of her knocks reverberated down the hall. The door opened, and she was greeted by Benjamin's wrinkled face sprouting from a ridiculously luxurious white bathrobe. A pair of sunglasses sat perched atop his head, and he held his folded white cane beneath one arm.

"To what do I owe the pleasure of this visit so early in the day?" he asked. His perfectly cordial tone would have sounded ironic and sarcastic coming from anyone else. Coming from Benjamin, the question merely rang with polite curiosity.

"There is something *seriously* wrong with my power," Alex told him without preamble.

Benjamin pulled the glasses down over his milky white eyes and peered at her. She wasn't sure what the blind man saw, but his expression darkened after a moment. "I see. Please, come inside." He turned to allow her room to enter.

Alex stepped inside the apartment and was struck again by how dark the room was kept. Shadows clung to the walls like cobwebs and the air tasted stale in Alex's mouth. She felt a strange chill in the air, as if the specter of death was looming just around the corner. Considering the patient in the back room, that might very well have been the case.

"May I interest you in anything?" Benjamin asked, sidling past her with fluid grace. "Coffee? Biscuit?"

"No, thank you," she said tersely. "I need you to explain what the hell is going on with me."

Benjamin clicked his tongue at her as he retrieved a mug from the kitchen cabinet. He poured a cup of coffee for himself. "You need to relax, my dear, and find your grace."

"My grace?"

"Your center of balance, your calm and happy place."

"I would be calm," Alex said through gritted teeth, "if I knew how to fix this. *Now*."

"Please, come join me." He pulled out a chair for her.

Alex glared at him for a moment before remembering he couldn't see it. Reluctantly, she accepted the offer and sat down with a wearied sigh. "When we first met, you said that I had spoken to you telepathically, that I had called out to you."

Benjamin murmured assent as he sipped from his cup.

"That isn't me," she argued. "I've only ever been a mind-reader. I didn't mean to call out to you, or whatever." Alex was unable to see past Benjamin's sunglasses as he stared at her.

"And yet you did," he said finally. "It would seem that your power has evolved to another level."

"Another level?"

"I have been working on a theory to explain these powers. You and I are connected, I am sure of it. Our abilities extend above and beyond those of traditional Sleepers."

"I'm not a Sleeper," Alex said.

"To become one would be a minor task to someone of your caliber. Untrained, unguided, you have already gained control of your ability and made it into part of your daily routine, wearing it as casually as one might throw on a cloak. I do not share in your power, but I can sense when it is in use."

"So you can sense that I'm not using it now."

"Precisely." Benjamin removed his sunglasses, and from the way his eyes searched her face, Alex suddenly felt that he could see much more than his blindness suggested. "I have said before that I am a Pathfinder—"

"And that I was a Reader, yes. Whatever that means."

He cleared his throat. "I am now reconsidering that position."

"Meaning what, exactly?"

"Within the context of my theory, we are all connected. You, myself, even Arthur Brennan. Our unique abilities suggest a web of interconnectedness, or in my working model, a tree."

"A tree?"

"From one trunk stem many branches," Benjamin said cryptically. "I believe that your jump from a Reader to a Speaker is akin to a squirrel leaping from one branch to the next. Same tree, new branch."

"Are you coming up with these terms out of thin air? Reader? Speaker?"

Benjamin smiled lightly. "There is a touch of madness to my method. Regardless, there is nothing to fear in this new power of yours. If you will pardon the pun, I believe you are merely branching out."

Alex resisted the urge to smack him. "But now I can't do either one!"

Benjamin idly drummed his fingers on the table. "This is a crisis of the conscience. Something disquiets your heart and mind, and until you can quell this inner turmoil, it is possible that you will be unable to access your powers again." His fingers stopped drumming and made a steeple beneath his chin. "Fascinating."

"Fascinating? Are you kidding me? None of what you just said makes *any* sense. I don't have any inner turmoil, so stop projecting your problems onto me. The only reason you think I have issues is because you can't deal with the reality that your grandson is never going to leave that bed!"

"And now we have come to the heart of the matter," Benjamin said. He sat erect in his chair and regarded her with a calm expression. "Tell me, how is your mother doing these days?"

"If you're trying to make me mad, you've succeeded," Alex said with deadly calm.

"You believe yourself incapable of love—"

"I've never told you that."

"Do you dispute it now?" Benjamin asked.

Alex remained silent.

"You feel true love for your mother, regardless of what you believe. She is alive today because of the love for her shared by you and your father. You both desperately seek a cure, yet you have conceded the fact that there is simply not enough time for her."

"How do you know all of this?"

"I knew your father, once upon a time. We still keep tabs on him."

Alex's spine crawled when he said that, since it meant Sleepers were almost undoubtedly involved more intimately in their lives than she had ever known.

"The love you have for your mother is your anguish," Benjamin continued. "Just as I grieve for my grandson, you too are suffering on your mother's behalf. It is the curse of the living to mourn the dead and dying."

Alex frowned. "That doesn't sound right at all. My mother wouldn't want us to be hurt because of her. No matter what she is going through, misery does *not* love company. She wouldn't believe that, at any rate."

"Do you want my advice?" Benjamin asked. "Go home and rest. Your power is like a muscle that has been pulled and stretched in unfamiliar ways over the past few days. I believe it will recover if you let it."

"That's it? Bed rest?"

"This is a new development, the likes of which I have never seen before. It will take time to understand more completely," Benjamin said.

Alex stared at him, dumbfounded. "I thought you were the Pathfinder. Can't you find the path that gets my powers back?"

"I am not all-knowing. That is—was—the power of another much younger than myself."

"Was?" Alex echoed. "What happened to him?"

"He died before his time," Benjamin said soberly.

Alex rose from the table and started heading toward the door. "Not very *all-knowing* of him."

"None of us may know the manner of our deaths, nor choose the hour of our passing. We can only live in the here, in the now, with what we know and what we have been given."

"Great," she said. "I'll put that on a bumper sticker."

"Alex," Benjamin called sharply, arresting her march out the door. "There is still the matter of directing Arthur Brennan toward our serial killer. Has he been made aware of the connection between the victims?"

"I'm working on it," she said shortly.

Benjamin sighed and walked over, using his guiding cane more for show than function. "I will speak to him myself," he said.

"I can handle this—"

"You have already proven yourself incapable of the task. You will arrange a meeting for us, and I will convince him of my sincerity."

"How will you do that? He's pretty high-strung, especially after he nearly died yesterday."

"And whose doing was that?" Benjamin asked mildly. Alex remained silent. "He will know the truth of my words. Your only task now is to put us in the same room."

"How do you know he will listen to me in the first place?"

"He trusts you. Was that not the point of your little exercise yesterday?"

Alex didn't bother asking how he knew about the staged attack. "I only spoke to him telepathically. How do you expect me to do that now?"

"Recover quickly," Benjamin commanded. "Lives depend on it, yours included."

Bastard.

"When do you want the meet to happen?"

"As soon as possible." Benjamin paused for a second. "Considering his current state, I can settle for noon. That should be sufficient time for the painkillers to take effect and mask his wounds."

Alex stepped out into the hall. "You really think he'll show?"

"He has every reason to," Benjamin replied. "As I said, lives truly do depend on us, and his hero complex will allow for nothing less."

Chapter Fifteen

High blood pressure and an erratic heartbeat caused the hospital to insist that Brennan stay overnight.

Clara had gone home immediately after being discharged, and Brennan didn't think he would be hearing from her anytime soon. The night had been pretty good up until the assault, though, and it was a shame that things could not have ended on a more normal note.

When he arrived back at his apartment, Brennan found Greg asleep on the couch with a packed overnight bag resting on the floor by his head. He smiled, feeling amused and slightly guilty that his nephew had been fully prepared to receive a text that was never forthcoming.

Brennan opened a kitchen drawer and retrieved the plain golden ring that lay inside. *One ring to rule them all,* he mused, slipping the wedding band back around his finger. It felt comfortable where it rested, like a piece of himself had been restored just by wearing it.

A small black box, rectangular and about the size of his palm, was nestled in the back corner of the drawer. Brennan stared at it for a long moment before shutting it away to the darkness again.

"G'morning, Uncle Arty," Greg mumbled. He rubbed his eyes as he sat up on the couch. "How was *your* night?"

"Best date I've had in years," Brennan replied dryly.

"Umm, what's up with the sling? I'm familiar with rough sex, but this seems extreme."

Brennan looked down at the arm that was braced against his chest. "That is actually a fascinating question." He paused. "Wait, you're familiar with—"

"Don't worry about it."

"You're using protection, though, right?"

Greg smirked. "No need for a gun, Uncle Arty. My dates are less aggressive than yours, apparently."

Brennan didn't even know his nephew was sexually active, but he also didn't care to think about it in too much detail. "How is the job search going?" he asked instead.

"I have a few irons in the fire."

"Meaning?"

Greg sighed. "I'll start looking today."

"Good," Brennan said, heading toward the bedroom. "I'm going to change out of these clothes, and then I'm meeting Sam uptown. Are you good to be on your own for today?"

"I could always use some extra cash for pizza or something."

"Get a job," Brennan guffawed, and he closed the bedroom door. He dropped his tattered suit jacket on the bed and slipped the loosened tie from around his neck. His right arm had recovered from its brief dislocation the night before, though his fingers worked stiffly as they undid the buttons of his white dress shirt. The other arm tingled as he gingerly shrugged out of his shirt and threaded his arm through its sleeve. Small burn marks traced along the outside of his arm, but they were not nearly as critical as he had previously believed. It was only at the doctor's insistence that he even bothered to wear the sling. For now, though, he felt comfortable removing the harness from around his shoulder. Goosebumps rose on his skin as his arm was exposed to the open air.

After he stepped out of the rest of his clothes, Brennan proceeded to the bathroom and turned the shower handle counterclockwise as far as it would go.

Hot water filled the stall as steam started forming overhead. His mirror was almost completely obscured before Brennan stepped beneath the spray. He groaned as the water splashed against open cuts and ran in rivulets down his legs. His shoulders flexed almost involuntarily, exposing as much skin as possible to the scalding water. It stung a bit, especially when some landed on his wounded arm, but the pain it brought was strangely welcome. Brennan turned his head and let out another low moan as the stiff muscles in his neck started to loosen up under the water's treatment.

Mmm, so your nephew had the right of it, he heard suddenly. *You like it rough.*

Brennan gripped the support bar in the shower stall as his feet slipped in surprise at hearing the voice again. *Who are you?* he demanded.

The woman who guided you to safety last night.

At least now he had a gender to work with.

Yes, I let that detail slip on purpose, the woman added, answering his unspoken realization and follow-up question. *Benjamin wants to speak with you.*

If he had been surprised before, now Brennan was floored—literally. His legs gave out, and he hissed in pain as his head slammed back against the ceramic wall.

"Uncle Arty?" Greg called from the other side of the door. "Are you okay?"

What did you say? he asked.

Benjamin wishes to speak, the woman repeated calmly. *Noon. He said you would know where.*

Brennan lifted himself up in the tub and attempted to regain some measure of composure. *What makes Benjamin think that I want to talk to him? That I want to have* anything *to do with him?*

There was a pause, and when the woman's voice returned, it carried a sharp edge. *What makes you think this is up for negotiation?* she asked rhetorically. *This is much bigger than the two of us.*

What are you talking about?

The serial killer. Her blunt declaration sent shivers down Brennan's spine, despite the warm water currently flattening his hair against his skull. *And you and Benjamin have history to resolve. He will see you at noon.*

Hey! I didn't agree to anything!

His outrage was met with silence, and he knew she had disappeared on him again.

"Uncle Arty?" Greg called again, knocking.

"I'm fine," Brennan said aloud. "I just slipped, but it's all good."

"If you say so." A minute later, he heard the living room television turn on.

Brennan remained sitting in the tub as hot water continued to spray the top of his head. A small waterfall cascaded from the incline of his forehead down to his chest as he contemplated the psychic savior's words. His power told him that everything she had said was true, a fact which made him less eager to meet with Benjamin. If a monster like Benjamin was coming to him for help, there was something seriously dangerous afoot, something which he was just barely beginning to comprehend.

Death is coming to Odols.

The ominous prediction echoed in Brennan's mind. Benjamin knew more about this string of deaths than anyone in the police department, he was sure of it now. He had known for *months* that this deadly game was set to unfold. As much as it pained him to admit, Brennan recognized that his old mentor—the traitorous bastard responsible for Mara's death—was now his best hope for gaining momentum in his investigation.

With slow, labored movements, Brennan grasped the shower bar and pulled himself up to his feet. He shut off the water and grabbed a fresh towel from the nearby rack as droplets formed on the lines of his face and arms. He dried himself off with little regard for his injuries, once more drawing on the pain as a temporary distraction from his current predicament.

Brennan returned to his bedroom and flipped open the laptop that was sitting on the bed. His CopAFeel inbox was empty, as he had expected, and he gave up any hope that he would hear from Clara again. With a resigned sigh, he opened his email and saw a new message from Sam. His eyes scanned the page quickly, picking out the crucial information in between thick blocks of joking banter about his dinner date last night.

He reached for his pocket, but stopped when he remembered his phone had been destroyed the night before. Brennan wondered briefly if his replacement plan covered unforeseen car bombs and shootouts. He wrote a brief response message to Sam, then closed the laptop and went about gathering a fresh set of clothes to wear. He opened the bedroom door as he buttoned his shirt. "Hey, Greg?" he called.

"Yeah?"

"I have to go buy a new cell phone," he said, emerging from the room. The sling somehow found itself left behind, and Brennan was not upset for its absence. "What are you going to do today?"

"Going to find a job," Greg replied glumly, and he sighed loudly. "You don't have to keep repeating yourself, I heard you the first time."

"If I don't say it over and over, then I know you will keep putting it off," Brennan countered. "Just looking out for you."

"Yeah, well, don't. I've got this." Greg cocked his head, and his frustration seemed momentarily replaced by curiosity. "What happened to your *old* cell phone?"

"It got blown up," Brennan said simply. He grinned in response to his nephew's puzzled look. "I can't explain, I have to meet someone soon, and I'd like to get the phone shopping out of the way before then."

"Meeting Sam?"

Brennan shook his head. "A contact about the case I'm working," he hedged.

"Oh. Cool. Have fun!"

Oh yes, Brennan thought. *Oodles of fun.*

ɸ ɸ ɸ

IT WAS VERY nearly noon when Brennan emerged from the phone store. The customer service rep very patiently explained that his service plan did not, in fact, cover incendiary bombs and covert assassination plots. She said all of this with a smile on her face, and Brennan realized she thought he was joking. Since he didn't have a better excuse he could give her, he was forced to buy a new phone at full retail price.

He purchased a newspaper from a man in a stall and boarded the shuttle to uptown. It was less crowded in the middle of the day, and few eyes met his as he sought out a secluded corner to sit down. He had roughly fifteen minutes before the shuttle would arrive at his rendezvous with Sam, but that was more than enough time to first meet with Benjamin.

Brennan slipped on a pair of dark sunglasses that he had brought from home and opened the newspaper to a particularly lengthy article on government spying. Next to the main article were a half dozen editorials on the subject, and Brennan figured an interested reader could easily spend a quarter hour reading the same open pages.

After one last glance around to confirm nobody was watching, Brennan promptly fell asleep.

Falling asleep on demand was one of the simplest skills he had acquired from his previous occupation. It was a necessity of the job; there was never any certainty of when a target would fall asleep, so Brennan and the other Sleepers needed to be capable of infiltrating the unconscious mind at the drop of a hat.

Slumber for a Sleeper was different, though. Instead of darkness for several hours followed by a series of intense hallucinations, all of which would be forgotten within seconds of waking up, Brennan entered a state of acute awareness and control even as the waking world slipped away.

In his mind, Brennan saw a beach that stretched endlessly to what he considered the north, east, and west. Calm ocean waves lapped lightly at the southern shore, and he dipped his bare feet into the water before returning to the warm sands littered with scattered seashells. All around him, on the shore and in the surf, rested rocks of varying sizes. Each one represented a sleeping individual, a mind that could be tapped into by a Sleeper. Some were massive boulders that cast wide shadows on the sand; others were small pebbles that fit easily between two fingers.

The Sleeperscape appeared differently to everyone, and Brennan was pleased that his presented itself as an idyllic beach. He hoped it spoke volumes about the state of his mind, even if his daily life was populated by criminals and liars.

"An interesting arrangement," said a sudden voice.

Brennan spun around to see Benjamin approaching him from the distance, his form wavering like a mirage in the heat. Even from a distance, though, his voice carried perfectly well, as if he were standing by Brennan's side. His steps carried him farther and faster than they should have, as if he were on one of the moving walkways used in long airport corridors. Within seconds, he casually strolled several hundred yards.

"I do not believe I have ever visited your 'scape before," the old man commented, looking around with those curious, blind eyes. His skin looked like dried parchment stretched thinly over his bones. "Interesting, indeed."

"You asked for this meeting," Brennan said sharply. "What do you want?"

"Straight to business, then. You always did have little patience for the niceties."

"You're testing that patience right now," he growled.

Benjamin's cheeks flushed, but he bit back whatever heated response had risen to the surface. "Straight to business," he repeated. "I did not kill your wife."

"I don't believe you."

"I urge you to stop listening with your ears and start listening with your power." Benjamin reached forward faster than Brennan could react, and the old Sleeper placed a finger above his heart. "Listen to my words," he said, "and know them to be true."

Something reverberated within Brennan, like a gong rung firmly in the distance, and he felt his body tremble to the core. A tingle rose up his spine like a climbing vine, shooting tendrils out across his back as it reached the base of his skull. The sensation suddenly exploded outward, unfurling like a set of massive wings.

"What the *hell* are you doing to me?" he demanded. It felt like he was witnessing the entire scene from above, and he stared down at the awestruck image of his own face.

"I know many paths, Arthur Brennan," Benjamin said imperiously. "I have tread where few men have gone before, and I understand more than you *ever* could." His hand shifted so his palm lay flat against Brennan's chest. "I am speaking to the root of your soul, to the power that resides inside your body. I will speak in no uncertain terms, so *hear my words*. I am not responsible for the death of your wife, nor did I condone any of my agents to strike her down."

Truth.

The single word echoed throughout the Sleeperscape, beating down upon Brennan and Benjamin with its sheer force of will.

"There is a very real and present threat to our organization," Benjamin continued. "There are rogues with Sleeper-level abilities wreaking havoc on our ranks, starting, I believe, with the unfortunate death of your wife."

Truth.

Brennan found himself back in his body, on his knees, staring up into Benjamin's unrelenting gaze. He didn't detect a single sign of deception, and for the first time in countless years, he believed the old man. Benjamin's hand left his chest, and the indescribable sensation of wings had faded without notice.

"Mara," Brennan sobbed, choking out her name. Feelings of remorse and guilt, a wellspring of repressed emotion, rose up and overwhelmed his system. Dark storm clouds gathered over the ocean as his body was wracked with uncontrollable shaking.

It was a long time before either of them spoke, but Benjamin seemed content to maintain the silence. He sat respectfully still as Brennan sobbed, embroiled in his rekindled anguish. Eventually, his tears no longer wet the sand beneath his face, and an unfamiliar sense of release washed through him, replacing the troubled grief with a sense of calm and purpose.

"How long?" he finally asked. "How long did you know?"

"You are referring to the comment I made at summer's end?"

"You said death was coming to Odols, but it had already arrived, hadn't it?"

Benjamin looked out over the ocean. "I have had my suspicions. Do you see out there, in the shallows?"

"I'm not interested in imaginary waves," Brennan said, his voice hollow.

"You will find it interesting and insightful."

Brennan's power supported the truth that lay in the direct reply, and he lifted himself into a sitting position. He followed Benjamin's raised arm and saw a curious aberration, something he had overlooked upon his arrival. About twenty yards out in the water was a massive whirlpool almost fifteen feet across.

"What is it?"

"That is all that remains of the most powerful ability I have ever seen."

Brennan let out a low whistle. After the performance he had just put on, to hear the old man make a statement like that spoke volumes. "I have to ask again, though…what is it? I've never seen a Sleeper's abilities cause anything like this, rogue or otherwise."

"It was not the work of a Sleeper," Benjamin replied mildly. "I met a boy who could absorb the memories of anyone he wished with a mere touch of his hand."

"That's…not possible."

"Look at yourself and reconsider what you believe to be within the realm of possibility."

"Does it ever get tiring, talking like that?"

A smiled touched Benjamin's lips. "The boy said something similar. This is simply the manner in which I choose to communicate." The smile faded. "He died shortly after absorbing the memories of his parents, and his sudden absence explains the disturbance you see now. It was even larger three months ago," he added with a sniff.

Brennan understood the general physics of the Sleeperscape, if indeed it abided by any set of rules. Every rock on his beach represented a node, a point at which he could enter a sleeping mind. Each node seemed to vary in size based on the life experience and importance of the individual, with the largest tending to be corporate executives, world travelers, politicians—in short, the worldly and wealthy.

"His name?"

"Jeremy Scott," Benjamin supplied.

"How old was he?"

"Just past sixteen years of age."

Brennan whistled low again. If the whirlpool he saw now was indeed a shrunken version, it meant the kid had had more knowledge in his head than anybody else within view, possibly within the entire reach of his Sleeperscape. Brennan watched the swirling waters continue to toss and turn, white froth bubbling violently at the center.

"It's shrinking," he noted. "But not gone."

"Memories linger long after the body has withered."

"Do you think one of the rogue Sleepers is responsible for his death?"

"The possibility crossed my mind, and it is not entirely surprising. They may have realized his potential, known that I was attempting to recruit him to our cause, and decided the best course of action would be to eliminate the threat." He coughed lightly. "What a waste."

The way he spoke gave Brennan chills, and it only served to remind him that whatever remorse the man felt for the boy's death, it was only insofar as the loss of such a unique power. "What do you plan to do now?"

"My objective has not wavered since the outset of this crisis," Benjamin said. "Your brothers and sisters await your return."

He shook his head. "I'm still out."

"Our Sleepers were not responsible for your wife's death, Agent Brennan. It is past time that you returned to the fold." He held his hands out openly, a magnanimous gesture. "When this serial killer is captured, you have my word that the full resources of our organization will be committed to realizing the justice you seek."

"Why is this case so important to you, anyway?" Brennan asked. "Sleepers always stayed away from official police business because it was too *mundane*."

"Have you ascertained the common denominator that links all of your victims together?"

Brennan stared hard at his old mentor. "No, but I'm guessing you have."

"Indeed." He waved a pointed hand between the two of them. "*We* are being hunted. Every target thus far has been an individual possessing some power or another. I was following each one's progress, naturally, watching their development, though it appears that this serial killer is capable of identifying and tracking our kind." Again, the way Benjamin spoke sent shivers down Brennan's spine.

The implications of his statement were unsettling. Not too long ago, Brennan had believed he was the only one with a special ability. He'd kept it a secret from the other Sleepers. Then, Greg showed some level of psychic ability, though that faded when he stopped using the Leviathan patches. Now, a telepath was saving him from armed attackers and Benjamin let slip that he possessed his own power.

"What can you do?" he asked. "I always thought that 'Pathfinder' was just a title of yours, like 'Agent,' but now…"

Benjamin's blind eyes remained focused on the distant waves. "I have never lied about what I am—nor *could* I, in present company," he said wryly. "I am the one who finds connections between things that others cannot. I brought others like myself together for a reason, with a purpose to protect this city from those who would do it harm. My mission is unchanged."

Brennan's brain worked in overdrive. "So every Sleeper has some kind of special ability," he concluded.

"Not all, but most. Largely, they believe they are unique in their power, as you did until recent events revealed otherwise." He turned and looked directly at Brennan. "I am aware that your nephew possesses some latent ability, though it has yet to manifest itself fully. The point I am trying to make is that none of us will be safe until this murderer is brought to justice. If you will not do this for me, then do it for your nephew."

Brennan felt himself being backed into a corner. "Why haven't you taken care of this yourself?"

"There is a private war going on that keeps our Sleepers quite busy," Benjamin said curtly. "Besides, this has become a police matter. A case with this high of a body count cannot be resolved discreetly, especially not since it has drawn the attention of the FBI."

That was news to Brennan. "The FBI?"

"Half a dozen connected murders over three months, all occurring in one city. It is a wonder they are not yet actively involved," Benjamin noted, his voice slightly ironic. "If you had agreed to speak earlier, I would not be spending valuable resources delaying their investigation."

"You? Why are you holding them back?"

"Take the cotton out of your ears, *boy*. The police need their killer, and the only connection between his victims is something that they cannot possibly comprehend. You must bring him in and force a confession out of him."

"I don't even know where to find him," Brennan protested. "The connection doesn't do me any good."

"It provides sufficient motivation to apprehend him, does it not?" Benjamin rose to his feet and brushed sand from the seat of his pants. "In any case, you have an appointment with your associate on that very subject. Perhaps he knows something that will be useful to your case."

Brennan had completely forgotten about his meeting with Sam. He felt Benjamin's presence receding, and he looked back to see that he was all alone on the long stretch of beach. Brennan closed his eyes and started taking deep breaths. Each inhale smelled less salty than the last, and after breathing out a dozen times, he awoke in the shuttle once more. He had wrung the life out of his newspaper, and his cheeks were damp. Brennan swiped at the sleep-inspired tears as he looked up at the digital map and saw that he had mere seconds to spare before arriving at his uptown stop.

He disembarked into a noisy shuttle station, and he threaded his way through the lunchtime rush to meet Sam just outside the building. His friend's expression soured as he approached.

"Why is it every time I see you, you're beaten up in some way?" Sam asked.

Brennan looked down at his body; all of his bruises and cuts had been covered by the long-sleeved shirt. "How could you tell?"

Sam gave him a serious look. "Walk with me. I've been meaning to tell you this for a while now, partner. I'm psychic." After a long moment of Brennan nearly gaping in stunned silence, Sam's trademark toothy grin resurfaced, wiping away any tension as quickly as it had spiked. "You're favoring your left side, and your gait is a little unsteady. Everything all right?"

Brennan told him about the car bomb, the multiple gunmen, and how the date had ended with a long wait in the sewer followed by a trip to the hospital.

Sam laughed at his misfortune. "You've got bad mojo, partner. Remind me never to take you out on any boats, or near any priceless pieces of art."

"Your constant confidence in me is inspiring, truly."

"That's a shame about the lady, though. Still, there are plenty of fish in the sea. You'll find the right one soon enough."

"There is actually something I've been meaning to talk to you about, Sam."

"Hmm, this sounds serious." He stopped outside of a respectable-looking pub, and he gestured to the sign bearing its name. "Mind if we grab a drink while we converse?"

Brennan looked up to see *The Eternal Tap* painted onto an old-fashioned swinging wooden sign. "You actually found it," he said in disbelief.

Sam grinned proudly. "You didn't give me much to go on, but this is where our man buys his beers. Just wait until you see the setup they have."

They walked inside, and Brennan took note of the pub's unique atmosphere. Several sturdy beams ran the length of the ceiling, and each table looked to be handcrafted from aged wood. It wasn't crowded, but there were enough people inside to make it feel lively and warm. A few booths lined one wall, but the favored seats were apparently the open floor tables and stools at the bar; almost all of them were occupied by men older or more muscular than Brennan.

Sam led the way to the last two open seats at the bar, which were unfortunately separated by a long-haired fellow who already seemed deep in his cup despite the early hour. The barkeeper nodded to Sam as they sat, and Brennan turned to him with slightly narrowed eyes.

"What kind of research did you do on this place?" he asked skeptically.

"Come on, Brennan, it's a bar!"

"A pub," the long-haired man corrected.

"Either way, did you expect me to come here and *not* drink? This is how you cozy up to the regulars."

"I got another suggeshchun," slurred their new friend. "How 'bout you shut the hell up? That'd make us pals right quick!"

Sam gave Brennan a look with raised eyebrows and signaled to the barkeeper to bring them three beers. After they arrived, Sam slid the extra glass over to the long-haired man. "We're going to be chatting a lot," he explained, "and I don't want to ruin your day. So how about you take this drink and trade places with my friend?"

He looked between Sam and the free drink and hiccuped. With a shrug, he motioned for Brennan to move out of the way, and he sidled over to his new seat.

"That was…effective," Brennan said.

"What can I say? You just need to know how to speak their language."

"Speaking of which, were you able to get a real name for our 'Johnny Appleseed'?"

"Mmm, that's a good lager," Sam said after taking a foamy sip. His proud grin returned. "Not only did I get his name, I got *several* names and numbers last night."

"You got his number?"

"Female numbers, Brennan. From women?"

Brennan sucked in his cheeks and took a long pull of his beer. "How are things with Bishop?" he asked tersely.

Sam sighed. "There's no harm done in looking around and having a little fun," he said, though he kept his eyes from meeting Brennan's.

"This is exactly the sort of thing that got you into trouble with her the first time around!"

"Reconciling with Bishop isn't progressing as quickly as I may have led you to believe."

"No kidding," Brennan scoffed.

Color rose in the base of Sam's neck. "What am I supposed to do when she shuts down like this? Live my life as a monk?"

His phone buzzed in his pocket, but Brennan ignored it. "You try *harder*. You're the one who messed up in the first place, so you shouldn't be surprised when she doesn't accept you immediately with open arms."

"Acceptance is exactly what she needs to learn, though. She has to accept that my past deeds are in the past, and I'll be one hundred percent ready to commit once she comes around."

Brennan shook his head. "I think you have it in the wrong order. Show her you're worth accepting, rather than waiting for her to 'come around.'" He let his friend stew on those thoughts for a minute before changing the subject. "So, what is Appleseed's real name?"

Sam seemed to recognize the reprieve and grasped at it. "Levi Kellogg."

"You're serious?"

"I swear to God! This guy's name might have walked out of two back-to-back commercials, but it is what it is. I think he joined the military just to escape the ridicule, though I can't imagine it was any better there." He snickered quietly. "Private Kellogg."

"If my parents named me after some pants and cereal, I'd probably want to go shoot a few people, too," Brennan said dryly. "How do you know he served?"

Sam nodded vaguely to the rest of the bar. "Buy a few rounds and these guys will spill their guts faster than a disgraced samurai committing seppuku."

"Iz 'at the numbers game?" asked the long-haired man suddenly. Brennan shook his head, and the drunkard turned away again to eavesdrop in solitude.

"Thanks for that mental image, by the way. What else did you learn about him?"

Sam drummed the base of his glass. "Kellogg was at the university the night Kelsi Woodill was murdered."

"How do you know? What was he doing there?"

"These guys confirmed it. They told me Kellogg doesn't have a steady job, so he takes work where he can find it. I'm assuming there was a manual labor gig that he found out about online." Sam shrugged. "He must have seen Kelsi on her way back from the party and made his move. She was a complete victim of circumstance."

Brennan frowned and said nothing. His discovery of Kelsi might have been by chance, but Kellogg had killed her for a very specific reason. Her ability—whatever it had been—was what ultimately cost Kelsi her life. The only questions that remained were *why* he was on this vendetta and *how* in the world he could spot those like Brennan among the ordinary citizens.

He pulled out his phone and checked the missed call; it was a familiar number. "I appreciate it, Sam," he said, rising from his seat.

"Leaving so soon? You haven't even finished your beer."

"There's a serial killer on the loose, and somebody else is going to die if I don't do something about it. Kind of have bigger issues to deal with, you know?" His nephew's habit of ending sentences with that question was rubbing off on Brennan.

Sam tipped back his glass and swallowed the remainder of his drink. "Way to make a guy feel guilty," he said. He slid off his stool and slapped a bill on the counter. "All right, let's go."

"I can't afford to pay you for another two days."

"Brennan, please, you're my friend. I'll waive my continuance fee for this one time," Sam said with a wink.

"Is there a discount for the standard rate as well? Seeing as how we're such great friends, I mean."

"I still have to maintain my income."

"By siphoning off of mine?"

Sam grinned. "Now you're starting to understand this whole 'friendship' thing. So where are we going?"

"First stop? The morgue."

Chapter Sixteen

Alex stared at the ceiling of her apartment and willed the room to stop spinning.

A morning of meditation, rest, and wine had culminated in her regaining control of her power once more, if for a brief period. She'd used that small bit of energy to send her message to Brennan, and the effort had left her completely drained. Benjamin told her that her ability was like a muscle, and it would strengthen with time and exercise. In the meantime, her body was telling her that the smart course of action was to lie on the couch and watch the overhead lights perform their impersonation of stars rotating in the heavens.

She knew that her idle recovery time was limited, though. Heinrich would be expecting the second half of his payment this afternoon—a time of day which had already arrived, according to the kitchen clock.

Alex groaned as she flipped over and grabbed the burner cell from the glass coffee table. It was a simple piece of plastic and circuitry, and the list of contacts was empty.

Alex trudged over to the bathroom and splashed some cold water on her face to shock her system into cooperating. She gasped sharply and felt her eyes widen in response, and her mind erupted with rapid-fire thoughts, returning to her usual state.

She dialed Heinrich's number from memory and waited until he answered. The shallow sound of breathing on the other end was the only indication that he had picked up, and his silence indicated clearly that she was meant to speak first. "Heinrich?" she asked. She cringed at how small her voice sounded, and she added more force to her words. "I have your money ready. When do you want to meet?"

"We will meet at the same spot in half an hour."

Alex looked down at her half-dressed self. "One hour, and I will text you with the address."

"You are proving to be a very trying client, Ms. Brüding."

"In this business, you can hardly fault me for being less than wholeheartedly trusting of you and your associates," she countered.

A pause. "This is true," Heinrich responded. "One hour."

Alex stayed on the phone for a moment longer before realizing he had hung up. The man had professional courtesy, but his *common* courtesy left something to be desired.

She quickly disrobed and changed into a set of more suitable clothes. From under the bed she retrieved a second briefcase, identical to the one from yesterday, with a comparable amount of money stored inside. After a brief glimpse in the mirror, Alex slipped on a pair of low-heeled dress shoes and proceeded out the door of her apartment toward the elevator.

Upon reaching the ground floor, she realized again how naked she felt without passively absorbing the sensory inputs of those around her. Alex asked the doorman to hail a taxi for her and returned her focus to the other people in the lobby. She could only guess at what lay behind each set of eyes, and she looked around the room with a sensation verging on paranoia. For so long, she had been accustomed to naturally seeing what others saw, hearing what they heard, and all the while being privy to their most intimate thoughts. This fresh loss of power was disturbing.

Oh yeah, she thought. *I'm exercising the* hell *out of my power when this is all over.*

Her taxi arrived, and Alex sent a text to Heinrich even as she told the driver to head to the Museum of Natural Sciences. She hoped a public setting would make Heinrich less likely to bring his goons, though she was certain a few were bound to be scattered in among the crowd. Still, she would take any precautions she could to mitigate the disadvantages of her weakened state.

Alex opened the briefcase and tucked the burner cell into a recessed groove in the interior lining. A cavity had been hollowed out, and it looked like a smooth layer of velvet to the casual observer. She closed the case again before the driver could see what was inside.

Time passed slowly, and Alex drummed lightly with her fingertips as she watched traffic roll by with all the speed of refrigerated syrup. She tried to keep her mind occupied on other things, and it worked to a degree. Still, she found herself attempting to reach out with her probe, yet even the pitiable distance between her and the driver might as well have been an unfathomable chasm for all the power she could muster. Her rest was insufficient, and she was going into a meeting with a contractual killer without any of her ability.

She knew Heinrich and his men were aware of her power to some extent, even if they had been stone-faced during their first meeting. Her probe hadn't been able to glean any information from them, and if she followed the logical connections, then it was almost certain that her father was responsible for training them to resist her. Somehow, in secret, he had managed not only to condition himself to mask his thoughts from her probe, but he had also passed on the technique to his favorite hired guns. She would have to talk with him about that particular issue, once she recovered.

That conversation would likely prove treacherous, though, and her smooth sailing through life might well founder if she confronted him about his secrets. The apartment, her expensive lifestyle, the fact that she never needed to work—all of these factors were conditional on her father believing she was an obedient daughter who was ignorant to the truth.

"Miss?" the taxi driver prompted. "We're here."

No, Alex concluded, still thinking of her father. *We won't be having that discussion just yet.*

She paid the driver and stepped out onto the curb. The sun was bright, and the air was warm with its light. A steady stream of tourists entered and exited through the revolving doors of the Museum of Natural Sciences, some of them stopping to take pictures next to the larger-than-life statues erected in the outer courtyard. Cameras and smartphones took hundreds of pictures per minute, another factor that Alex had considered when picking the location. Heinrich was unlikely to bring many men to such a public venue, where their faces might be captured and immortalized in online albums forever.

Alex turned around and looked across the street at her true destination: the Jardin des Anges.

The Jardin des Anges was an enormous botanical garden that covered a full city block with its soaring trees, peaceful streams, and carefully planned pathways that wound in fluid loops and curls around the aromatic flowers. It was a favorite destination for couples and tourists, though the latter group's numbers lagged as the seasons shifted. The summer rush had passed, and there would not be another boom until the dead of winter.

Alex, with her briefcase in hand, crossed the street and walked into the Jardin, grabbing a thin informational pamphlet as she entered. She was several minutes early for their meeting, which gave her just enough time to navigate through the Jardin to one of the only stone structures standing amidst all of the greenery.

It was a tall, rounded tower with windows looking out from the second story. Once upon a time, the only way to reach the upper floor was to climb a vertical ladder, though that proved to be unsafe with children, especially in winter. The city council had a curved staircase installed, and the safety concerns were eliminated. Alex ascended slowly and stopped at the top of the steps. For some reason, large slices of the floor were made of thick, foggy glass, giving certain sections an ethereal feel to them. She took a hesitant step and found the glass to be just as secure as the stone.

Each of the five windows bore a unique sigil of stained glass, an image of nature plucked seemingly at random. A snowflake, a flower, a peach, a lake, and an open field. Curiously, the window depicting the field was opaque in the area surrounding its image, whereas every other portrait of glass was clear.

Alex shrugged and pushed open one of the tall, curved windows, providing a direct line of sight to the Museum of Natural Sciences. She reached into her purse and retrieved a small makeup mirror, flipping it open and thanking her stars that the weather was clear today. She cupped the mirror delicately from behind and angled it to catch the sun as it beat down from above. Hundreds of yards away and across the street, a small but clearly visible circle of light swayed erratically across the courtyard. It caught a few tourists in the eye and probably caused a bit of lens flare for others, but Alex quickly gained proficiency in its control. She snapped the mirror shut and commenced waiting.

Below, she could hear sightseers making noises of fascination at the assortment of plants collected in the Jardin. She rested comfortably in the wide windowsill, her eyes scanning the street for black SUVs or Heinrich's distinctive shiny, bald head. She was once again reminded of how much easier this would be with her power; she would have simply co-opted the sight of several commoners and carried out her surveillance that way. For the time being, she would have to make do with being like everyone else.

Her idle vigil didn't last long. At exactly one thirty, a black sedan pulled up in front of the museum. A thick-necked guard stepped out and quickly scanned the surrounding area before opening one of the rear doors. Heinrich's bald head emerged, his eyes hidden behind a pair of dark lenses as the sun followed its course through the sky. Several more men clad in dark clothes spread out to cover the other entry points, awaiting her arrival.

Alex flipped open the pocket mirror and quickly found a good angle with the light. A corresponding circle appeared in the far courtyard, and she waved it around in front of the suited men to get their attention. The man closest to the vehicles pointed, and Heinrich visibly frowned at the light on the ground before his eyes snapped up toward her position. It was unlikely that he could see her directly, but her mirror would shine distinctly for anyone with a clear view. She traced a short trail with the reflected light, drawing it toward the entrance to the Jardin before jumping back to where Heinrich stood and repeating the cycle. His men began to retract, drawing toward the cars, but he waved them off with an arrogant flick of the hand. A second car arrived behind the first.

More men? Alex wondered.

A tall man emerged from the newcomer sedan, and Alex was shocked to recognize her father. She wished she could reach out and discover what the hell he was thinking, but that would be impossible until her power recovered. She could only watch from the tower as he reached out and shook Heinrich's hand. The bald man gestured, and they both started walking toward the entrance of the Jardin. Alex noted with satisfaction that only one of Heinrich's men followed beyond the leafy gate.

The odds were as good as they could be, and though her father's appearance was a wrench in her otherwise flawless plan, Alex had time to compose herself before they arrived. When his head appeared as he ascended the stairs, she met his disapproving gaze with a solemn look of her own. Heinrich smirked as he watched closely for his gambit to pay off.

"What do you think you're doing?" her father asked. His voice was colored with anger, but he kept the emotion from playing out on his face.

"Expanding the family business, it seems," Alex said mildly. She tried to sound nonchalant, and it worked in drawing her father's ire even more.

"I don't have time for this. You have no right using my money to hire *my* men."

"We are nobody's men," Heinrich put in, his voice quiet but firm.

"You were paid to keep our dealings a secret," Alex said, not quite glaring at him.

"He pays me more to tell him secrets." Heinrich crossed the room and sat next to her, uncomfortably close, letting one hand rest casually on the briefcase. "Our bargain is fulfilled. You will pay me, and I will leave you two to sort this out."

"Your orders were to scare Brennan but leave him *unharmed*."

Heinrich shrugged lazily. "In the heat of battle, anything can happen."

"Your obligation is fulfilled, Heinrich. You can go," James said to him. He continued staring at Alex, as if daring her to object.

She worried at how rapidly she had lost control of the situation, and she decided to go out with her head held high. "I won't forget this," she said, narrowing her eyes at Heinrich. "A good deal broken by bad faith cannot be mended by another built upon a poor foundation."

He smirked again and rose with the briefcase in hand. "Words and noise," he said dismissively. "When you are worthy of my respect, you will have it." With that, he left, sparing a parting nod with James before descending the stairs.

Alex frowned at her father as he approached her. How could he let Heinrich walk all over her? She deserved to be treated better than that, yet he hadn't said a word as the mercenary took her money and waltzed right out.

"What is wrong with you?" James asked, peering at her intently.

She folded her arms across her chest. "I was only using the same men you've been hiring for years."

"Not about that, I don't care about Heinrich and his men. Money is just pieces of paper."

"A lot of pieces of paper," she pointed out.

"Regardless, we have more. I could ask you *why* you hired him, but I suspect I don't want to hear the answer. But what is wrong with *you*? I have been thinking aloud to you for several minutes and you haven't *heard* a single word I've said."

Alex tried to keep her shock from showing. "How did you know?"

"I saw it on your face the moment we walked in. What happened?"

"I'm going to get better, it's just temporary. Benjamin said that in time—"

"Hold on, did you say Benjamin?" Her father's eyes frowned as lines gathered at the sides. "Short, old man? Pretends to be blind?"

She nodded.

"I cannot stress how important it is that you stay away from him, Alexis. That man is dangerous."

"That's funny, he said the same thing about you."

"What are you talking about?"

Alex didn't care anymore. Her power was gone, her money was lost, and soon the detective would be killed by her father's vengeful henchmen. Then there would be nothing to prevent the serial killer from continuing his streak, a deadly trail of bodies that might soon include her own. "Benjamin told me that he has had you under surveillance for a long time. And I know *exactly* who he is, Dad, so you don't need to try and protect me from him. Why would he put eyes on you? He's a Sleeper, and possibly their leader. If that man is worried, then what does that make *you*?"

James pursed his lips and looped an arm around her shoulder. "I am your father. I will always have your best interests at heart, unlike that withered assassin."

Alex shrugged off his hand. "Just like how you trained Leviathan to resist me? Yeah, I know about that," she said, watching his face for any reaction. He was impassive, in control, as always. "And if they know how to block me out, then they must have had one hell of a teacher. How long have you been deceiving me?"

"I have always been honest with you. No secrets, remember? You're so powerful, more so than I could have ever hoped for. I'm the proudest father in the world."

"Platitudes won't make me any less upset with you. I'm going home now."

James rose and straightened his suit jacket. "Yes, you are. With me."

"To my apartment, I meant."

"I know what you meant, but the result is the same. I'm worried about you, Alexis. Your decision to hire Leviathan out from underneath me is disturbing, and until your power recovers, I don't feel comfortable leaving you on your own."

Alex looked out the window and saw a flash of black disappearing, the edge of another suit as it entered the tower. A few seconds later, Kern's familiar face appeared as he climbed the stairs. The butler's age showed in his movements, but he smiled politely as he gestured for her to join him. She spared a glancing glare at her father before rising and smoothing out the wrinkles in her dress.

"Fine, Dad. I'll come home with you, but just for tonight." He nodded, and she walked ahead of him at a crisp pace. "Besides, it will be nice to see Mom again."

Chapter Seventeen

"This place seriously creeps me out," Sam said. "I don't know how anybody can work here."

"Hey, I'm standing right here!"

"Sorry, Wally."

"It's Wallace…"

Brennan drew his jacket in tighter against his body. He secretly shared Sam's sentiments, and he would gladly have traded the pervasive cold of the morgue for the dry heat of a roaring fireplace right now. Winter was coming, and there would be plenty of time for bracing against the cold soon enough.

"Wally, why did you call us here?"

The pathologist frowned. "Me? I thought you were just visiting because we're friends. I didn't call you."

"I did," said a harsh and familiar female voice.

Sam and Brennan turned to see Bishop coming from the stairwell with two suited men in tow. They were big and muscular, though neither was quite as tall as Brennan. "Lieutenant," he said respectfully.

"My Queen," Sam said, bowing at the waist. "How lustrous your luscious locks look in the limpid light of the...lights."

"Shut up, Sam. Brennan, these men are with the FBI. They—"

"We would like a few moments of your time," one of the agents said, extending a hand as he stepped forward. His voice sounded like wet gravel crunching underfoot. "Special Agent Pascale," he said by way of introduction. "My partner is Special Agent Jun."

"You both have the same first name? How *special*."

"Shut up, Sam," Brennan and Bishop said in unison.

Pascale looked down his nose as Sam. "You aren't with the department anymore, McCarthy, but don't think you're off our radar."

"I'm quaking in my boots."

"Four, seventeen, eight," Pascale said cryptically.

The smile slid from Sam's face, and he affixed Agent Pascale with a wary stare. "How do you know about that?"

The agent smirked and looked briefly to Bishop, who nodded. "Agent Pascale, he's all yours."

"Detective Brennan, if you would follow me."

"What's this all about?"

"We can discuss this further in private."

Brennan exchanged looks with Sam and Wally before following the two agents to the elevator. When they reached the second floor of the station, Agent Pascale marched directly to Bishop's new office and let himself in. He motioned for Brennan to sit while his partner shut the door and closed the blinds. Agent Jun folded his hands and stood impassively by the door.

In the morgue, he had feared being reprimanded by Bishop for disobeying her orders and getting involved in the serial killer case. Benjamin had said the FBI were closing in, but Brennan had hoped the old Sleeper could keep them occupied at least for another day or two. "This is about the serial killer?" he guessed.

"You aren't officially assigned to that case," Pascale said. "We're here regarding your handling of the Leviathan drug cartel. More accurately, the fact that you broke into a government-owned building and murdered several civilians."

"Armed gangsters, actually, if it matters."

"They had your partner, and you felt justified taking their lives because they were criminals, is that it?"

"Exactly."

Pascale steepled his fingers beneath his chin. "What am I going to do with you, Detective? You broke a dozen regulations and could have been killed yourself. Now there's a serial killer on the loose, and you want to play renegade cop again. We can't have you getting in the way of our investigation."

"Bishop wouldn't be alive if it weren't for me," Brennan said through gritted teeth. "And I saved countless others by getting Chamalla off the streets."

"But you didn't, did you? There are a dozen copycat drugs out there now, each more deadly than the last. More people are dying from the patch than ever before. We have a procedure for handling these situations for a reason."

"Right. No operation done 'by the book' has ever gone belly-up. I saved Detec—*Lieutenant* Bishop, and I put a stop to Leviathan. You're going to bring me up on charges for doing my duty to protect and serve?"

The agent sighed and leaned back in the ergonomic chair. "Here's the situation: your lieutenant made it clear that you are not to be involved. I don't know her reasoning behind it, but I agree with the sentiment of it." His eyes darkened a couple shades as he glowered at Brennan. "Your already checkered past has many of us in the bureau worried."

"My checkered past?"

"You turned on your father just as he was reaching the peak of his career. He was poised to take over the organization, and then he was suddenly gunned down by a rival outfit? Our best agents couldn't get into their ranks, and Joseph Brennan had a way of inspiring loyalty in his followers—not a single one of them would speak to us." His voice lowered, and Brennan had to lean forward to hear what he said next. "Everything is classified, of course, but we know only someone intimately involved in Brennan's affairs would have had the necessary information to betray him. And now you're sitting on the largest estate this side of the county."

Brennan's eyebrows knitted together in a deep frown. There were more complex reasons for what he had done, for why and how he had—

Betrayed your family, whispered the dark voice of truth.

"No," he whispered.

"What did you say?"

Brennan glared fiercely at the agent. "I said no. You aren't taking me off this case, and you have no grounds to. There are greater stakes than you realize, and a lot of people are going to get hurt if I don't help."

Pascale's eyes narrowed. "What do you mean, the stakes are greater than we realize?"

"Greater than *you* realize," Brennan corrected him. He hooked a thumb over his shoulder. "I don't know about strong-and-silent over there; he may be a genius and have figured all this out already."

Agent Jun's mouth twitched with a suppressed smirk, but he said nothing.

"The official story," Pascale said, swallowing his anger, "is that you improperly handled the Leviathan debacle. This is true enough, even if it has made you something of a hero within the precinct. If I find you snooping around this investigation, I will personally charge you with obstruction of justice."

"This is outrageous! You can't seriously expect me to—"

"Watch yourself, Detective." Pascale rose from his seat, and Jun silently opened the door. "Please, leave me to my work. There is a serial killer stalking your streets, and I have less than twelve hours before he leaves his next victim."

Brennan scowled at the smug agent and retreated from the room. As soon as the door closed, he rushed to his desk and grabbed a plastic cup. He set its mouth against the door to the office and pressed his ear flat to listen at the base. It was a rudimentary trick, but effective for the circumstances.

"Do you believe him?" asked a deep baritone voice. Brennan assumed that Agent Jun finally chose to speak.

"Not for an instant. His family has bred nothing but conmen and cowards. Follow him; in due time, he will reveal himself as one or the other."

The door started to open, and Brennan retreated behind the divider that separated the office from the open farm of detectives' desks. Agent Jun emerged and scanned the room with alert eyes, his face a neutral mask. He looked ready for anything and bored by everything.

Brennan waited until the agent was out of sight before making his own exit, taking the stairs down to the morgue. He opened the door to find Sam getting an earful from Bishop, though it appeared their fight was coming to an end. They were not quite standing apart from one another, and Sam was murmuring something to calm her down. Bishop met Brennan's eyes as he emerged from the stairwell.

"We can talk about it more tonight," she told Sam before turning away. "Brennan, what did they say to you?"

"Special Agent Past-His-Prime warned me to stay away from the case, or there'd be trouble."

"So if you had just done what I told you in the first place—"

"Dammit, Noel. There's more to this than either you or Pascale realize."

"Enlighten me," she said coolly.

"I...can't really talk about it."

"You want me to let you keep hunting after this ghost named Kellogg? Fine, be my guest. I've done all I can to keep the feds and the chief from having your badge, but you don't seem to realize the situation I'm in." Her hands left her hips, and her tone softened. "I appreciate what you did for me, back at the hospital, but now I'm your boss, and I can't have you getting yourself and civilians in harm's way."

"I'm touched by your concern," Sam said over her shoulder.

"Part of the job description is being 'in harm's way,'" Brennan argued. "Generally *in the way* of it getting to someone else."

"Again, your valor is noted," Bishop deadpanned. "But hang up your cape and get on board with the team. If you have information, you need to come forward with it, not go all dark knight with your trusty companion."

"Hey, I am no one's Robin. Unless you're up for a little bird-watching tonight," Sam added, moving within inches of her again.

"I'd probably catch the avian flu, knowing you," she told him. "Or the STD equivalent. Brennan, the point I'm making here is that maybe Agent Pascale is right. Maybe you need to step back from this one. We have a name now. Your approach was…unorthodox, and I can't condone you keeping secrets from me, but we're closer today than ever before. The only reason I haven't suspended you for disobeying orders is because we need to show unity in a time of crisis, now more than ever."

"But you're still taking me off the case?"

"I'm sorry," Bishop said, and it sounded like she meant it. "You acted against my orders, and I have to show strong leadership if I'm going to keep this promotion." She strode past him purposefully toward the elevator.

"Lieutenant," Brennan called. "Answer me one thing. Did our time as partners mean anything to you?"

She looked back at him with a sorrowful expression. "Of course it did."

"Noel," Sam called louder. "Did *our* time as partners mean anything to you?" His eyebrows wiggled suggestively as he made air quotes.

Bishop rolled her eyes, got into the elevator, and left the pair of them alone.

"Hey, where did Wally go?"

"He said something about you and I being dry tinder and our newly minted lieutenant being a raging forest fire." Sam shrugged. "Little man can be downright poetic when he wants to be."

"So he ran away at the smell of smoke," Brennan said. "Smart man."

"Smarter than the two of us."

"What did Pascale mean earlier when he said those numbers to you?"

Sam started walking toward the elevator, shrugging off the question. "It doesn't matter. But you and I need to have some real talk. I have a couple questions that need answering."

"I guess I should have seen this coming."

"We've skirted around it long enough," Sam said. It was one of the rare moments when he was serious, without a trace of a smile on his face. "How did you know where Bishop was, back when Leviathan took her?"

"Do we have to do this here? Now?"

The elevator doors opened, and Sam turned to looked at him directly. "Yes, we do."

Brennan sighed. "Let's take the stairs. The elevator has a camera and mic." Sam raised his eyebrows but stayed silent. He followed Brennan to the concrete stairs which held a chill of their own, separate from the morgue. This was an empty space, full of chilled city air and dank, damp spots of condensation. It was an uncomfortable place to be in, and it was optimally bereft of surveillance equipment. "You want to know the truth?"

Sam crossed his arms and nodded. "And don't feed me some line about a confidential informant. You're brave, but not suicidal. I know you wouldn't have gone on the word of some complete stranger. Do you have someone on the inside of Leviathan?"

It was an intriguing guess, and Brennan quickly thought of a half dozen lies that could be spun to accommodate that theory. But why would an insider give information that would leave him jobless once Leviathan was dismantled? Maybe he just had a crisis of conscience? Then there was the explanation of how they met, how the information was exchanged without interference—

No, Brennan thought. *This is Sam. He deserves to hear the truth.*

"Greg is…psychic," he said slowly.

Sam stared at him skeptically. "Your nephew is psychic? Like, a mind-reader?"

Funny you should mention that, I just met one the other day. He didn't know the mystery voice in his head, not even her name, but she had saved him when he and Clara would otherwise have died. She was responsible for bringing him and Benjamin together, too, where the truth of his wife's death was revealed. Brennan had a lot to owe to the unknown woman.

"Well, not all the time," he said. The words started to flow on their own. "Greg has had visions before, and he told me he could help find Bishop if I gave him a patch, so I—"

"Roll that back a bit. Your nephew is secretly a drug addict—whose top pick is a hallucinogenic, I might add—and you just *believed* he could find Bishop if he had a dose of the good stuff? What the hell were you thinking?"

"Keep your voice down," Brennan warned. "Sound carries really well here."

"There's a bit more perspective to this situation than worrying about being overheard." Sam moved in closer, though, and dropped his voice. "Do you realize you supplied a minor with an illicit substance?" He rubbed a hand through his hair. "So the entire rescue hinged on his *word*, which brings me back to my original point: Why the hell did you believe him?"

Brennan bit his lip and glanced around before answering. "Because," he whispered, "I'm just like Greg."

"You're psychic? Do you know what I'm thinking right now?"

"That I'm crazy?"

"Wow! We have a winner!"

"It doesn't work like that," Brennan said. "Not exactly. He would take the patch, and it—I don't know, it unlocked something in him. He had visions that sometimes came true. My own power confirmed it when Greg said he could help, so I gave him the patch. Trust me, it was the last thing I wanted to do, but there wasn't any other choice. It was either that, or wait to hear the report of her body being found a day or two later."

"Your power?" Sam started to climb the stairs. "I'm talking to a crazy person. Brennan, you need to get your head looked at, because this joke is—"

"Tell me anything," Brennan dared him. "Or better yet, I'll ask questions and you'll respond, and I will *know* if you are telling me the truth."

Sam grinned good-humoredly. "Fine. I'll play this game. Nothing to lose but a few minutes of my time, right? After that, I'm going to the Eternal Tap for an endless lager."

"If you're not convinced in five minutes, I'll pay for us both."

"Good to see your sense of humor isn't tied to your sanity." Sam cleared his throat. "Fine. Ask away."

"What is your favorite color?"

"Green."

True.

"Why?"

"Because it reminds me of my Irish heritage."

False.

"Why?" Brennan repeated. "The real reason."

Sam frowned, and then blushed slightly. "I saw a green flash at sunset when I was growing up in California. It was something rare and beautiful, and I guess it stuck with me."

True.

Brennan nodded. "Good. Why did you lie to me a couple nights ago when you said you were meeting up with Bishop?"

"You're already assuming I lied then."

"Fine, I can backtrack. Where did you go that night, after our pool match?"

"I went over to Bishop's with a bottle of wine—"

"No, you're lying. I'll ask again. Who did you actually meet up with that night?"

"You can't possibly know that I'm lying," Sam argued, his frown deeper than ever. "You're guessing based on some other information."

"The question still stands."

"I was meeting another woman, all right? Is that what you want to hear? I met a sexy redhead who rocked my world until the sun came up."

True.

"I only wish that weren't true," Brennan said sadly. "Do you believe me yet?"

"No," Sam said, and it was the truth. "I love you, partner, but I think you're absolutely insane."

Brennan leaned against the handrail and looked up at his friend. They had been close for years, but it was an easy thing for guys to get along. It was another matter entirely to transcend that superficial acquaintanceship into something that would last for years. Brennan realized he was about to discover what that threshold entailed. "How about a game Greg told me about? Two truths and a lie? You tell me two things that are true about you and one lie, and I'll determine which is the lie."

"A one-in-three chance that you'll get it right? Hardly definitive proof that you're a psychic."

"I'm not psychic," Brennan said. "I can just tell when someone is lying to me. Do you want to play?"

Sam shrugged and then nodded. The internal struggle he must have been going through was almost palpable. Brennan saw that deep beneath the armor of suspicion, his best friend desperately wanted to believe in his sanity. There was something more, though. "Go ahead."

"I need a moment to think." True to his word, it was less than a minute before he came up with his answer. "I am the youngest of six siblings, my dad rode a motorcycle when he was younger, and I have always wanted a lemur."

"You don't have any siblings."

"Won't you even consider the other—?"

"Nope, because I know that one was false. I know it the instant you say it."

"All right, I was going easy on you the first time. I'm *obviously* an only child. I have another round ready."

"Go for it."

"I was a big fan of anime as a kid, I have never known true love, and there are only a handful of people I count among my true friends."

A surge of pity flowed through Brennan as he looked at his friend. "Who do you love?"

"You think it's the second one?"

"I know it is."

Sam sighed. "I don't know how, but you're right."

"I already told you *how*, you just need to believe me. Who was she?"

"Look, it was a long time ago, and suffice it to say that she isn't around anymore. I don't want to talk about it, because nothing is going to bring her back!" His hands balled into fists as he paced up and down several steps. "I don't know—I don't believe that you can actually know the truth from lies. This is too much to process."

"It was a lot for me to digest at first, too."

"You're, like, a superhero. My best friend is Fact-Man."

Brennan grinned. "I really hope that isn't my moniker. And you don't need to talk about her if you don't want to."

"I don't even know if I could," Sam gasped. "I've never talked about this with anyone."

"Same thing for me."

Sam seemed to get himself under control, and he took two steps up the stairs before looking back at Brennan. "We're still going to work the case, right?"

"There's too much at stake to be taking idiotic orders right now."

"Hey, that's my lady you're talking about," Sam warned. "Though in this case, I'll have to agree with you."

"You do? You don't still think I'm just being crazy?"

"Hard to believe that you're a human lie-detector, but even harder to doubt it after what you just did. You are *absolutely* crazy, though."

"Why is that?"

"When Bishop hears what you're up to, you are going to get reamed. Still, I'll be by your side tonight. Even if you're a freak, you're still my best friend."

Truth.

"You told Bishop about Kellogg?"

Sam flinched. "It was unavoidable, partner. She wanted to know what we found out on our own, and this whole thing is bigger than us. Even if she doesn't want you or me on the team, she'll still need all the help she can get. She just can't ask for it."

Brennan followed his logic. "She knows we're not going to let this go, but she also can't officially sanction our involvement. And if we get caught by Pascale and his prototype android, she'll deny any involvement."

"She'll throw us under the bus to keep her position," Sam said. "Brutal, but necessary. Better us than her, right? No sense in all of us being taken down for insubordination."

"I understand," Brennan sighed. "It doesn't mean I like it, though. Machiavellian political maneuvering was never my strong suit."

"Nobody ever suggested otherwise."

"Did you get anything useful out of her in return?"

Sam shook his head. "They didn't have Kellogg's name until I gave it to Noel. I'm sure that they're gathering all the intel there is on him now, but they won't have anything actionable for a while."

"Dammit. Are you able to reach out to any of your private contacts? Maybe one of them can track down some useful information."

"It's possible," Sam said, but he sounded dubious. "But with the full resources of the department and now the Bureau weighing in, I doubt we'll get a jump on any leads."

"Better late than never, right?"

"I guess you're right. I'll make a few calls, but we probably shouldn't be seen together. With your current in-fed-station, I'm worried I'll catch something."

Brennan smiled. "Fine, I'll leave first and lure them away. Let me know when you become useful."

"This is how feelings are hurt."

The fresher air of the precinct hallway felt good on his face as Brennan left the clammy staircase. He felt even better when he emerged onto the busy sidewalk of afternoon rush hour. It was Friday, and people were taking off early from work. They would be going home and getting ready, either for a crazy night out or a relaxing night in. Brennan looked at the passing faces, none of them grabbing his attention. How did Kellogg select his targets? How could he find the special ones, the ones with powers like Brennan's?

He felt eyes on him. There was no way of knowing for sure, but Brennan sensed somebody was watching as he crossed the street and let himself into his apartment building. He climbed the stairs two at a time and resisted the impulse to check the mid-landing window. If Pascale already had eyes on him, then that meant fewer people would be watching Sam as he left the station.

Brennan's injured hand fumbled around with the apartment door key before it slid into the lock. He could hear something playing as he entered, but the sound abruptly died off as Greg pushed a button on his keyboard. "You're home early," he said quickly. The pullout bed was unfolded, and he wore a plain white t-shirt that looked like it had been put on in a rush—it was backwards and inside-out. A blanket covered his lower half, and the laptop rested over his lap.

"Did I interrupt something?"

Greg cleared his throat. "Um, no."

"Right."

The two looked at one another for a moment, and then Brennan turned left into the bathroom and closed the door behind him. He decided to give his nephew a moment to compose himself and spare either of them further embarrassment.

His reflection looked as haggard as he felt. It was frustrating to be sidelined by both Bishop *and* the FBI, even if the former's orders were only on paper. His love life was virtually nonexistent, and he wasn't entirely convinced it didn't deserve to stay that way. His loyalty to both Sam and Bishop was strained by their recent actions—Sam's sexual indiscretions and Bishop's bout of case-blocking—and it seemed that they were all reaching a critical point in their bonds to one another.

Most of all, he resented the fact that each new line on his face brought him one step closer to being the spitting image of his gangster father.

Brennan turned on the tap and let the ice-cold water numb his fingers. He cupped his hands and splashed shallow bowls of water against his face in an attempt to remove the worry lines. The hairs on his back stood on end as the cold shock jolted his system, but the hint of his father's face still stared back at him from the other side of the glass.

He dried off and opened the door, walking to the kitchen to make dinner. A quick glance confirmed what he suspected would happen; Greg was fully dressed now, and the bed was once again concealed beneath the couch cushions. His nephew darted into the bathroom, and Brennan heard him turn on the shower.

It'll be a cold one, he guessed. He turned a dial on the stove and gathered ingredients while he waited for it to heat up. A tray soon held a pine tree-shaped layer of packaged dough for crescent rolls, a jagged arrow of doughy goodness. He quickly browned a quarter pound of ground beef in a pan and mixed it with taco seasoning. When it smelled ready, he lined up the seasoned beef along the middle line of interconnected doughy triangles and sprinkled cheese on top. The tips were grabbed with care and stretched up over the beef, securing it into a meaty bûche de Noël that he placed in the oven to cook.

The simple meal promised future heart attacks, but it was soul food, something which Brennan was desperately craving. Greg was still in the shower, so Brennan took a moment to retrieve his laptop and check his messages. There was no update from Sam yet, and while that wasn't particularly surprising, he still felt nervous about each minute that was lost not pursuing Kellogg. Still, there was nothing to be gained from worrying over what he couldn't change.

There was a message from CopAFeel, and Brennan opened it a little too eagerly. Unfortunately, it was just an automated message that listed a few new potential matches to his profile. It seemed like Clara wasn't keen on setting up a second date after their first had ended with gunmen and vomiting in the storm drain.

And who says I don't know how to show a girl a good time? he thought bitterly as he closed the laptop.

Greg emerged from the bathroom in an exhale of steam. "All better," he announced.

"I don't even want to think through the implications of that."

His nephew sniffed the air. "Dinner smells good."

"It's a family recipe. I'll teach it to you sometime."

"Why would I learn to cook when I have you to do it for me?" He walked over and sat on the couch. He began contentedly flipping through television channels, though his head was turned slightly in Brennan's direction.

"About that," Brennan started. "Have you found anywhere to work yet?"

"It's a brutal job market out there, you know? I have a few places I'm interested in, but I don't know if they'll hire me."

Brennan crossed his arms. "You'll never know until you try. Well, at any rate, I don't want you going out tonight."

"Why don't—oh, is this about that serial killer?" Several more channels passed under his thumb.

"Greg, this is serious. We're hunting him, but for now it's better if you stay home. He's targeting specific individuals. People like us."

"I'm not a Sleeper," Greg said, sounding bored. "And neither are you. So what's there to worry about?"

Brennan sighed. He sat down heavily and rested an arm on the back of the couch. "There's more to all of this than Sleepers and non-Sleepers," he explained. "With enough experience and training, anyone can become a Sleeper."

"Even me?"

"Yes, but that's beside the point. I don't know what it is, exactly, but your gift of foresight isn't Sleeper-related. It's something much greater than that, and this serial killer is tracking people like us."

"Like us?" Greg slowly lowered the remote and gave him his full attention. "What can *you* do?"

"This isn't important right now—"

"No, no, I think I'd like to hear it."

"All I want is for you to stay home tonight with the door locked. Hell, even push the couch in front of it."

Greg gulped, but otherwise kept any emotions from showing. "If you don't tell me what you can do—and what the hell we *are*—then I am going to walk all over the seediest neighborhoods while wearing a t-shirt that has 'I'm a psychic' written in bold print."

Brennan shifted his jaw around and stared sternly at his nephew. He knew the odds were slim that the FBI might already have ears *inside* his apartment, but paranoia was an old habit from his Sleeper days, and it was a tough one to break. "What I'm about to tell you can't leave this apartment."

"What is it with you and secrets? You said the same thing before you told me you were a Sleeper."

"Promise me, Greg!"

"All right, fine. Your secret is safe with me, Batman."

True.

Brennan exhaled loudly. "We are...different."

"Thanks, sensei. I got that much."

"Sensei Batman is talking, so your attitude needs to take a backseat for a second."

Greg frowned, looking chagrined. "Sorry."

"I didn't mean to snap at you, it's just...this is important." He took one last breath and took the plunge. "I can tell when people are lying to me. Anybody—*everybody*—at any time."

"But I've lied to you tons of times and you never knew." Brennan gave him an even look, and Greg's eyes widened in comprehension. "Oh. Umm...shit."

"Yeah."

"So I can see the future and you can see...what? The truth?"

"More or less. But what I'm saying is, these kinds of gifts aren't exclusive to Sleepers, or even common among us."

"Us?"

"*Them*," Brennan amended.

"You said us," Greg continued. "Did you...are you *one of them* again?"

Brennan wiped a hand over his face. "It's complicated, okay? I've found out some things that have shifted my perspective on them a little bit."

Greg scoffed. "A little bit? This is a complete one-eighty!"

"Focus! This serial killer isn't hunting normal people, or even Sleepers in particular. He's hunting people with *powers*, people like you and me."

"You and *I*."

"Sensei Batman hates grammar Nazis," Brennan warned. "Particularly when they're wrong."

Greg leaned deeper into the couch and scratched his head. "So you're saying I shouldn't go out tonight?"

"I'm forbidding it."

"You do realize this means I'll have to put my job hunt on hold, right?"

Brennan shifted to lock eyes with his nephew. "Greg, this is a dangerous man, and we've made him desperate. I need you to take this seriously."

"Uncle Arty, I *am* taking this seriously. But if I have to cower in fear every time some bad guy wants to take a shot at you, how do you expect me to deal with my *own* problems? How do you expect me to survive in a city where dangerous stuff goes down every day?" His lips spread in his foolish grin. "I'd rather *live* and go out with a smile on my face than be fearful of every creaking stair and dark alleyway."

"Maybe I don't need to keep you in the city after all," Brennan mused.

"What's that?" Greg eyed him suspiciously. "Are you sending me somewhere?"

"It might be worth it to look up more information on the Scottages out in the valley," Brennan suggested. He watched as his nephew's eyes lit up with excitement, even as he kept the true reason for his suggestion to himself. It would give him the opportunity to investigate the death of Jeremy Scott, and the search for housing information would provide a decent distraction for Greg. Two birds with one stone.

Greg reached eagerly for his laptop. "I'll start looking it up now!" He inhaled deeply and made a show of licking his lips. "Dinner smells ready."

"Oh, I forgot!" Brennan leaped up and ran to the kitchen. He slipped on a padded glove and grabbed the tray from the oven. The taco log was a work of perfection; steam rose from between the openings in its golden, flaky crust, carrying with it the aroma of cooked meat, melted cheese, and spices.

He called out to Greg. "Come on over and make yourself a plate," he said. "We might as well eat while I wait for Sam to get back to me."

Chapter Eighteen

Alex waited for Kern to come around and open her door.

It had been a long drive home, and the tension in the air was palpable. Her attempt at cold-shouldering her father had melted away several miles ago, and now she wanted little more than to collapse into her bed with the help of a little wine.

Or a lot of wine.

Her power's absence kept her on edge. It was unnerving, not knowing what others were thinking around her. She hadn't realized until now just how heavily she had drawn on its insights. How she longed to escape into another person's eyes, to hear another person's thoughts besides her own. It was impossible, though, and she now trusted her safety to an aging manservant, her never-aging father, and the relative security provided to her by being miles from the city.

And I will have my mother, of course, Alex added. Nobody could hear *her* thoughts, but she felt guilty about excluding her from the mental checklist. *Not that she can do much protecting.*

On top of that, she knew that her temporary protection of Detective Brennan had come to an end. Heinrich and the rest of Leviathan would be coming for his blood, and there was nothing she could do to warn him. Perhaps Benjamin and his Sleepers could still stop the serial killer even after Brennan was dead. It was the best she could ask for if she ever hoped to live securely in the city again.

The car door opened, and Kern reached out a hand to help her up. He dutifully walked ahead of them to get the front door as well. "Thank you, Kern," Alex said, touching him on the shoulder. It was an action she'd seen her mother do on occasion when she was younger, a kind gesture for a fatherly figure.

"Of course," he replied. Kern looked to her father. "Dinner will be ready within the hour."

"I'll be in my study until then."

"Very good, sir."

Alex left them in the foyer and took the curved flight of stairs to the second floor. Her room lay at the end of the hall, directly above the converted room where her mother now resided. She hung her jacket on a nearby hook and fell onto the plush bed, not even bothering to take off her shoes. The comforter felt good beneath her head, and sleep tempted her with ease. Her eyes were heavy, and it felt like much longer than a day ago that she had lost her powers.

I don't want to be here.

The thought pushed its way into her head, and Alex frowned up at the ceiling. She wanted everything to go back to normal. Or, at least, *her* version of what was normal. Only one good thing had come of the past few days, and that had been the brief realization that she could grow and adopt other abilities. That bit of experimentation had ended, though, when it short-circuited *everything* she could do, including the simplest bit of telepathy.

Still, this was the best place for her to recover. She *did* want to be here. It must have been the depression talking, or else she was crazier than she'd thought. She certainly didn't want to be in the city right now, not with a serial killer on the loose.

Her bedroom windows faced the west, and the setting sun threw harsh bolts of light into her face. Alex pulled a pillow over her head and tried to not think about anything. That set her on a dangerous path of thinking about not thinking, and the subsequent thoughts about *that* conundrum. She wasn't used to being stuck in her own head.

How do normal people do it? she wondered. She quickly discarded the thought. There was a reason she lived in a luxury apartment above the rest of the city; she was special, an elite, truly above the rest of the city's inhabitants. The only person with abilities comparable to hers was her father.

"And Benjamin," she sighed. The old man and his Sleepers were nearly on her level—but only *nearly* so. Now that she knew they were real, she could defend herself from their psychic probes into her sleeping mind. She would take what they could offer while developing her own powers, and when the time came, she would be the strongest of them all. "For that to happen," she said aloud, "I need to rest."

As hard as she willed it, though, sleep didn't come for her. It was a major setback in her plan to become the ultimate Sleeper. Sleep seemed like a necessary component in the job description.

Alex slipped off her shoes and crawled further onto the bed. She yawned, hoping to trick her brain into thinking it was later in the day than it actually was. The heaviness in her eyelids returned, and the comfort of the mattress increased fivefold. She closed her eyes for the briefest of moments.

"Miss Brüding," prompted Kern's polite voice from the doorway. "Dinner is ready."

Alex groaned loudly enough for him to hear her. Her eyes were closed and her face was still covered by a pillow, but she knew the sun had set. It was a cool, dark evening. The table was set for two, and there was a visitor in the driveway who would soon need attending to.

Poor child.

She bolted upright in bed and stared at Kern. "Did you say something?"

"Dinner is—"

"No, no," she interrupted impatiently, "after that."

Kern shook his head. "I don't believe so, no, Miss." The doorbell rang, and Kern turned his white head to glance down the hall. "If you will excuse me."

"I told you to call me Alex," she called after him. She heard his amused chuckle echo down the hall, and a similar feeling spread through her chest. It hadn't originated from her, which could only mean one thing. Alex reached for her power and she felt it there, waiting, as if she were dipping the tips of her fingers into a placid pool of icy water. Goosebumps spread along her arms and her hairs raised on end.

She moaned appreciatively as it swept over her body. Same as taking a dive into a frigid lake, Alex quickly became readjusted to its presence, swaddling herself in the cocoon of extrasensory awareness. She jumped into Kern's mind, seeing through his eyes and hearing through his ears.

A large man was at the door. He wore a faded leather jerkin over an outfit of jeans and a camouflage shirt. His broad chest was barely contained by the worn material, and a messy crop of dark hair jutted from his head. Flecks of silver shined at the temples. "Is James in?"

"I'm sorry, sir, but Mister Brüding is preparing to sit down to dinner."

"It's urgent," the stranger said. "I need to speak with him as soon as possible."

Hmm, sounds intriguing, Alex thought, and she sent a probe toward the newcomer. Instantly, she was met with a flare of violent purple light, as if she had come up against a force field. In fact, that was *exactly* what had happened. She watched through Kern's eyes as the stranger shifted his gaze, glaring up in the direction of her bedroom.

"I wouldn't do that again, if I were you," he said to Kern.

In her bedroom, Alex shivered. She had the distinct impression that he knew she was watching through the butler's eyes. She knew that he knew she had just tried to read him, and he had been more than prepared. *Just like Heinrich and his men,* she thought, glowering at the idea that so many "others" had been trained to resist her.

She withdrew her probe from Kern and slipped out of the business attire she had worn to the meeting in the Jardin des Anges. It was wrinkled now, and there were more suitable outfits to wear around the house. When she had changed into something more comfortable, Alex walked down the hall and took a different staircase than before, one which avoided the foyer and emerged into the kitchen. From there, she moved to join her father in the dining room.

"Alexis," he murmured, drawing her in with his arms. He kissed her lightly on the crown of her head, and she returned his warmth briefly. She hadn't forgotten the secrets he was keeping, though, and she realized that he would still think she was powerless. Perhaps she could question him during dinner, when his guard would be down.

"I think someone is here to see you," she said in lieu of a proper greeting.

James nodded. "I know who it is. Why don't you and Kern get started without me?" he suggested, and he pulled out a chair for her to sit. "The sooner I can deal with him, the sooner he'll be out of our hair."

"Go do what you need to," Alex said, playing the part of the dutiful daughter.

He smiled at her, though it didn't quite reach his eyes. He strode purposefully down the hall, into the foyer, where he relieved Kern of his job in delaying the visitor. Alex felt Kern's gratitude wash through his body. Her perception felt even stronger than before. She had to keep herself from grinning like an overexcited fool; Kern was loyal, but that loyalty extended more deeply to her father than to her. If he realized her powers had returned, the news would soon reach her father's ear.

Alex forced her own smile as Kern appeared, looking affable and concerned at the same time. "It is not my place to speak ill of your father's acquaintances," he said, "but that man has an air of darkness about him."

"You think so as well?" she asked. Alex had no feelings about the man yet, other than distrust, but if she planned on having a source of information close to her father, she could do no better than their faithful butler. They already had a connection; now she needed to solidify his allegiance, and that started by creating common ground.

"Oh, yes," Kern said enthusiastically, before he cleared his throat. "But I forget myself. If I may have your plate…?"

She handed the dish to him, and he disappeared into the kitchen, returning a minute later with a full complement of meat, potatoes, green vegetables, and a biscuit. In his other hand, Kern carried a bottle of red wine, one of the older vintages that her father kept in the basement. "Is tonight a special occasion?" she asked.

"Any time that you are home is a special occasion," Kern said, smiling faintly.

"Oh, Kern, you're such a flirt."

He poured her a modest portion of wine, two fingers' worth. Kern had grown up in the age of scotch and brandy, and it seemed the habit for portioning drinks in such a way had never left him. "It is true, Miss—*Alex*," he amended, catching her stern glare. "It has not been the same since you moved out, and with Mister Brüding so occupied with his research, your presence has been sorely missed."

Alex smiled, with feeling this time, as she raised her glass to him. "With all the trouble in the city and *the clock* winding down, perhaps it's time I returned home for a bit," she said. There was no need to clarify which clock she meant; there was only one scale of time that mattered in any way to her father. "I can spend these final few months with Mom," she added in a whisper.

"I'm sure she would be delighted to have your company," Kern said.

There was the sound of raised voices in the other room, though the incident passed too quickly for Alex to hear what was said. A moment later, the door slammed, and she heard her father's steps approaching as he returned to the dining room.

"Derrick forgets himself," he said by way of explanation. He glanced at Kern as he took his seat. "If Mr. Scott shows up unannounced in the future, I give you permission to handle him as you see fit."

"Of course, sir."

Alex looked between the two of them in confusion; Kern was too feeble to shovel snow from the driveway, much less fend off unwanted guests. She resisted the impulse to probe them for information, though. Thus far, her father had only permitted her to see what he *wanted* her to see. She didn't want to set off any psychic wards like the ones she had found inside of the other man.

Everyone and their mother can resist me these days, she thought grudgingly. She kept the anger from showing in her eyes, though, as she looked up at her father and smiled. "Have you made any progress with the treatment?" It was a hopeless question, but the cure had become her father's obsession.

His expression soured. "No breakthroughs yet. There just isn't enough *time*," he growled. "And with

SymbioTech breathing down my neck, I can't hire Leviathan to do anything untoward."

'Untoward' was a diplomatic term for kidnapping people to use as test subjects, but Alex understood why he was speaking obtusely. "Kern, could you excuse us for a moment? I'd like to speak with my father in private."

"Of course, Alex." James glanced curiously at the casual usage of his daughter's name, and Kern's sagging cheeks reddened. "Miss Brüding," he said, bowing slightly. He stepped out into the front hallway, closing the door behind him as he left.

"I wish you wouldn't tease him like that," James said, cutting off a piece of steak. "He is a man of discipline and obedience. If you take that away, what will be left?"

Alex sighed. "You're right. Servants are made to serve."

"That isn't what I meant at all. Kern wasn't always a servant, but he has always had discipline in his life. He follows orders. I've ordered him to refer to us with respect, and he feels most comfortable when carrying out orders." He paused to chew and swallow another mouthful. "Now, you wanted to talk to me about something?"

She folded her hands on her lap, trying her best to look humbled. "I'm sorry I hired Heinrich without first consulting you," she said. "I knew of no one else, and this was a job that only he and his men could perform on such short notice."

James merely nodded. "What job was this?"

"I hired them to fake a hit on a detective," she explained, "so that he would trust me after I saved him."

"You may need to wind back the clock on this story."

Alex took a deep breath and began anew. She explained how she had sensed a presence of extreme fury in her building, and how she had followed the disturbed thoughts to find the enraged man. James's eyes darkened as she mentioned her conversations with Benjamin, but he remained quiet and let her continue. The rest of the story came in a blur. Leviathan's attack. The brokered meeting between Brennan and Benjamin. The loss of her power.

She kept two details to herself. First, she never told him that her power was evolving, that she could "jump between branches," as Benjamin had called it. Second, she didn't disclose the true correlation between the murder victims. She wasn't sure why; call it foresight, or call it a gut instinct, but she didn't feel right revealing that particular piece of information.

Her face remained placid as she hid those facts from her father. She hadn't missed the dark look that had passed over her father's face, either. "So what is the history between you and Benjamin?"

James stared at her for a long moment. "Why did you think attacking the detective was the best way of earning his trust?" he asked.

Alex shrugged. "He thought he was in imminent danger, and I appeared to save him. I figured he would trust me implicitly the next time I showed myself."

"And what does it matter if he trusts you?"

"Well now that I *know* about the Sleepers—thanks for the warning, by the way—it could be useful to have influence over a detective, particularly one who has distanced himself from Benjamin."

James rubbed at his chin. "And he didn't see your face in either instance?"

"No, I called him anonymously on his cell," she explained, lying on multiple levels. "Why?"

"That's just as well. These Sleepers can't be trusted, Alexis."

She gave him an irritated look. "You have to answer my question now. Why does Benjamin have people watching you? Did you used to be one of them?"

To her surprise, her father laughed out loud. It was a sound she seldom heard. "*One of them?*" he asked incredulously. "I may have lived a long time, but I do not yet have a death wish."

"A frail, old man and his crippled grandson don't seem too dangerous to me," Alex muttered.

"That *old man* is the grandmaster of their order."

"Grandmaster?"

James waved a hand dismissively. "A self-appointed title, basically worthless. But it does mean he was the first of them, the one who brought them all together. Your detective is one of them. There are countless others. My *threat*, as you and he both call it, is simply that I know they exist."

"Detective Brennan seemed pretty adamant against meeting with Benjamin. Whatever happened between them, I think he's on the outside now."

One of her father's eyebrows raised in surprise. "Now that is interesting," he murmured. "Nonetheless, they met. I have little doubt that he has been roped back into the old man's schemes."

Alex eyed her father with suspicion. "So you really have nothing to do with Benjamin aside from being really old and knowledgeable?"

"Not as knowledgeable as I would like, not by half," he said, his eyes unconsciously wandering in the direction of her mother's room. "I know enough secrets, though, that Benjamin would like to see me dead."

"Could he do it?" The question blurted out from her lips. "Is it even possible for you to die?"

James flexed a hand, and she watched as veins rolled from the movement of the muscles. "It was a long time ago, but I used to look younger. I am old, but not eternal." He gave her a tired smile that crinkled the skin around his eyes. "I imagine my blessing will run out eventually."

"Hopefully not too soon."

"Are you truly worried about this serial killer? There's nothing to fear, Alexis. If Benjamin is half the strategist I believe him to be, then Detective Brennan will be able to put an end to these deaths. Until then, you'll be safe here."

Alex took a sip of wine, which depleted her meager portion by half. "I just have one more question to ask before we can bring Kern back in."

"Go ahead."

"Why did you train Heinrich and his men to resist my power?" She prepared herself for the inevitable answer, the one that would break her spirit. Her father feared her, and he had actual *henchmen* who could fight against her if the need arose.

James frowned at her. "I didn't teach them to resist *you*." He reached out and took her hands between his. "You have to understand that there are others out there like us, and some of those people could very well have the same abilities. Can you imagine what your gift would be like in the wrong hands? What *mine* would cause? An ageless tyrant, or an all-knowing one…either would be disastrous." He patted her hands and rested back in his seat. "So we must be cautious, and learn to moderate ourselves. The path onto which Benjamin leads his Sleepers is a dark one, and I refuse to be taken down by his folly."

Alex seldom heard her father speak like this. The words he used, along with the way he spoke, harkened back to another century. James Brüding was an old man, older even than he let on, and the world had changed drastically since his youth. The sudden change in his parlance made her both nervous and alert. Clearly, Benjamin's appearance in her life had put him on edge.

"What will you do about Benjamin?"

"I thought you already asked your last question," James said, arching an eyebrow. "You are normally not so talkative."

"Is it a problem?"

He pursed his lips before responding. "No," he said. "It is simply a change."

Alex persevered in her questioning. "So? What can we do to stop Benjamin?"

"Stop him?" Her father gave her a level look. "Why should we need to stop him? His business is none of ours. Once the murders are resolved, I suspect

Benjamin and the detective will resume their feud, and we will remain out of the crossfire."

"That's it?" she asked in disbelief. "We stand by while they duke it out?"

"Of course," he said, sounding shocked. As he stared at her, she reevaluated her own reasons for being involved. Why did it matter so much? The detective meant nothing to her, and Benjamin was only as useful as far as what he could teach her. The more they spoke, the more she realized that her father might just be the source of information she needed. Benjamin was an unnecessary component in her life. More than that, he was a danger to her and her father.

"It…makes sense," she said, nodding to herself as if it would reinforce her belief. That confidence was shaky, but growing. Her father was the only one she needed…until she didn't.

And then what? she thought. She loved him. But would he be as interesting to her, or as tolerable, if he had nothing to offer beyond human company? She could find that anywhere. Alex looked at her father, and neither of them moved for a long moment. It occurred to her that, had their roles been reversed, he could be reading her mind at this very instant, hearing her confused, *despicable* thoughts.

"I think I'm full," she told him, pushing her plate away.

"Kern!" James called, and the butler appeared in the doorway.

"Yes, sir?"

"Dinner was delicious, thank you," he said, gesturing to his own plate.

"I will give your compliments to the chef," he said dryly, and the two men shared a smile. Kern cooked, served, and cleaned every meal under their roof.

"Alexis?" her father prompted.

"Thank you very much, Kern," Alex said graciously.

He set about clearing their plates, and James put a hand on his daughter's back as they stood and walked toward the foyer. "I hope you are feeling well," he said to her. "Your ability will return, don't worry. Once it does, you will feel more like yourself."

Alex smiled weakly. She had already forgotten her lie, and the urge to correct him was smothered just in time. "Thanks," she muttered.

James glanced wistfully down the hallway toward Alex's mother's room. "I have to work."

"I understand."

"Breakfast in the morning?" he asked, leaning forward to kiss her forehead.

She leaned into the embrace, feeling fatigue rush over her unexpectedly. "Sounds good," she said. "I'll let you know when I'm awake."

"The stairs are old," he reminded her.

Alex winced. "Right. You'll hear the creaking."

She took to the steps two at a time, bounding toward the upper landing. It felt strange to be home again. There were some things that had become permanent memories, like the knowledge that there were fourteen steps between the first and second floor, or the fact that the flight she was ascending moaned with each footfall. Other things, though, had changed since her last prolonged visit home. Floorboards that had been sturdy before now groaned beneath her weight. The banister wobbled slightly as her hand trailed along its length. Dust dwelled in corridors that were once well-trodden by her mother and father.

The room at the end of the hall had always been hers, and yet now it wasn't. Everything remained the same, but it felt foreign after so many years away. The industrial browns and whites and silvers of *her* apartment would never be at home in the lilac-colored corner room of her parents' house.

Her life had changed so much since her childhood. *Armed thugs, Sleepers, Mom's illness...,* she thought, running down the list in her head. Suddenly feeling ashamed, she reached out to touch upon her mother's mind. A whirlwind of sensations flooded her consciousness, and she had to sit down before she could begin to process it all.

Stephanie Brüding's mind and body were both a wreck. Her skin felt clammy, sweltering beneath the covers despite the cool breeze and gentle sunlight coming through the windows. The bed was soiled again, since her body refused to listen to the brain's commands. But her brain wasn't giving any commands today; all cylinders were firing, but nothing was being produced. There was nothing besides the pain. She was nobody. The mirror reflected a face that wasn't hers, not one she could recognize. There was nothing going on in there.

Nothing but pain.

In that moment, Alex wanted to die.

With an effort of will, she pulled away from the dying woman, retreating into the young shell of her own body. Her throat had instantly dried, and her hands trembled as she tried to calm herself. No matter how she reminded herself that the thoughts weren't her own, though, the tremors remained.

How could her mother live in such a state? If only her father had enough time to work on his cure, then they could put an end to her suffering. As it was, the next few months were going to be a long and arduous descent for all of them.

Alex collapsed back in her bed, and the weariness felt from her mother's frustration quickly brought sleep down upon her head.

Chapter Nineteen

"Brennan, we've got something."

The call came before the taco log was three-quarters consumed, and Greg gave a mock parting salute as he guided another steaming bite toward his mouth. Brennan shook his head at his nephew's black hole of a stomach as he left. He met Sam in an alley a few blocks away from the apartment. A light autumn rain began to fall, and they took shelter beneath the overhanging roof of a Chinese take-out restaurant.

"What'd Bishop tell you?"

Sam wiped some water from his eyes. "Kellogg has been routinely paying out rent for multiple apartments, and as far as we can tell from electrical and plumbing bills, he's been living among all of them for months."

"So there's no way to pinpoint him to one spot. They'll have to split up to find him…" Brennan frowned. "This sounds familiar."

Sam nodded. "Multiple objectives, multiple police task forces? This is right out of your playbook against Leviathan."

"They know how catastrophically *wrong* that went, right?"

"I tried to dissuade them, but it makes as much sense now as it did back then. Bishop backs it, and those FBI agents are on board as well." Sam leaned in close. "But this is an opportunity for us, too."

Rain started to fall more heavily, and Brennan huddled closer to hear Sam's words. "How so?" he asked. "I'm on probation and you aren't even on the force."

Sam pulled on Brennan's jacket sleeve. "Come on, let's walk as we talk. There isn't much time."

"What do you mean?"

The light of the street lamps was muted by the steady downpour, and their steps were silent as they made their way south, away from Brennan's apartment and the police station. "They broke everyone into teams of two," Sam explained. "Each pair is taking one of Kellogg's residences."

"And we're headed to one of them?" Brennan guessed.

"Exactamundo!"

"What kind of head start do they have on us?"

"I called you as soon as I heard about it, partner." He faced Brennan, who saw a grin plastered on his friend's face. "They assigned Pascale and Jun to check out the location we're headed to. Can you imagine the egg on their face if *we* beat them to Kellogg?"

Brennan returned his smile. "How far is it?"

Sam nodded ahead of them. "About ten blocks that way. And if I know our boys in black, they'll take the shuttle or, better yet, try to drive there."

"What are we waiting for?"

Brennan pulled the collar of his jacket up around his neck and the two of them took off at a loping jog. Sam set a steady pace for them, and Brennan was grateful for the exercise regimen he had set for himself months before. While he still carried a few extra pounds, the breathlessness never quite emerged, and he found his legs striding powerfully beneath him.

Each step carried them forward a little bit more, and the blocks disappeared beneath their feet. Sam's pace made it easy to avoid slipping on the rain-slick sidewalk, and startled, umbrella-wielding passersby hurried out of their way.

"Explain to me why Bishop is on board with this plan," Brennan said. His breath came out in small huffs of white mist in the cool night air. "She of all people understands the magnitude of that mistake."

Sam's breathing was barely labored, as if he ran like this every day. "The orders came from higher up. The chief, or maybe even the mayor. With the elections coming at the end of the year, he can't very well have a serial killer loose on his watch, can he?"

"So it's politics," Brennan grumbled. He wasn't sure Sam even heard him, his voice was so low. "What's the game plan here? We go in, hope he's there, and cuff him?"

Sam shrugged, which was an impressive thing to do while still jogging. "That was basically my plan," he said. "If Kellogg is there, then great. We'll take him down, and they can't fault us for bringing a mass murderer to his knees. Hell, we'll probably even get medals. If the place is empty, we'll make ourselves scarce before Pascale and Jun show up."

"We'll be cutting it close."

"No way," Sam said, waving him off. They dodged around a young couple that was walking briskly without the protection of an umbrella. The traffic light was red in their direction, but their pace was too determined to be broken. Brennan awkwardly twisted to the side to avoid being hit by a car just starting to move, and Sam *slid* across the hood of the car. For the second time that week, he seemed the spitting image of James Bond.

"You're lucky that car's hood was wet from the rain," Brennan shouted as they continued running.

Sam laughed. "I know, right? That was actually way harder than I thought it would be."

The flow of traffic worried Brennan. It actually wasn't too terrible tonight, which meant Pascale would have an easier time navigating the streets. He wouldn't have been surprised if the car they had just avoided had belonged to the men in question.

Luckily, though, Sam slowed to a halt in front of an old brownstone duplex. A few of the lights were on, but it seemed like the sort of neighborhood where people didn't want to attract too much attention to themselves, and the majority of the rooms were dark.

"I don't have a search warrant," Brennan said.

"How exactly do you think I do most of my work?" Sam asked, producing a set of lock picks from inside his jacket. He set about inserting them in sequence into the lock, adjusting them with practiced ease as the tumblers fell into place. Even through the rain, Brennan heard a distinctive click as Sam turned his picks and the doorknob in unison. "After you."

Brennan unsnapped his holster strap and placed his hand on the grip as he shouldered his way through the entrance. The room inside was dark; the only illumination came from the street lamps outside as their light filtered through the cracks in the boarded windows. A couch and chair sat in solemn silence in the room to the left. A hallway continued to what looked like the kitchen, and Brennan could just make out a set of stairs leading up to another level.

"You get the hallway, I'll take the second floor?" Sam suggested, keeping his voice low.

"Ha ha," Brennan said bleakly. "You went high last time. Check out the kitchen, and then meet me upstairs."

Sam gave a mock salute and pulled his own, private sidearm. He stepped slowly and methodically down the hallway, his lean form a shadow among shadows.

Brennan tentatively placed a foot on the first step; it held his weight without protest. Like an animal stalking its prey, he ascended the staircase swiftly and silently, his back to the wall with the gun raised ever so slightly. His eyes had adjusted to the dim lighting, and details came to him in shades of gray. Not quite fifty of them, but enough to distinguish family photos on the walls from the dulled phosphorescent stars clinging to the ceiling of one bedroom.

He opened a door in the center of the hall, but there was only a small bathroom beyond. That only left one room to be explored, the one directly above the living room.

There was a faint hint of light showing through the space at the bottom of the door, and Brennan felt more than heard the thrum of electrical equipment inside. Something was happening in that room. His hand reached for the doorknob, and just then a loud thump came from the stairs behind him. He whirled around, weapon raised, and Sam held up both hands with his gun turned sideways.

"Woah, Brennan, it's me!" His voice obviously struggled not to shout, and it came out as a harsh whisper.

Brennan lowered his pistol. "Sorry," he said. "You spooked me."

"Well now that *both* of our hearts are pounding," Sam grumbled, "let's see what's behind door number three."

The metal knob was cool against the skin of his palm as Brennan gripped and twisted it. He leaned hard against the door as he entered like a bulldozer, and Sam followed close behind. Armed and alert, they swept the room with their eyes and weapons, but Kellogg wasn't anywhere to be seen.

"That's disappointing," Sam said, allowing his arms to drop to his sides.

"Hang on." Brennan leaned forward and squinted his eyes. There, on the far side of the room, was a faint, blinking red light. He flipped on the small flashlight attached to his gun and pointed it at the dot. A small camera came into view, and its lens was a peculiar shade of crimson.

A small television flickered to life, and a man's face appeared on the screen. It was a face that Brennan recognized, even though he had only seen it once before, on paper.

"Detective...Brennan, was it?" Levi Kellogg asked on the screen.

"And associate," Sam chimed in.

"Where are you, Kellogg?"

"Far away from your current location," Kellogg said. His eyes remained trained on Brennan, who looked around the room warily. "Though maybe I should say current locations, plural."

"That doesn't sound good," Sam muttered under his breath.

"He knows we're storming all of the—"

"What I *know*, Detective," Kellogg interrupted, "is that the microphone mounted to the camera is a powerful one. What I *know* is that you will never find me."

"Pretty confident for a man whose cover was blown in a day."

"Yes," mused the man on the screen. "After a day in your hands. I wonder why that is."

Sam glanced at Brennan. "What does he mean?"

"No idea."

"Come now, Detective, we both know that's not true." He leaned forward, his face nearly pressed against the screen. His pale features shone as he glared out at them with serpentine eyes. "I see you for what you really are. Why do you freaks insist on living among us? Why am I the only one who can identify you as an imminent threat to humanity's survival?"

"You're insane," Brennan told him.

"I'm insane?" Kellogg looked to Sam, as if in search of support. "He calls *me* insane? I can see your aura, Detective Brennan, and it is just like all the others. Black, to the core. Your corruption spreads like the plague, and I am this city's deliverance."

Brennan felt a tingle in the small of his back, the same sensation that had emerged when Benjamin confronted him in his Sleeperscape. He remembered the feeling of wings that had sprouted from across his shoulders…He was no angel, but to hell with anyone who called him part of a corrupt plague.

"I am doing *everything* I can to save this city from people like you!" Brennan yelled.

Kellogg's visage smirked from behind the glass. "People like *you* destroyed it. I set up this little distraction to get the police off my case, but to find one of *you* among them...this will be a treat indeed."

"What are you talking about?"

"Uhh, Brennan?" Sam holstered his sidearm. "We need to go."

"Sam, what are you—?"

"Do you know what my specialty was in the military, Detective Brennan?" Kellogg asked. "What kind of skills I got while I was over there?"

"Arthur, we've gotta *go*!"

Brennan turned to look at his friend. It wasn't often that Sam called him by his first name, and his tone now spoke of anything but good news. Sam nodded to the side, and Brennan followed his gaze. On the floor, tucked almost out of view, was a colored cable running between several tightly closed gray packages. As his eyes traced the length of the cable, he saw more packages arranged in a semicircle around the perimeter of the room.

Attached to each squat gray block was a small metal charge.

Kellogg's face split in a cruel grin. "Keep a spot cool for me in hell, Detective."

"Sam, run!"

Brennan pushed his friend out of the room and slammed the door shut as he followed closely behind. The opening to the stairs was too far away; Brennan body-checked Sam into the banister, jarring it loose, and it broke free entirely as he added his own weight to the impact. They fell almost ten feet before landing on the bottom-most step in a tangled mess.

An earth-shattering rumble shook the house, and the room upstairs exploded into flames. The burning door burst outward and slammed against the wall before it came crashing down toward their heads. Sam pulled the two of them out of the way just in time, though the flames caught quickly on the peeling wallpaper and old wooden stairs. Black smoke started to envelop them.

Sam flung open the front door, and they were greeted by a gust of clean air and the sight of a nondescript black SUV pulling up in front of the house. "We have to leave through the back," Sam coughed.

"Why?"

"Pascale and Jun just arrived."

Brennan shouldered his way past burning debris from the blast upstairs. Nothing was being spared by the roaring, gaping hunger of the inferno. Flames licked their heels as they blazed a trail down the hallway, through the small kitchen, and out the back door. Rain fought off the smoke that tried to follow them. Sam fell to his knees, hacking up ash as his lungs tried to clear themselves. Brennan wiped at his mouth with a dirty hand as he gulped in deep breaths of fresh air.

"Come on," he urged Sam. "We need to keep moving."

"Kellogg is a psycho."

Brennan nodded in agreement. "A psycho who *hopefully* thinks we're dead. If he has the place under surveillance, though, he'll spot us if we stick around. Plus, we don't want Pascale to see us and start asking all the wrong questions."

Sam stood slowly and contemplated the rain and soot that marred his clothes. "I just had these cleaned."

"You can put it on my tab."

They took off across the backyard and vaulted the metal fence at full speed. It wasn't something he would have attempted several months ago, but Brennan had adrenaline pumping through his veins, and he jumped with youthful vigor into the shadowed alley.

Brennan heard sirens approaching, but their sound was echoed a dozen times over. It didn't make sense to send so many fire engines to combat a single house fire. "Over there," he said, pointing to the fire escape of a nearby building.

Sam took off at a sprint, jumped to grab the lowest rung, and leveraged his weight to pull down the raised ladder. They wasted no time in climbing up to the metal landing above, then ascending the stairs until they reached the roof. "What're we doing up here, anyway?" Sam asked.

"Listen," Brennan told him. In the distance, the alarm of more sirens wailed through the rain. He strained his eyes to see what his nose and ears were already indicating. After a few moments, Sam made a startled noise and pointed, and Brennan looked to where his finger indicated. Against the well-lit skyscrapers, the black smoke became easily visible. Brennan counted the sources.

Another dozen buildings—presumably all of Kellogg's other residences—blazed like beacon fires in the night sky.

Chapter Twenty

I DON'T WANT to be here.

The thought kept reverberating in her head, even after Alex had determined it wasn't her own. It was late, she was tired, and yet she lay awake in bed with her brain in overdrive as she thought about solutions for her mother's ailment. Every way she calculated, though, the answer remained the same: there was too little time and too much of it.

There simply weren't enough hours in the coming months for her father to find a cure, to find a way to synthesize his own ability and transmit it to her, and yet each of those hours was another sixty minutes of unending agony for Stephanie Brüding.

Alex had glimpsed that pain for an instant, and it had driven her to wish for death. In that moment, she had understood what must be done. But how could she rationalize it to her father?

Her mother was no longer her mother. The body that was dying downstairs was just an empty shell; with the mind ravaged by the disease, her mother had ceased to exist long ago. Now, a breathing corpse waited to be relieved of its suffering. Stephanie's body waited to be laid to rest.

She took shallow breaths in the dead of night, and each exhale sounded exponentially louder than it actually was in comparison to the silence of the rest of the house. Water trickled down the gutters that rimmed the house, and only a light rain remained of the deluge that had claimed the evening.

She isn't the woman she used to be, Alex reasoned with herself. *Your mother left a long time ago.*

That's still her body.

And it doesn't even work! Who really benefits from keeping it alive? You and your father? Your sentimentality is torturing her.

Alex rose quickly and sat by the window. She pressed her forehead against the glass and let the cool sensation calm her nerves. The dark thoughts slowly receded, but they didn't fade entirely. More importantly, their reasoning was sound.

She didn't want to put her mother through any more misery. Her father might find a cure, but that would still be many months away from testing, if it even worked at all.

"No," Alex sighed softly, "this is something I need to do on my own."

Silence enveloped her like a cloak as she stepped out into the hallway. Alex called up her memories of the past few days and sidestepped the weak portions of the floor. The boards stayed quiet beneath her feet as she made it to the banister and crept silently down the stairs. She kept to the outer edges of the steps, where the old wood would be least worn and creaky.

A low moan met her ears as she reached the ground floor. Alex turned her head instinctively, in the direction of her mother's pained cry, but she needed something else first. Her feet carried her to the kitchen, and she took off one of the long black stockings that covered her feet and legs. The tiled floor was cold to the touch, but its brisk embrace kept her alert, so she welcomed it. Goosebumps climbed the right side of her body as she slid the stocking over her hand. There was no questioning her conviction now.

A wooden block held all of the sharp cooking utensils, and Alex slid a long, narrow slicing knife from its sheath.

Alex was a mute ghost as she padded half-barefoot back to the most dangerous part of her mission. The hallway to her mother's room was fraught with loose floorboards, any of which would willingly emit a haunting groan under the slightest bit of pressure. Alex removed her other stocking to keep her steps even, and trod carefully as she navigated the hornets' nest of hardwood.

She had gleaned everything she needed to know from the minds of Sam and Detective Brennan. In each of the five previous murders, a knife from the victim's own kitchen had been used as the weapon of choice. One fatal stab wound that severed the spine. The incisions were precise, so she would have to do it right the first time. There was no margin for error.

Her trusted memory served her well, and she stepped over the threshold of Stephanie's room without incident. The weak cries of pain had only grown louder as she approached, and now she quite clearly heard the sound of sobbing. Alex peeked around the door frame and saw the woman weeping into her pillowcase.

Stephanie had removed the pillow and was now crying openly into the limp piece of fabric, using it like a tissue to dab her eyes and wipe her nose. The room was too dark for her to make out these details herself, and Alex feared she was dipping unconsciously back into Stephanie's mind.

Keep your distance, she reminded herself. Alex stepped further into the room, and Stephanie still showed no sign of being aware of her presence. It wasn't until she sat on the edge of the bed that Alex earned any reaction from the dying woman. Red, watery eyes looked away from the pillowcase and stared up at her in wonder.

"Mom, are you there?" Alex asked.

Stephanie's eyes held no recognition for her daughter. Her brow furrowed, a confused look passing over her face before it was replaced by a blank, complacent stare. In another instant, the vacant expression was replaced by a flashing grimace of pain. The tendons in her neck stood in sharp relief as she gritted her teeth in agony.

A dozen panicked, frustrated thoughts flew through Alex's mind, all of them radiating from the shell that used to be her mother.

"It's okay," Alex murmured, shushing her quietly. She brushed the sweaty strands of flaxen hair from Stephanie's face. A thought occurred to her as she calmed the woman down. "There now, that's better. Would you like to see the fireflies?" She didn't know if there were even any fireflies left this late in the season, but she figured it didn't matter. When she had been alive, her mother had loved to watch the little lightning bugs flying around the yard under the pale moonlight. Perhaps there was still some sentiment of those precious moments lingering in what remained of her brain.

Stephanie nodded numbly. No smile graced her lips, but a calm seemed to descend over her features. Alex nodded encouragingly and slipped a helpful hand beneath the woman's arm, gently lifting her from bed. Stephanie looked down as she eased out of bed. "You aren't wearing any socks," she commented. Apparently she didn't feel the material of the stocking slipped over Alex's arm.

"It's actually quite warm," Alex lied.

"Oh, is it? Well, all right, then."

Alex fought the revulsion she felt at seeing how thin Stephanie had become. Her splotchy skin stretched over knobby bones that looked painfully arthritic. Her condition had accelerated all forms of decay, not just mental, and Alex knew that the basic impulse of pain was a difficult stimulus to ignore. Her mother had been lost when the disease had taken away all higher functions of the brain, and this woman needed to be released from the crippled body she now inhabited.

"Here, stand with me by the window," Alex said. "Isn't this nice? Can you see the moon from here? Point it out for me."

Stephanie's eyes were weak, but it was impossible to miss the glowing orb peeking out from behind the passing storm clouds. Now, a childlike smile spread across her face as she struggled to raise her arm and point. Suddenly, she turned her head and stared hard at Alex, confusion returning to her face. "Who are you?" she demanded.

"My name is Alex. I'm your daughter."

Stephanie smiled at her, but her tone was patronizing. "I think I would recognize my own daughter," she said. "You must be mistaken. Besides, that isn't my little girl's name."

It was hard to describe the feeling that came with those words, but it hit Alex in the gut like a heavy fist. There was no remnant of her existence inside Stephanie's mind, as if the last two and a half decades of her life had never happened. Not even her name lingered in the annals of the frail woman's memories.

"Of course," Alex said, shaken. "Don't worry about it. Just keep looking at the fireflies. Do you see them out there?"

There were none, but Stephanie's addled brain apparently provided the image anyway. "They're beautiful," she marveled, her eyes raptly focused on the dark yard outside. The light rain outside continued to drizzle, and its soft pitter-patter masked the slithering sound of the slicing knife sliding from its place in Alex's back pocket.

Carefully, she placed one covered hand on Stephanie's shoulder and shifted into a more solid stance. While Stephanie watched the faux fireflies, Alex steadied the blade in her grip. *One chance*, she reminded herself. It needed to conform to the pattern to look legitimate. Alex took a deep breath and thrust her arm forward.

The white bathrobe and the thin skin beneath parted smoothly under the pressure of the knife. Stephanie's mouth opened in a wide circle of shock, though Alex imagined the pain couldn't be any worse than what she had been experiencing for the last few years. To be safe, though, Alex covered the woman's mouth with her free hand. Stephanie's surprised gasps came out muffled, nearly inaudible.

"There now, that's better," Alex whispered. Blood spilled from the wound, something she hadn't anticipated, but it was thankfully absorbed by the fabric of the stocking around her knife hand. The stocking on Alex's other hand slid slightly on the floor as she removed the knife and gently eased Stephanie to the ground. The woman looked content, and it was obvious that she was being freed of her pain with each beat of her struggling heart.

Alex took a risk and extended her psychic probe. This time, she was not met with a wave of panic or agony, but rather a deep sense of calm understanding.

She stared into the eyes of the body that had once held her mother's soul, watching as they fluttered to a close.

Thank you.

The thought came through with perfect clarity, and Alex's heart swelled. She had helped free someone from pain. It didn't matter that the risk was enormous that she might be caught during the act. She had survived the ordeal, and now that it was over, there was only one logical explanation for the police to believe.

It was another senseless murder, just one in a string committed by the now-infamous Odols serial killer…

Chapter Twenty-One

A TOTAL OF thirty-eight men, women, and children had perished in the flames.

Brennan stared at the final tally with a sickening mixture of pity and disgust roiling in his stomach. Only three members of the police department had been caught in the fire traps, but the timed nature of the assaults meant that fire companies had been suddenly stretched beyond their limits trying to fight a dozen simultaneous blazes. It took the better part of the night to put an end to the chaos, and by then, thirty-five civilian lives had been lost.

Thirty-six, he amended, bringing the total body count to thirty-nine. Another body had been reported earlier this morning, one which matched Levi Kellogg's modus operandi. Stab wound to the back, a quick death, murder weapon taken from the victim's own household. It seemed that Kellogg used the incendiary diversion to continue his streak of precise assassinations. Now that he had been seen, though, there was no doubt in Brennan's mind as to who the next victim would be. And with the noose tightening around his throat, Kellogg wouldn't give them the luxury of two weeks' time before the next attack.

A yawn forced its way from his mouth, and Brennan hid it behind his hand as inconspicuously as he could. He and the rest of the force were sitting together in the large conference room while Bishop, Pascale, and Jun stood at the front, coordinating the discussion of how they should proceed.

"I'm telling you, Jun and I weren't even at the apartment yet when it blew," Pascale was saying. In every other case, it had been the officers on-scene who set off Kellogg's devices. Nobody yet knew that Sam and Brennan had been present downtown. "No other bodies were discovered at the scene, though. So what set it off?"

Brennan felt Pascale's stare land on him as he asked that last question. He feigned another yawn and kept his eyes trained elsewhere.

"It could've been a damn cat, for all that it matters now," Bishop argued. "Kellogg knows that we're onto him, and he's clearly escalating in response. Last night's fires are proof of that."

Pascale scowled and addressed the whole room. "Who is he targeting? We need to establish a pattern if we're going to have any chance of catching him. Come on, people, I'm open to any ideas."

"He killed three of our own last night," one of the officers said. "Maybe he's attacking law enforcement."

Jun shook his head. "We have to assume that last night was an anomaly. Every murder for the past three months has appeared random, but they must be linked somehow." His eyes darted to Brennan before glancing away again. "The explosives were meant exclusively for us, which means he thought we were getting close enough to be a threat."

Pascale pointed to an image projected onto the large white screen behind him. "These red spots indicate the locations of the bombs that went off last night. The yellow dots are the locations of where the bodies of the murder victims were found. As you know, each victim's body was found *inside* their own home."

"Kellogg is making a statement with these murders," Bishop added. "He believes he can reach anyone, at any time. The overlap of these areas, however, suggests that he was only comfortable operating within a certain radius."

"The two-week gap between murders also indicates that he took his time to stalk each victim and learn their daily routines," Pascale said. He clicked forward in the presentation, bringing up a picture of an older woman lying on a hardwood floor. A dark pool surrounded her torso, and a bloodied knife was on the floor nearby. "This is Stephanie Brüding," he said, clicking through close-ups of her face and body. "It seems Kellogg used our tactical strike as an excuse to go outside his radius. This happened almost five *miles* outside the city limits."

Brennan watched the uniformed officers' reactions as that news sunk in. Kellogg was loose, no longer bound by the fragile social contract he had made by establishing his two-week routine. The previous murders had taken place all over the city, but at least they could be assigned as uptown, downtown, east, or west. This woman's death, far outside the city, changed the whole game.

"He knew we were getting close, so he changed his pattern," Agent Jun said. "We need to regroup and assume he *isn't* going to give us two weeks to respond to these latest attacks."

"So what's the plan?" Brennan asked. A few heads turned to look at the erstwhile outcast detective.

Pascale paused before responding. "We've already sent Kellogg's photo to be disseminated among the major news networks. There's a hotline being set up to receive reports of sightings, and you will all be broken off into teams to canvass the city neighborhood by neighborhood." He clicked the remote in his hand, and the presentation screen went black. "Lieutenant Bishop will give you your assignments. That is all."

The agent left without another glance, with Agent Jun following just a few steps behind.

Brennan stood to leave, but Bishop waved a hand at him, beckoning him toward her. "What's up?" he asked.

"Can I talk to you alone for a minute?"

"Whatever you need, Lieutenant."

Bishop scowled. "None of that, Brennan. We're friends."

"Are we? Because the way you've been acting the past couple weeks had me fooled."

"Now you're just being childish," Bishop argued, but her face softened. "Those FBI agents came here for you, but they aren't telling me what it's all about."

"I have a pretty good idea," Brennan said darkly. "Pascale mentioned my father specifically before he sent me home yesterday."

"That would make sense…so you think they're worried you'll turn out like him?"

"He did some pretty awful things when he was around. Like father, like son, I guess."

Bishop placed a gentle hand on his arm. "You're a good man, Brennan. I didn't know your father, obviously, but I do know you. Pascale will have to suck it up and deal with the fact that you're on board."

Brennan stared at her for a moment. "Does this mean you *want* me to work the case now?"

"It seems I have no choice," she sighed. "I was trying to protect you from Pascale and Jun while they were sniffing around the department, but what was it you said to Wally? 'All hands on deck'? We need that now." Bishop glanced around to make sure nobody was listening in on their conversation. "And one more thing, Brennan…I haven't properly thanked you for coming to rescue me from Leviathan. I know it has been a couple months, and we haven't talked about it since then, but maybe that's for the best."

He frowned. "Why do you say that?"

Bishop's voice dropped to a whisper. "Now might be a good time for you to use those contacts of yours again."

Brennan thought about how Greg had used one of the Leviathan patches to receive his vision. It had been a risky move, and even though it had paid off in the end, there was no way he could risk Fracturing his nephew by attempting it a second time.

"That might prove to be difficult," he told Bishop.

"Don't you dare get all coy on me, Brennan. I swear to God, I will have your badge if you hold anything back from me now."

"What happened to us being friends?"

She sighed. "That's dependent on us being open and honest with each other, especially when it comes to catching a serial killer. Seriously, I don't know why you *wouldn't* want to use…well, whoever it is, to help us."

A flash of insight came to mind, and Brennan realized that he *did* have somebody he could go to without endangering Greg's sanity. "Fine, Bishop, I'll give them a call. But only because there are no other options."

Bishop held her hands up and shrugged. "That works for me," she said, continuing to stare at him expectantly.

He coughed. "I, uh, kind of need privacy for this sort of call. Permission to go back to my apartment, Lieutenant?"

She dismissed him with the wave of her hand as she turned back around to give the uniformed officers their assignments. Brennan quickly slipped out of the conference room and down the stairs, taking care not to meet any of the inquisitive glances directed at him as he plowed through the lobby doors. When he unlocked the door to his apartment and stepped inside, he stopped short at the sight of the tall woman he found inside.

Strawberry blonde hair fell to the bottom of her shoulder blades. She held a framed picture in one hand, and the expression on her face was one of mixed curiosity and amusement. Her head turned to face Brennan as he entered. Trouble was promised by the gleam in her eye and the curl of her lips.

"Who are you?" Brennan demanded.

"You don't recognize me?" she asked, her tone plaintive even as she continued smiling. The voice sounded familiar, but he couldn't place where he had heard it before.

His hand drifted to the holster at his waist. "No, but you seem to know who I am. I don't appreciate having strangers barge into my house."

But it's hardly a house, now, is it?

Brennan flinched at the sound of her voice in his head, and he realized why it seemed familiar.

The grin on the woman's face widened. "Ah, there it is," she said. "Took you long enough, little hamster, but I see your wheel is finally turning."

"You're the woman from the other night!"

She snapped her fingers. "Exactamundo." Her impression of Sam was eerily on the money.

"And you obviously know my friend," Brennan continued. "I take it you're the mystery woman he has been seeing?"

"We should get you a puzzle book, because you are connecting dots all over the place today."

Brennan frowned. She seemed amused, and he suddenly felt as if he were being toyed with, like a captured mouse being batted around by a cat.

The woman smiled dangerously. "I *did* call you a hamster, so the rodent imagery certainly fits."

His hand still hadn't left the holster. "Who are you?"

She held her palms out in a placating gesture. "No need to fear me, Detective. I'm here to offer my services."

"Who *are* you?" he asked more forcefully.

"My name is Alex Brüding," she said, taking a step forward. "I see you recognize the name now."

"Brüding…your mother was the most recent victim." Brennan let his hand drop to his side. "I'm sorry for your loss, but I don't see why you broke into—"

"That man—Kellogg—could be coming for any of us next. You and I both know the kind of people he is targeting."

Brennan nodded. "I was about to call Benjamin, but you'll do."

"You sure know how to make a girl feel wanted," Alex said, and this time her complaint sounded genuine.

"I, um…sorry?" He felt uncomfortable apologizing to the woman who had broken into his apartment. "I could use a mind-reader. But shouldn't you be home right now?"

"I don't feel safe there," Alex said, crossing her arms. A less observant eye wouldn't have noticed that she was cradling herself ever so slightly.

Truth.

"Besides," she continued, "if I can't be protected in my own home, what's to keep Kellogg from coming after me next? I would rather take the fight to him than wait for a knife to find my back. I can't stand by and do nothing." Alex took a step closer. "Please, I need this."

Brennan nodded, deeply impressed. "All right, then, you're on the team."

"Team Sleeper…I like it."

"That's not what—"

Alex tapped her temple. "You were thinking it, not me."

"Hmm." Brennan looked around the apartment and voiced the question he had been holding. "Where is my nephew?"

"I haven't seen him," she replied, which was confirmed by Brennan's power. "He's probably looking for a job, like you told him to."

"Stop reading my thoughts," Brennan said sternly.

Alex grinned. "I was running out of reading material anyway."

In spite of himself, Brennan felt his mouth returning her smile. This woman had saved his life and had put him in contact with Benjamin so the truth about his wife's murder could be revealed. Everything was running against them now, and Brennan knew it was just the calm before the storm, but it felt incredibly good to have something to smile about.

"Seriously, though, I'm sure he is fine," Alex said. "You have to focus on the priority here, which is stopping Kellogg."

Brennan breathed out slowly. Kellogg had killed Ms. Brüding's mother and had seen Brennan's face. It seemed likely that either he or the telepath would be the next one chosen to die, so if Greg wasn't near them when shit hit the fan, that was a good thing, wasn't it?

"*I* think it's a good thing, but that's just me."

"And I thought I told you to stay out of my head."

"Old habits," Alex said, shrugging as she contemplated the picture frame again. "Your wife was beautiful. It seems we've both lost someone we loved."

Brennan took the framed photo from her hands and placed it back on its shelf. "You'll learn to accept it with time."

Alex nodded slowly before affixing him with her intense eyes. "I have to ask, though. Mara, Clara…both pretty brunettes, about shoulder-height with you? You certainly have a type."

He sighed. "And you've been through my emails…I can see why Benjamin values you so much."

"Not your emails. I was there the night of your date," she reminded him. "She was with you when I found you under fire in the alley. And as for Benjamin, I hardly know him. He values *you*, Detective."

"Only as far as I am useful to him." Brennan wiped a hand over his face, the earlier humor he'd felt now completely dissipated. "If anybody asks, you're under my protective custody."

"What's the nature of our relationship that I would come to you for help?" She shrugged at the gaze Brennan gave her. "What? I've picked up a lot of things along the way. They'll be curious why I came to you for protection rather than staying at home, or going to the station, and you don't have a good response for that."

Brennan didn't bother telling her again not to read his mind. Everything she said was true. "In that case, we'd better not get spotted by anybody. But we won't be able to get much done by staying here. Kellogg knows where you live, and I wouldn't be surprised if he uses my name to track me down soon enough."

Alex nodded. "I think I can find Kellogg," she admitted, "but we're going to need some wheels. Where are you parked?"

"I don't have a car."

She smiled lightly. "I know…it was a joke. You need to get on board with this telepathy trick, or maybe you aren't as quick and interesting as I thought you'd be."

A nervous laugh escaped his lips as Brennan turned sideways and gestured for her to step out first. He caught a whiff of her floral perfume, and her light hair nearly brushed against his face as she breezed past. As he locked up, she continued down the hall, pausing only for a second to glance back at him.

"Keep your thoughts to yourself."

ϕ ϕ ϕ

BRENNAN MADE SURE nobody was watching them as he and Alex climbed into the back of a taxi. The driver seemed confused at their lack of direction, but Alex handed him a thick wad of bills and told him to start driving in an outward spiral. He raised an eyebrow at that, but the money in advance kept him from asking any more questions. Brennan kept one eye on the meter and the other trained on the strange psychic. Her eyes closed as she cupped her knees with her hands, and Brennan felt the subtlest thrum of energy charging the air around her. He glanced toward the front of the car, but if the driver felt anything, he didn't give any indication of it.

Alex started to mumble, and Brennan closed the glass window to provide a modicum of privacy. "This is a new sensation," she said. "I've never read so many people at once. It feels…incredible. And overwhelming."

"How so?" Brennan asked.

She breathed in sharply. "I can hear and see and feel everything they do." She shuddered. "It's cold outside."

It was a tad chilly, but they were wearing jackets and the heat was on.

"I can still hear you," she continued, sounding annoyed. "And let's see how *you* deal with the cold when you're experiencing it a hundredfold."

Brennan retreated to his side of the taxi and stared out the window. There were hundreds of people walking by at this hour, and this was just one street out of an entire city. *Are you sure you can find Kellogg among all of this?* he asked, knowing Alex was still listening.

It'll be easier if you aren't constantly distracting me.

Chagrined, he leaned his forehead against the cool glass. It helped clear away some of the thoughts clouding his mind, which would in turn help Alex by providing less of a distraction. An idea occurred to him, and he thought back to the days of his Sleeper training. He envisioned a massive wall around his brain, a dome that shielded anyone from prying into his thoughts. It was a trick he had been using to keep Sleepers at bay for years, but now that that threat had passed, he realized he could repurpose it to block his thoughts from Alex while she worked her magic.

Learning how to create a mind-shield had been a laborious process all those years ago. Like a physical structure, there were plenty of ways a shield could be undermined by a Sleeper's psychic attack. It required a solid foundation, usually built from the memory of a loved one. The foundation had to be molded from something that was immutable and unchanging, something that the person believed in wholeheartedly. Brennan chose the day he and Mara had been married.

The next part required two components: building blocks for the dome, and mortar to hold those blocks in place. Each brick was fashioned from the dark deeds Brennan had committed as a Sleeper; their nature would also dissuade any curious telepaths from probing too deeply once they sensed that darkness. For the mortar, he poured his enduring faith that he had acted in the interest of the greater good. For each life he took, he had saved many more, and that belief was what held him together. It would serve the same function for his mind-shield.

Finally, the centerpiece that would sit at the top of the dome, the keystone. This was the most difficult part of the shield's construction, the one which prevented most from creating something that lasted. It required something of all three qualities: love, action, and purpose. Ironically, it was the first piece Brennan had ever collected.

The betrayal of his father to a rival crime boss. The keystone memory fit snugly into its slot, and Brennan felt his ears pop as the shield, completed, washed away the psychic pressure emanating from Alex. The low thrum of power was still there, but he no longer felt it crackling across his skin or causing the hairs on his arms to raise.

Alex opened her eyes wide and stared at him. "What did you just do?" she asked.

"This is me helping," Brennan said. "Now, look for Kellogg."

She shook her head. "He could be moving, or else he's just outside my radius. Even being everywhere at once, I can't find him, and this is going too—" She broke off, and Brennan heard something vibrating.

Alex took out her phone and scowled at the number before she answered. "Dad, this isn't a good time."

He could only hear one side of the conversation, but Brennan knew better than to try to listen in.

"No, Dad, I already told you," Alex said, turning her head away. "We obviously aren't safe at home, so I'd rather be in the city. No, I need to do this. I'm not coming home." There was a pause while Mr. Brüding spoke for nearly a whole minute, and Alex's voice was softer when she responded. "I know you told me not to get involved, but I can't sit around and do nothing. I'll be home when I can feel safe again."

She hung up before her father could respond.

"I take it he isn't pleased," Brennan commented.

"That would be an understatement." Alex turned to him, and he could see the angry gleam in her eyes. "My mother was murdered. Why can't he see that I need to know Kellogg is brought to justice? And how can he ask me not to get involved, especially when I can do something to help?"

Brennan nodded slowly, not wanting to alienate his only real chance of finding Kellogg. "I trust you," he said. "Your father needs to learn to do the same. You're old enough to make your own choices. And for what it's worth, I think you're doing something incredibly brave by being out here."

Alex stared at him, seemingly stunned by the compliment, and her cheeks reddened more rapidly than her mouth could respond.

"On another note," Brennan continued, "I want you to stop seeing Sam."

Her words finally found themselves. "Fair enough."

"That…was really easy. You don't need any further convincing?"

"No," Alex said with a shrug. "I was getting bored with him, anyway."

"Oh." Brennan looked outside his window again in a bid to escape the uncomfortable silence that followed. When he finally glanced back, Alex had resumed her near-meditative state. Her eyes moved rapidly beneath her eyelids, but she was otherwise completely still.

Her power couldn't touch him, but Brennan still felt its influence persistently lapping against the mind-shield like the tide of the ocean. Their taxi turned and further widened its route, riding along the circumference of an ever-expanding circle. They rode on in relative silence as the sun started to fall toward the tips of the western skyscrapers.

A phone vibrated, and this time it was Brennan who patted at his pockets in a hurry to answer. He spared a quick glance at Alex, but she seemed unfazed by the distraction as he answered. "Sam?"

"Where did you go?" Sam's voice was hard to hear over the buzz of activity in the background. "Noel said you were all having a big meeting, but by the time I showed up, you had already split."

"Sorry, Sam, I'm with one of my old contacts now," Brennan said, skirting the truth.

"I don't know who you've been talking to, but I hope they have something good." Sam's voice lowered, and the tone changed in a subtle way. "Brennan, I wanted to say that I'm sorry. I know I've been giving you a hard time these past few months, pushing you about how you get your information. You obviously know some people I don't, though, and they've proven themselves to be trustworthy."

Brennan gulped after hearing his friend's apology. Even though he had finally told Sam that Noel had been found by Greg while patched with a psychoactive drug, he didn't have the heart to tell him that his partner now was a near-omniscient telepath, the very same woman Sam had been regularly sleeping with for weeks. "Don't worry about it," he said simply. "What's all that noise in the background?"

Alex's eyes opened. "Stop the car," she told Brennan urgently. She opened the small glass window and spoke to the driver before Brennan could even respond.

"They think they have a lead," Sam was saying. "Security cameras caught Kellogg entering a building on Eighteenth and Guerricke."

Brennan faintly heard Alex relating the same information to the taxi driver—slightly before Sam said it over the phone. Her psychic probe was just barely ahead of the FBI resources at OPD's disposal. "We're close to the location," he told Sam, confirming it with a glance at the driver's GPS. "Stay at the station, Sam, you've done enough."

"I hear you loud and clear."

"Uh, you don't need any further convincing?" Brennan asked. He saw Alex smirking out of the corner of his eye.

"Hell no," Sam said, elongating the first word with feeling. "This dangerous crap is exactly why I left the force to begin with. I'll go check in on Greg while you do all the heavy lifting."

"He wasn't at home when I left."

"But I already have the spare key in hand, and I don't mind the walk."

Brennan smiled. "Fine, go ahead. Lock up when you're finished raiding my liquor cabinet."

"A man's work is *never* finished, you know that."

He ended the call and glanced at the rising cab fare meter. It was a good thing that Alex was covering the tab. They drove the last several blocks in silence, but Brennan could sense his partner's rising excitement as they approached Eighteenth Street. Her eyes remained riveted on the large, tiered skyscraper that marked their destination.

The taxi pulled up alongside the curb, and the two of them stepped out into the shadow of the building. It was a large corporate office center, and the name of SymbioTech was hung in bold, steel letters in the middle of the expansive lobby.

"Why would he come here?" Alex asked.

"You're the telepath, you tell me."

"I'm not going anywhere near that. The only thing jumping into that psychopath's head is a bullet."

"We're here to capture Kellogg, not execute him," Brennan reminded her.

Alex gave him an unrepentant look. "He's a murderer. Doesn't he deserve to die for that?"

Brennan waited for the helpful voice in his head to speak up, but it remained silent. His power apparently didn't extend to moral dilemmas. "How do you think that will look to OPD?" he asked instead.

"After what happened this summer, I would have thought you'd be used to standing in blood."

"Is there something you want to say to me?"

Alex waited until Brennan had waved his badge at the security guards before responding. "I've been inside your head. Your moral high ground is shaky at best, *Sleeper*. You have killed before, so I don't understand why you hesitate to do so now when faced with the man who murdered my mother and kidnapped your nephew."

False. True.

"What was that?" Brennan demanded as his steps faltered. "Where's Greg?"

Alex pointed straight up. "On the thirty-first floor, your nephew is kneeling on the ground. His heart rate is up, and I'm not getting any visuals from him, but otherwise he seems fine. For now."

"Why didn't you tell me earlier?"

She shrugged. "I didn't know until now."

Something about that statement didn't set right in Brennan's stomach, but he didn't have time to worry over it right then. "And what about Kellogg?"

"Same floor," Alex reported. "He was just with someone, but now I can only sense Kellogg." She placed a palm to her temple as they boarded an elevator. Her eyes looked around at the walls with a heavy dose of distaste. "I think it's this *place*. It's messing with my ability."

True.

This day was getting weirder and weirder. "Can you get anything more from Greg?"

The elevator started to rise, and it looked like Alex was recovering more with each floor. "His ears are working just fine, but whatever he's hearing is muffled. His wrists are chafing, but so far any bruises are self-inflicted. My best guess is he's being kept blindfolded in a small room."

"Like a storage closet?"

"Most likely. It would make sense for the distorted noise and feeling of claustrophobia."

Brennan raised an eyebrow, more impressed than skeptical. "You can read all of that from him?"

"All of that and more."

The elevator doors pinged open, and their conversation ended as a well-lit hallway presented itself to them. It was a late Saturday afternoon, but the office still wasn't entirely deserted. Brennan and Alex slowed their pace to appear casual as the telepath's eyes grew vacant. He knew she was tapping into the senses of everyone on the floor, processing their own sights and sounds as quickly as she would her own.

"Down that hall," Alex said, indicating it with a faint nod.

"Take the long way around and blend in," Brennan ordered. "If he tries to run your way, you need to stop him."

"What about your nephew?"

"If Kellogg took him, and they're both on this floor, then it stands to reason that he will want to keep Greg close. When we find Kellogg, we'll find my nephew."

She regarded him blankly, her eyes still vacant, before she continued down the main hallway alone.

Brennan turned down the side corridor and kept from meeting anybody's eyes for too long. Not that anybody was paying particular attention, but it never hurt to be careful. Kellogg seemed to have a supernatural sense of when he was being hunted. He slowly slid a hand under his jacket and his fingers wrapped lightly around the grip of his holstered gun.

There were a few curious gazes as Brennan passed, and he realized that an unfamiliar face among the small weekend workforce might be an instant red flag to them. He dropped the grip he had on his firearm and forced a smile that was meant to reassure them. They didn't look convinced, but nobody rose to stop him.

Brennan felt a burst of psychic pressure, and he realized Alex was attempting to contact him. He considered dropping the mind-shield, but he stopped himself at the last second. An uneasy feeling spread through him, and even though he wasn't sure why, he suddenly felt that letting the psychic into his mind was a bad move.

He continued his search, clearing several more offices before turning another corner. If the layout of the building was consistent, this was the hallway in which he hoped to trap Kellogg. The only other avenue of escape was past Alex, who currently sought vengeance for her mother's death.

A quick glance around confirmed that nobody was watching, so Brennan drew his gun and kept it half-concealed in the sleeve of his jacket. The lights flickered overhead, and the hairs on his arms raised as electricity hummed through the air. A moment later, a loud cry of pain issued from down the hall.

"Alex!" Brennan yelled, breaking into a run. Startled employees began fleeing in the other direction, and he had to either dodge around them or shove them aside to make headway. "Alex, I'll be right there!"

The lights dimmed heavily, and another wrenching scream filled the air.

In the corner office at the end of the hall, Brennan finally spotted Kellogg.

He looked disheveled and out of place, despite the business clothes he now wore. The fabric of the sleeves was stretched to its limits over his ridiculous arms. His hair was cropped short, nearly to the skin. A long, sparking cable was held in one hand, while the other gripped the ridge of a large rolling office chair. Brennan could only see the legs and feet of his hostage.

"Hold it right there," Brennan ordered, his gun trained on Kellogg's back.

Kellogg spun around to face Brennan as he entered the room, and his eyes danced with frenzied nervousness, at extreme odds with the man on the television the night before. He positioned himself behind the chair, using its occupant as a shield.

"How did you find me?" Kellogg asked.

Brennan, though, was too distracted by the blindfolded figure seated in the chair. "Greg?"

His nephew whimpered in response. Another length of cloth was wrapped over his mouth, effectively gagging him. Burn marks showed on the exposed skin beneath his torn shirt.

Kellogg drew a knife and pressed it against the soft flesh of Greg's neck. "I don't want to hurt him, Detective, but I will if you so much as take another step."

"Drop the knife and step back from the boy."

"No," Kellogg said, shaking his head. "I have a message to deliver to the citizens of this city."

"The murders? The bombing? Enough lives have been lost already," Brennan said. "Message received."

"You don't understand, Detective. Then again, how could I expect you to? You're just another drone in the system."

"Whatever you think you know, you're wrong. You've taken innocent lives—"

"Innocent?" Kellogg asked, sounding incredulous. His face contorted in a grotesque mask. "I can't stand the very sight of you…*things*. Corporate executives. The chief of police. The *mayor*. Do you know what all of these things have in common? They're positions held by the rich and powerful. And how do you think they got those resources? By oppressing the masses with their abilities and corrupting the system that is meant to protect the innocent."

"Is that why you were here today, Kellogg?" Brennan asked. "Were you stalking your seventh victim?"

Kellogg's eyes narrowed. "I've only cleansed this city of five of the corrupted. But my mission is far from complete."

"From where I'm standing, you have two options. Either surrender yourself to me peacefully and stand trial for your crimes, or I'll shoot you where you stand." The plastic grip of his gun groaned slightly as he tightened his hold on it.

"You won't kill me," Kellogg said confidently.

Stepping into the building, Brennan would have agreed. He had wanted to take Kellogg in alive, in spite of everything the ex-soldier had done. Now, with Greg's life on the line, that resolve had all but disappeared.

"When I was overseas, the enemy combatants were obvious," Kellogg continued. "They were all around me, and my purpose there was clear. But now that I'm home, and I see a new enemy, *still* all around me…I can't live with that reality."

"There are no enemies here, Kellogg, except the one holding the knife and the live electrical wire." Brennan glanced at the open door to the closet in the corner. There were scuff marks on the floor between the closet and the chair where Greg was now seated. "If you come with me to the station, now, without any more deaths, you'll have a chance to say your piece."

Kellogg jerked his head from side to side. "No," he said shakily, "that's not true." A bead of blood appeared on Greg's neck, sliding down the length of the blade. He started to press in harder. "You're trying to trick me, I can see what you are!"

"No, stop!" Brennan yelled. He turned his gun sideways and held up both hands. "Stop. I'm putting down the gun, okay? Watch, I'm putting it down."

The knife didn't move, but Kellogg watched warily as Brennan knelt and placed the gun on the ground. "Kick it back into the hallway, away from you," Kellogg ordered.

Brennan slid it backward with his foot, his blood rising with each skittering sound of metal against hard tile. *Where the hell is Alex?* he wondered, taking a step into the room. He dropped his mental barrier and sent that thought out broadly. "I did as you asked, Kellogg," Brennan said. "Do a courtesy for me and put the knife down."

"I don't think so. Do you know what the difference is between you and me, Detective? I am a man of action. I fight for what I believe in, and I know which side I'm on."

"So what does that make me?"

"Last night, I would have said you were simply another pawn in their game. But you strike me as a reasonable man. You made the news this summer." Kellogg smiled smugly. "No names were dropped, but I did a little digging and found out what you did. Tried to take patches off the street and pissed off a lot of powerful people in the process."

"Petty drug lords don't scare me," Brennan said.

Kellogg frowned. "You don't get it, do you? I'm not talking about dealers and addicts here. It's the bosses upstairs that you've upset, the ones who benefit most from having corruption spread through our streets. When the chief of police can stand in front of the press and say that Chamalla is the next big crisis, that benefits both him and the mayor."

"I don't understand. How does that—?"

"Maybe I overestimated you," Kellogg said, his voice full of disappointment. "I thought *you* of all people could see past all the bullshit. The people in charge are fearmongers, and they thrive on leading the public from hysteria. Without chaos, how can they institute order? Without crime, how can they deliver punishment? This city is dying, and it's those with power who stand at the helm."

Something clicked in Brennan's brain, a cog turning that was previously gummed up with ignorance. "When you say 'power,' you mean—"

"People like you, yes. The freaks, the conquerors. Humans two-point-oh." Kellogg was breathing heavily now as emotion overcame him. "I'm the only one who can see the heart of the matter, the root of the problem, so it's my responsibility to save humanity."

"I've done nothing but help this city," Brennan growled. "And if you can see us, then you are *one* of us. Your power is seeing others with power."

Kellogg shook his head, and there was a subtle shift in the features of his face. There was something akin to acceptance, even though he was clearly living in denial. "I'm not like you," he said proudly. "Your power corrupts, while mine has given me clarity. And purpose."

"Then do it," Brennan dared him. "Fulfill your purpose and kill me. I'm the one with power, not the boy. And look! I'm unarmed." He took a step closer. "So go on, then. Do it!"

Kellogg snarled and pushed Greg out of the way, the rolling chair careening toward the far wall. He lunged at Brennan with the knife, and two things happened in that moment.

First, Brennan went deaf as a gunshot fired from almost directly behind his head.

Second, a red lotus blossomed on the shoulder of Kellogg's dress shirt as a long sniper round cut through his body like a fan blade through the air. Blood soaked the material as his snarl was replaced by a slack-jawed look of utter shock. As Kellogg fell to his knees and then the ground, Brennan noticed a sister wound on Kellogg's other shoulder, this one with a smaller entry point and less immediate blood.

Brennan cupped both hands over his ears and swayed into the nearest wall, losing all sense of balance with his hearing. The ringing that exploded in his skull was deafening all on its own, and he looked up deliriously to find Agent Jun standing over him. The grim-faced agent stared at Brennan for a moment before moving in to slap handcuffs around Kellogg's wrists. It seemed like a moot point to Brennan, but he wasn't in any condition to object.

Actually, Alex spoke in his head, *a moot point is a subject still open to debate.*

Where the hell have you been?

Letting the cavalry know where to find you, she replied, sounding testy. *You're welcome, by the way.*

Oh, I'm welcome? I needed you here, *with me. I could have been killed!*

And I would have fared any better, without a gun? Besides, you're still alive. She paused for a second. *Everyone is alive, it seems.*

What? Brennan stared blearily at Agent Jun and Kellogg while the ringing in his ears slowly faded away. Jun had secured his pistol, and he was reciting the Miranda rights while keeping one knee firmly pressed against one of Kellogg's wounded shoulders. "He's still alive?" Brennan asked.

"For now." Jun looked up at him with a solemn expression. "I only shot him once."

Wind whistled through the hole in the glass window pane.

Comprehension washed over Brennan. He made a mad dash to grab Greg and wheel him into the hallway, staggering away from the line of sight of whatever sniper was posted on the adjacent roof.

Kellogg followed shortly after, pushed from behind by Jun.

When you say 'the cavalry'…

Not the FBI, Alex finished simply. *I sensed them closing in behind us, though, and had to make myself scarce.*

Why? Are you a criminal?

There was an almost imperceptible pause that followed the question.

I was thinking of you, actually. How would you have explained my presence?

Somebody took a shot at Kellogg, Brennan said, feeling like he was finally putting the pieces together. *If I had been just a foot closer, that round would have hit me, too.*

Another pregnant pause.

Ask the question that's on your mind, Detective Brennan.

Brennan breathed out slowly. *Kellogg didn't kill your mother.*

That wasn't a question.

Maybe that's because I already know the answer. Why did you do it?

Today is a win, Detective. A murderer is going behind bars, and you get to live another day.

Brennan bristled at her words. *So you want me to just let you go?*

Alex's response was swift and cutting. *You don't have a choice.*

Chapter Twenty-Two

Alex severed the connection and looked over to Heinrich.

The thick, bald man was disassembling a high-powered sniper rifle and stowing it away in a hard plastic case. His eyes met hers for a moment, and a shadowed look passed over his features. She couldn't read his thoughts, but there was resentment plain on his face. The other men, a half dozen in total, seemed impassive about her presence.

Behind him, James Brüding stroked his chin thoughtfully. "If I didn't know any better," her father said, "I would have guessed you were aiming for the detective, with Kellogg merely being an obstacle in your way."

Heinrich continued stowing his gear. "Two birds with one stone," his deep voice rumbled.

"One of those birds killed my wife," James said, his tone darker than Alex had ever heard before. "And your gambit didn't pay off. That shot was hardly fatal."

"Then we'll take him out during the transfer back to Washington," Heinrich said, sounding unconcerned.

James pursed his lips before responding. "We will," he said. "You won't."

With a two-fingered wave, he motioned to one of Heinrich's lieutenants, who promptly stepped forward with a silenced pistol. The sound barely registered louder than a hoarse cough, and the command of Leviathan shifted to the gunman himself. A jagged crescent tattoo wrapped around one ear, and he couldn't have been much older than Alex. However, his rigid bearing spoke of previous military training, and he turned now to receive his orders from her father.

"Very good," James murmured quietly. "Take care of the body and then get set up for the inevitable transfer." To the group at large, he said, "Matheson is your leader now. If you have a problem with that, feel free to step forward."

Not surprisingly, the men found little issue respecting the new chain of command.

ɸ ɸ ɸ

"What was that about back there?"

Kern was driving them each home, starting with dropping Alex back at her apartment in midtown. It would be a slower drive with rush hour traffic, which afforded her the time to voice the question she had been muffling since the exchange of power on the rooftop.

"Why don't you just read me and find out?" her father asked. He sounded genuinely curious about why she wasn't employing her powers.

She knew now that he could deceive her, if not hide the truth entirely. "I want to hear it from you," she said. "Talk to me."

James shifted in his seat, cradling a glass of champagne poured from one of the towncar's resident bottles. "Leviathan is mine, Alexis, and their leadership lost sight of that. Independence from government oversight is one thing, but independence from *me* is something else entirely, an aberration that I will not tolerate. Your mother's death—" He broke off for a moment, and Alex could hear the pain in his voice as it cracked with emotion. "Her passing struck me hard, and I wanted vengeance, I'll freely admit it. Life has been unfair as of late. SymbioTech's acquisition of my company, in addition your mother's...decline, has worn heavily on my soul. To think that her killer yet breathes pains me in ways you cannot imagine."

His speech had dipped into the formal parlance of his upbringing—whenever that had been—and Alex trembled at how the words affected her. This was a man with power and purpose. Her mother's passing—an event which long preceded her body's death—had been her father's crucible, and he had emerged all the stronger for surviving it.

James clenched one hand into a fist as he lifted the champagne glass with the other, draining it in one ambitious gulp. "I was wrong about our purpose here, Alexis," he said, gazing meaningfully into her eyes. "We are not silent observers, nor should we be humble in the face of danger. There are more men like Kellogg out there. Those who would wish us harm simply for being born the way we are. This city is dying—" He reached out and grasped her hand. "—but we are the cure."

Alex smiled at her father, and another question came to mind. "Don't you think it's a coincidence that Kellogg was at SymbioTech tonight? Who do you think he was meeting with?"

"You couldn't read in on them?" James asked, sounding both surprised and disapproving.

She shook her head. "Something about the place was throwing off my ability. It's like they were using a psychic radio jammer."

James frowned, but he squeezed her hand encouragingly. "Whoever it was, I intend to find them."

"And then what will you do?"

"Discover the nature of their meeting, and take back my city by any means necessary."

Chapter Twenty-Three

Greg's body was becoming a patchwork of burn scars.

The chemical burn on his arm from the patch was healing more slowly than the singed remnants of his electrical torturing. While those marks were fading fast, the square patch on his arm looked like the deep tan that followed a severe sunburn.

Emotional scars from that night were going to take a little longer to get over.

Brennan sat on the couch with a half-empty glass bottle of Coke in his hand and something mindlessly playing on the TV. Greg was paying attention, but Brennan was lost deep within his own thoughts. Two weeks had passed, and no more stabbings or bombings had occurred. Kellogg was in the custody of Agents

Jun and Pascale, and Alexis "Alex" Brüding had made herself scarce, as promised.

He knew where she lived, both inside and outside the city. It would be a simple matter to march up to her door and slap handcuffs around her wrists.

And then what?

The infernal question reared its ugly head each time his thoughts ran around this circle, and there was no good answer. Lacking any evidence to the contrary, her mother's death had been framed perfectly as the final murder of the now-infamous Levi Kellogg. Psychic conversations aside, she had never admitted to committing the murder. Approaching her now and bringing her into the station would only open the chance for her to play the tortured victim. Her mother just died, and now a detective who was known for being unstable wanted to pin her as an opportunistic copycat killer?

Brennan's badge would be on Bishop's desk within the hour.

He gulped down the rest of his Coke and contemplated opening another. At least his drinking problem was less expensive than most, and with significantly less damage to his liver.

A knock at the door startled both Brennan and Greg out of their contemplations.

Brennan took a moment to peek through the peephole, and he sighed as the worst of his fears were confirmed. He opened the door to find Agent Pascale standing on the other side. Jun was positioned to his left, outside of the peephole's frame of view.

"Detective," Pascale said by way of greeting. His eyes scanned the interior of the apartment in one quick sweep. "It seems you're off the hook."

"Excuse me?"

Agent Jun coughed and pushed his way forward. "With regards to the busting-up of the Leviathan drug ring, you have been cleared of all possible wrongdoing," he said, frowning at Pascale.

The older agent didn't back down. "A half dozen men lost, and more drugs on the street than ever—"

"That's enough," Jun said firmly.

"So I'm still a detective?" Brennan asked.

Agent Jun nodded. "Lieutenant Bishop will reassign you to active duty, and you won't be barred from any cases going forward."

"That's great news and all, but why was I kept off this one for so long in the first place?"

Pascale stepped across the threshold and jabbed a finger in Brennan's chest. "Because you're a dirty son of a—"

"That's enough!" Agent Jun repeated, pulling his partner back into the hall.

"He's just as bad as his father," Pascale continued. He turned to Brennan. "We *know* you were in that building the night of Kellogg's explosives, just before we arrived."

"He also cornered Kellogg when nobody else was even close," Jun reasoned quietly.

"Because he was in on it!" Pascale's attention was fully focused on Brennan, who expected fists to start flying at any second. "You and Kellogg were working together, admit it!"

Jun ignored him. "When a significant number of officers are wounded or killed in action, an independent inquiry is organized to investigate any suspicions of misconduct."

Brennan eyed him with suspicion. "They called in the FBI for an Internal Affairs matter?"

"The situation had…extenuating circumstances, where you were concerned."

He put more pieces together. "Because of my father."

Jun nodded. "Your family's history on the wrong side of the law has caused certain parties to have reservations concerning your right to carry a badge."

"So the inquiry was less about the actual case and more about me," Brennan grumbled, displeased.

"We were wrong to be suspicious of you."

Pascale scowled. "Speak for yourself."

"There's, uh, one other thing we have to tell you," Jun said. He coughed self-consciously and produced a small plastic bag from within his jacket. "This entered into our investigation as evidence after the death of your sister."

Brennan accepted the bag and looked through the clear, flimsy plastic to see a shaped lump of metal inside. A key, one which he vaguely recognized. Jun took it back and coughed again, his cheeks an even deeper red.

"You are your sister's next-of-kin, so ordinarily all of her possessions would be transferred over to you," Jun continued. "However, her living will was very specific about this key in particular. Is your nephew here?"

Greg shot up from the couch. "My mom left me something?" He sidled his way past Brennan and took the bag from Jun. He looked down at the key and frowned. "What does it go to?"

Brennan glanced between his nephew and the key before turning to the agents and smiling. "Is that everything, Agent Jun?" he asked, purposely ignoring Pascale.

Jun nodded and stepped back. "Enjoy the rest of your day, Detective."

The door closed quickly behind the men in black, and Greg gave him a curious look. "So what's the big deal with the key?"

"It belonged to my parents, your grandparents," Brennan explained. "I didn't know that Maddy had the key, though I guess it would make sense that she did."

"And the lock it opens…?"

Brennan shrugged off the sudden discomfort. "That's the key to the, err…mansion."

Greg's jaw visibly dropped a few inches. "I don't think I heard you properly. Did you just say you're living in a cheap apartment in the city when you could be living in a freaking *mansion*?"

"Hey, this apartment isn't cheap!"

"Compared to a house that has *wings*?" Greg countered.

"It's a long story, but I wasn't exactly the golden boy of the family. I couldn't have moved back even if I wanted to." Brennan helped himself to another Coke before sitting back down on the couch.

Greg sat beside him, and a silent moment passed between them, during which a wide smile spread slowly across his face. "So," he started, drawing out the word. "Now that I legally own a mansion, I guess I don't have to live here anymore."

"I guess not."

"So when can we move me in?"

Brennan grinned. "We? You're a grown man now, obviously."

"Well, I just need a ride there, since I don't know where it is. After that, it'll be full independence living in the lap of luxury."

"Uh-huh," Brennan said dubiously. "And how will you buy groceries? Or pay the utilities? I'd be surprised if the old place is even furnished anymore, so you'll have to get a bed, too…"

Greg held up his hands in surrender. "All right, fine. I will *allow* you to be a paying tenant in my mansion." He paused to consider something. "Since when did our family have a mansion?"

"That's another long story," Brennan sighed. "What makes you think I'd want to move? This place has to be a thousand times easier to maintain in terms of upkeep, not to mention rent."

"Are you crazy? The rent here is insane, and whatever nest egg you saved up from being a Sleeper can't last forever. Also—*lest we forget*—the homicidal Leviathan thugs know where you live."

Brennan rubbed his chin. "You think Leviathan knows about this place specifically?"

"They would have to, right? You killed a half dozen of their men while rescuing Bishop, and then you escaped again from their ambush the other night. Wait, we're sure it was Leviathan, right?"

"I haven't pissed off any other gangs, to my knowledge."

"Right. So odds are good that they'll have this apartment on their hit list soon enough."

Brennan sighed and looked around the room. It wasn't much, but this place had been his home since before his and Mara's wedding. The commute to work couldn't be better, and despite Greg's earlier argument, the rent was lower than a lot of places in center city. Not by much, but enough that it afforded an extra pizza or two each month.

Before long, he was thinking about where they could pick up boxes for packing, and Brennan knew that the battle was lost. He didn't want to return to the home of his youth, the birthplace of some of his darkest memories and deepest regrets, but it simply wasn't safe for them to remain here. While taking refuge in a Scottage in the valley had been a pipe dream, the family mansion was a very real and imminent future for them.

The only thing left now was to recognize the gift fate had given them and to accept it.

Chapter Twenty-Four

Alex swirled her glass of wine in one hand as she gazed down upon the city.

The floor-to-ceiling windows afforded her an amazing view, and the sunset this evening was no exception. Fire spread across the city as the amber rays of the sun reflected rampantly off the mirrored sides of the skyscrapers that dotted the landscape. She emptied the cup of its last finger of wine and felt her mind become mercifully less poetic.

If the pattern of the last few weeks persisted, she would not be getting any sleep tonight.

All around her, neighbors grumbled at their spouses and thought about only the darkest portions of their days. Everybody was in a generally foul mood, a collective disgruntlement that was only getting worse, and Alex had a pretty good idea of what was behind it.

PATIENT DARKNESS

When the last violent hues of red disappeared behind dusky clouds, she put on a decent outfit and left her apartment. The elevator dinged, and Alex pressed the button for the sixteenth floor.

Benjamin didn't seem surprised by her appearance outside his door. "To what do I owe the pleasure?" he asked. He was dressed comfortably, but not yet in sleep attire.

Alex pointed toward the back bedroom. "You need to take care of that."

Well-worn wrinkles appeared as Benjamin frowned back at her. "*He* is not an object or an animal to be thrown away or put down," he said sharply. "I do not carry so little faith in my loved ones as you do, Ms. Brüding."

"That isn't your grandson anymore. Not in the way that has any meaning."

"All life has meaning."

Alex sighed. "He's only in pain now, and you know it. And he obviously isn't pleased that Brennan is still alive."

"All the more proof that the man he once was still exists," Benjamin said mildly.

"His negativity is affecting everyone in the building, like a contagious darkness spreading from one head to the next. He's patient zero."

"I thought the wellbeing of others was not your concern."

"Yeah, well, *I* can't get any sleep, either," she said resolutely.

Benjamin crossed his hands on his cane. "You must learn to manage stress if you wish to live as we do." At the look on her face, he continued, "I will see about moving him to a more secluded rehabilitation facility. Would that satisfy you?"

"It will have to do."

A moment of silence passed, and Benjamin took a slight step back into his apartment. "You did not come all this way just to tell me that," he said solemnly.

Alex felt her lips spread in a vulpine grin.

I think it's time we began my training.

Epilogue

"I AM PLEASED to see you again, Arthur."

Father Dylan ushered Brennan into his private office, and Brennan was struck by the room's lack of decoration or ornamentation. There were few personal effects aside from framed photos of the holy man with several groups of people. The photos looked like they were taken during religious retreats.

"What brings you here this evening?" Father Dylan asked, waiting until Brennan was seated before taking his own chair.

"I was hoping to ask you something of a rather personal nature."

"Of course you may. Please, speak your mind."

Brennan hesitated for a moment and realized he was wringing his hands. "I'm not very good at this sort of thing. It's been...well, god knows how long since my last confession."

"It may seem a long time to you, but He is always listening."

"That's a comforting thought," Brennan said dryly.

Father Dylan's smile was gentle. "It should be."

"I don't know how I should start..."

"Take your time."

"Have you ever felt conflicted?" Brennan asked. "I mean, when you know what you are doing is right, but the way in which you do it is not always so just?"

The priest inclined his head and steepled his fingers. "What is causing you to feel this turmoil?"

"You're keeping up with the news, I assume?"

"Indeed. Dreadful things must have happened to that man to guide him on such a path," Father Dylan said solemnly.

Brennan felt his hair raise on end at hearing such a generous view given to the mass murderer. "He's going to be in federal custody for the rest of his life...and I'm not sure that that's enough."

"You want to kill him." It wasn't a question, but Father Dylan also managed not to make it sound like a judgment.

"Yes." Brennan paused. "No. I don't know. The lives I took in my line of work…they were always justified because I believed in what I was doing."

"And now your belief is shaken?"

"No, it's not that. It's…well, Kellogg believed in what *he* was doing, too, and he thought he was right. We've both left our share of bodies in our wake, but I'm a free man today because of…what? Enough people backing me up, and not enough people backing him? What if the mob thought that blowing up buildings and murdering innocents was the only way to achieve their goals?"

"Murder is never justified," Father Dylan replied, his voice firm. "I am sorry that yours has been a difficult journey, and I am grateful that you do not have to undertake it alone."

"You mean Bishop?"

Father Dylan nodded. "Noel will always be by your side, Arthur, just as I know you will always be by hers. I do not believe it was coincidence that crossed your path with hers."

"My path has led me through some dark alleys, Father…and I'm afraid the darkest of them may be yet to come." Brennan breathed deeply through his nose and exhaled through his mouth before glancing up at the priest. The old man's eyes held an inviting warmth. "Recently, I experienced a…thing," he started slowly.

"I don't even know how to describe it. Energy flowed through me, and it felt like wings were spreading outward from my back. I've never felt more powerful than I did in that moment, and in a flash, I knew exactly what I needed to do. My role in catching Kellogg became clear, or at least the drive to do *something* was reinvigorated."

The priest's face was grave, and Brennan noticed for the first time just how many lines actually showed on that usually jolly face of his. "There may be an answer to explain what you are feeling," Father Dylan said, "but I fear you will not be pleased to hear it."

Brennan sat up a little straighter. "Tell me what you're thinking."

Father Dylan cleared his throat. "There are stories as old as storytelling itself that depict a chosen one, a hero borne of legend that succeeds in performing great feats where others have failed. Greek demigods are the ones you might be most familiar with, such as Hercules and Achilles."

Brennan shook his head. "Last I checked, neither one of my parents was a Greek god."

"These are not the only examples, though," Father Dylan argued. "Gilgamesh, a great king who defeated terrible monsters before succumbing to his own dark quest for immortality. According to some Mormon beliefs, John the Apostle—a man who performed miracles in his time—still walks the earth as he waits for the Second Coming." The priest smiled wryly as he said, "Even today, we have comic books that depict the epic battles of such heroes. They have a wellspring of power within them, and gifts that cannot be explained by the average man."

"Are you suggesting that I'm some kind of…superhero?" Brennan asked.

"That is for you to decide. Personally, I have not witnessed such a thing, but I would not be surprised to find that it is true," Father Dylan said, the smile on his face widening. "I believe that God has, over time, selected individuals to be his Chosen, those who perform great works in our world."

Brennan frowned. "But with the exception of John, all of those figures eventually gave in to darkness or death. Even the superheroes have their off days when they nearly destroy the earth."

"And why should they be any exception, hmm? Everyone has villains they must face, inner demons they must quell, even the best of us." Father Dylan leaned in confidingly. "It is how we choose to address these monsters that matters most."

"So if I'm one of the Chosen, then I'm destined for great things?"

"You have already accomplished great things," the priest countered. "You disbanded a violent gang of drug peddlers and stopped a misguided fool from immolating half the city. Ask the question you truly have in your heart."

Brennan breathed out slowly, and his heartbeat seemed to slow to a crawl. His wife's murderer was still out there, and Benjamin had promised that he could help. There was darkness there, Brennan knew, patiently waiting to consume him. Just as it had consumed Kellogg. "If I break the law in my pursuit of justice, how am I any better than the criminals I put down?"

"You mean put *away*?" Father Dylan asked mildly. Brennan met the question with a frown, and the priest sighed. "The Chosen have always had an unorthodox life compared to their contemporaries. I believe you are a good man, and that you will remain in His favor as long as the core of who you are remains true."

Brennan ignored the growing sensation that was spreading across his back. "And if I am changed in the process?"

Father Dylan regarded him sadly. "Then you will be one of the Fallen."

TOM SHUTT

ABOUT THE AUTHOR

What Tom wants you to know:

TOM SHUTT WRITES paranormal suspense with generous helpings of humor and a sprig of mystery thrown in for good measure. Sometimes he dabbles in fantasy, but in all cases, he strives to push the boundaries of modern fiction in search of good answers to hard questions.

He lives on the perpetually rainy East Coast with some cats, dogs, and a basement full of mistresses. His favorite authors are Jim Butcher, George R. R. Martin, Jonathan Stroud, and Eoin Colfer. He knows how to hide a body from the police, and the research for his novels has likely landed him on a few security watch lists. He enjoys reading, gaming (*Halo, Civilization, BioShock, Call of Duty, Minecraft*), playing pool, chasing deer, hunting deer, riding deer, and lying about what activities he does with deer. His favorite shows include *Supernatural, Game of Thrones, iZombie,* and anything created by Joss Whedon.

What Tom's family wants you to know:

TOM LIVED WITH more clarity, passion and dedication than most of us can ever hope to achieve in an entire lifetime, let alone just 25 years. He was hilarious, wise, thoughtful and loving. While he's left us behind physically, he's also left behind a collection of written works to keep us connected to him until we meet again. Until that day comes, we will miss him every moment.

Made in the USA
Middletown, DE
14 September 2019